THE FAMILY AFFAIR

James Gainer

Raider Publishing International

New York   London   Cape Town

ISBN: 978-1-61667-078-8

Published By Raider Publishing International
www.RaiderPublishing.com
New York London Cape Town
Printed in the United States of America and the United Kingdom

THE FAMILY AFFAIR

James Gainer

1

ONE YEAR AFTER STEPHEN'S ACCIDENT, RICK CAME TO STAY
with me. He was my sister Julie's stepson by her fourth
husband.

"It's just for part of the summer while he finishes his
internship at UCLA. You won't even know he's there.
He's great kid. *Please*," she begged from her San Diego
phone line. "We missed the deadline for campus housing,
and you're only a forty-minute drive from the school."

Reluctantly, I agreed. After all, she was my sister. I
kept my reservations to myself. I wasn't used to having
anyone around since Stephen's death; it would be difficult
relearning to share my space.

* * *

I LIVED AT THE BEACH— HERMOSA BEACH, TO BE EXACT. A
SMALL community, just thirty-five minutes west on the 405
from Los Angeles. I loved it there. It was quiet, but it had
great restaurants and an unpretentious style. Stephen and I
built our house right on the beach, but we had lived there
together for only a few months before the accident
happened. Stephen was out surfing when the tide went
from calm to angry. He was a strong swimmer, but the
water was stronger. It exhausted him and took his life.

That was another reason why I was concerned about
having someone else in the house; it was our special place—

1

mine and Stephen's. Rick was family, though— sort of— and so I agreed.

*   *   *

I WAS JUST COMING AROUND THE BEND WHEN I SPOTTED A RED Jeep parked in my driveway. When I pulled up next to it, I discovered it was unoccupied except for a duffel bag and a laptop. *Rick's?* As far as I knew, he wasn't due to arrive until Sunday— two days away. I hoped I hadn't misunderstood my sister's plans.

I quickly let myself in the front door and went immediately to the back of the house, to the main living area: a huge room with the kitchen, dining, and living room areas all open to one another. The entire back wall was made up of glass doors that opened out onto a huge deck and views of the beach and ocean. Flipping a switch, I flooded the deck area with light and went outside to look around. *No one.* I thought. *Maybe it wasn't Rick's car. Maybe it was a friend of my neighbour who parked in my driveway by mistake?*

I went back inside the house, leaving the doors open to let in the warm night air, making a mental note to check with my neighbours later on. For now, I turned on the CD player and flooded the house with U2's "A Beautiful Day". I poured myself a glass of wine and headed upstairs to shower off the last of a long day. I turned on the shower and checked my voicemail while I was waiting for the water to get to just the right temperature. *No messages. Typical.* I hadn't heard from my friends much since Stephen's death. They all seemed to have become uncomfortable around me. They just didn't know what to say.

The water felt amazing as I entered the shower, washing the stress of my day down the drain. As I lathered my body, I felt the tightness and strength of my muscles. I worked hard at staying in shape: weight training, as well as running twenty or thirty miles a week. My cock jumped to attention as I ran the soapy sponge over my pubic area. I lathered up really good and continued massaging the length of it, stroking it, harder, faster, my breath speeding up as I headed for the release of my orgasm. I cried out as I climaxed against the shower tiles.

Spent, I stood under the showerhead for a couple of minutes and then turned off the water. Once I opened the door, I realised I was not alone. I let out a scream.

"Jack, it's me! *Rick*. Don't be alarmed." His husky, yet soft, voice came to me through the foggy haze.

"What are you doing here?"

"Um, I'm living with you for the summer, remember?"

"I mean, what are you doing in my bathroom? I thought you were supposed to arrive on Sunday?"

"Julie didn't call you?"

"No," I said, searching for my towel.

"I needed to come early to meet with my teaching group before Monday's class."

He handed me a towel. I quickly wrapped it around me, but still couldn't see him completely through the steam, except to know that he was taller than I was.

"Can we finish this conversation downstairs in a few minutes?" I asked.

"Sure," he said, but he made no effort to leave the room.

"Can you wait downstairs while I finish up in here?"

"Oh, *ya*. Sorry."

Finally, he left.

I don't know why he's embarrassed, I thought when he was gone. *I'm the naked one.*

I had to sit down. I suddenly felt sick. *Why did he come into my bathroom? How long had he been there? Did he hear or see me masturbating? How loud did I moan during my climax? Was he watching?*

I reassured myself that he probably just walked in as I was getting out of the shower. Quickly, I finished drying off, and put on a pair of shorts and a t-shirt. Then, I headed downstairs, running my hands through my wet hair.

Rick wasn't in the living room or kitchen when I arrived. Then I saw him, standing outside leaning against the deck railing, staring up at the night sky. I felt the blood rushing straight to my groin. I hadn't seen Rick for at least ten years because he lived with his mom in Seattle. The last time we met, he must have been only thirteen or fourteen. My, how he had grown.

The more I stared at him the harder I grew. He was tall— at least six-foot-two— lean and muscular. He was wearing a tank top and a pair of cut-offs, which showed off muscular arms and legs covered by a very fine layer of golden blond hair, the same colour as the hair on his head. His jaw was strong, and it set the foundation of his face. He had nice high cheekbones that off-set clear blue eyes. His hair was medium length, messy, but styled.

I just stood there staring. I couldn't move. My feet felt like they had lead in them, and my hard-on continued to strain against the fabric of my shorts. Then it happened. Rick took his gaze from the night sky and placed it on me— assessing me, just the way I had assessed him, for what seemed like hours.

Say something, I thought. But I couldn't snap out of my haze.

"Jack," he said as he came closer to me. "I'm sorry about upstairs. The back doors were open, and I called out your name when I came in, but I guess you couldn't hear me over the music. I was just trying to find you, to let you know I was here."

"It's okay," I stammered as I put the cooking island between the two of us, hiding my slowly shrinking hard on. "Sorry I wasn't there to meet you, but, as I said before, I wasn't expecting you today. My sister isn't the most reliable person at times."

He smiled and agreed with me.

"Want a drink?" I asked. God knew I needed one.

He held up his hand to show me a Corona. "I helped myself. Hope you don't mind."

I did, but I wasn't going to let him know, since he was going to be staying here, and I had to get used that. I poured myself another glass of wine and suggested we bring his things in from his car. He was here to stay.

* * *

HE GRABBED HIS DUFFEL BAG AND I TOOK HIS COMPUTER IN. I then took him back upstairs to show him his room. The guest room was directly across the hall from my room. It was large and bright and had its own en-suite, a feature I made sure he noticed. I put his computer on the desk under the window.

"This is great! So much better than the dorm room I've been living in."

"I'm glad you like it," I replied. "Let me show you the rest of the house."

I gave him a tour. We went back downstairs to the main part of the house. I showed him the den, office and the other rooms. He stayed close to me, too close. With every step through the house I was constantly aware of his body, his breath— an awareness that made my body tingle with excitement and fear.

"What's downstairs?" Rick asked as we concluded the tour, gesturing to the staircase.

"Downstairs is completely off limits," I replied, a little too quickly. The tone in my voice made Rick take a step backwards, a shocked expression registering on his beautiful face.

"I'm sorry. I didn't mean for that to come out the way it did. Downstairs is off limits. Please respect that."

I quickly brushed past him, going in the direction of the kitchen. The truth was I couldn't even bring myself to go downstairs. The lower level of the house had been Stephens's office. His space. Stephen had been a landscape architect a very successful landscape architect. He personally was responsible for most of the beautiful landscapes seen up and down the Pacific Coast Highway. He specialised in gated communities. He worked from home; the office downstairs was at one time completely furnished with the latest in computer and design equipment. When Stephen died I gave the whole business to his assistant, a woman named Sheila. I took no payment for the equipment or client lists. The only condition was that she had to move the office out quickly. I couldn't have her, or the business, around.

After Sheila moved the office out, I moved Stephen's old things into the space, including the surfboard he was using the day of his accident. Then, I sealed the room, covered the windows with heavy paper, double bolted the doors, and then hid them from sight by covering them with an antique armoire. I thought I could make the pain of his death disappear.

"Jack, you okay?"

I was suddenly aware that Rick had followed me into the kitchen area. *How long had I been zoned out?*

"I'm good," I replied, brushing the tears from my face, not turning to meet his gaze. Getting my composure and strength back, I asked him if he was hungry.

"Starving," he said. "I haven't eaten since lunch."

"Why don't you grab another beer from the fridge and go hang out outside. I'll make us some appetisers."

"Sure."

I kept my back to him as he took another beer from the

fridge and left the room. I felt relieved to be alone for a moment, to finish getting myself back together. I didn't turn around until I was sure Rick was back out on the deck. Then, I reached for my wine glass and took a very large swallow of Chianti. I felt it immediately. I hadn't eaten much that day. Composed again, I focused on the task at hand: preparing food for myself and my houseguest/step-nephew. I opened the fridge to retrieve my usual Friday night dinner: pate, various cheeses, fruit, cold cuts, and stuffed olives. I then opened the pantry where I chose a couple of different kinds of crackers. I was just finishing up arranging everything on a platter when the phone rang.

Without looking at the caller ID I picked it up. "You are a bitch, and you so owe me."

"What? Me? Now why would you greet your darling sister in such a way?"

"Cut the innocent act, sis, you know exactly why."

"Whatever could you possibly be talking about?"

"Um, let see— Rick showing up two days early, and you conveniently forgetting to tell me?"

"Didn't I tell you? I'm sure I did."

"No, you didn't tell me, and I think you didn't tell me on purpose. What gives?"

"Oh, darling, we know each other far too well, don't we? I just decided you could use a little shake up in your completely structured, semi-boring life," she said, baiting me.

"I am not boring!" I said, a little too loudly.

"Not boring then. Predictable."

I was just opening my mouth to respond when she continued, "What are you doing right now?"

"Talking to my bitch of a sister."

She laughed. "I am going to tell you exactly what you're doing, and how you spent your day. You started your day by running on the beach for probably ten miles, finishing at about 7 a.m. Then you had a shower, and a breakfast of fruit and yogurt. You left your house at precisely 7:45 a.m. Since the weather in the L.A. area was beautiful today, you drove the forty-five minutes it takes you to get to the studio with the top down. You made one stop, exiting Hermosa Beach before hitting the 405, and that was at Starbucks for your once-a-week latte. How am I doing so far?"

Not waiting for my reply, she continued to rattle on, "You arrived at the studio at approximately 8:30 a.m. because traffic is a little lighter on Fridays and you managed the freeway in good time. After arriving in your office, you checked your voicemail, while your computer warmed up. You then did a bunch of boring writer stuff until lunch, at which time you started to clear off your desk, pack away files, and change your voice and email messages to vacation messages, because this was your last day of work for six weeks. At approximately 12:30 p.m., briefcase in hand, you headed towards your car for the drive to West Hollywood, where you met with your team of writers for the customary end of season lunch. You ate half the salad you ordered and had a glass of white wine. Lunch wrapped up at 3 p.m., ending with a toast you made to celebrate your team's 'job well done'. You then gave out gifts and their season-end bonuses. Since it was still early, you headed to Melrose Avenue to finish the afternoon with a little shopping. I suspect there is a new pair of shoes in your closet? You drove home the long way via the Pacific Coast Highway, taking your time, avoiding getting home too early. When you arrived home you promptly opened up a bottle of Chianti, put on U2 and headed for the shower. Somewhere in that time you discovered Rick and settled him in the guest room. And now at 7:30 p.m. you are starting your second glass of Chianti, and I would suspect there is a platter of appetisers sitting on your kitchen island waiting to be taken out to the back deck to be devoured. How did I do?"

I was silent for a moment. "*Jeans*," I said. "New *jeans* in the closet, not shoes. How do you know that much about my day?"

"Jack, you have nearly the same routine every day. This being Friday, I know you don't cook; you always have appetisers for dinner, which you eat on your deck. You sit out there staring at the ocean until the bottle of Chianti is finished before you allow yourself to go to bed. The only part I had to guess at was what you did after lunch."

She paused. "I'm worried about you. You're in this rut since Stephen died. All you do is work and come home. You don't see your friends anymore. You don't go out unless it's a required studio event. You are the most boring person, in the most glamorous industry."

"Great. My sister thinks I'm boring," I responded, hurt.

"What I'm trying to say is that you've stopped living. Stephen died, not you."

I bit my tongue so I wouldn't lash out at her. She always had a talent for pushing the right button at the right time, and I wasn't about to let her know she was successful.

Before I could think of a response, Rick walked in from outside.

"Rick is right here. I'll pass you to him." It was a good excuse to wrap things up with her.

"It's your step-monster," I said, handing the phone to Rick.

"Hello, Julie? Yah, the drive down was awesome. Your brother has a great place."

That was all I heard of Rick's conversation. I picked up the appetisers and the bottle of Chianti and headed outside, giving Rick the opportunity to talk to Julie in private.

                    *   *   *

I SET THE APPETISERS AND WINE DOWN ON THE TABLE IN FRONT
of the outdoor sofa and made myself comfortable among the
pillows. I just sat there staring into the night, replaying the
conversation I had with Julie. *How dare she bring Stephen
up like she did?* She really knew how to get to me.

"I'm not boring," I said. "Am I? Maybe a little crazy,
sitting here having a conversation with myself."

I closed my eyes, forgetting about everything. I wasn't
sure how much time had passed before Rick came back
outside.

"Julie said she'll call you tomorrow."

"Joy," I replied sarcastically.

"Were you guys having a fight?"

"Let's just call it a conversation that was almost a little
heated. It's what siblings do."

"Wouldn't know. Don't have any," Rick said.

"Ah, that's right. You're one of a kind."

Rick eyed up the appetisers.

"Please, help yourself," I said, handing him a plate. He
picked at some fruit and cheese, avoiding the pate.

"Is this how you always eat?"

"Friday night ritual," I answered. "You don't like?"

"Well, I'm usually not into chick food."

"Chick food? Are you calling me a chick?" I asked, a
little stunned.

"No, you definitely are *not* a chick, but you eat like one.
Have you seen what's in your fridge?"

I was about to protest, but he continued, "There's
nothing but yogurt and fruit. What do you survive on?"

I was a little pissed. This was only his first night here;
he should have been on his best behaviour. Instead, he felt
comfortable enough to criticise me, even though he had no

idea who I really was.

"You have rollerblades?" I asked

"*Ya,* in the back of my Jeep."

"Go put them on. We are going out," I said.

2

THE NIGHT WAS AMAZING AS WE BLADED DOWN THE boardwalk along the beach and on towards the pier at the centre of town. The moon was almost full, causing the ocean to shimmer in its reflection.

"Where are we going?" Rick was asking again.

"I told you, to get you some 'man food'."

"But where?"

"You'll see when we get there."

"Why couldn't we have driven?"

"Stop whining. You're starting to sound like my sister. It's a fifteen-minute blade, and we have both been drinking, so there is no way we were going to drive. Besides, it's a beautiful night, so stop complaining, you big baby."

He shot me a look; I just grinned back.

The boardwalk started getting more active the closer we got to the pier. Soon, we were engulfed in the crowd, part of it. Rick was now following me, instead of being at my side. I had to slow our pace to avoid accidents with pedestrians. I could smell all the different aromas coming from the restaurants on the boardwalk. My stomach started to growl in anticipation. I spotted an empty bench, pulled up, and sat. Rick sat right next to me, his eyes darting in every direction, taking in a Friday night at Hermosa Beach.

I opened the backpack I was carrying. "Time to change. Can't go in on wheels," I said as I handed him his shoes.

I quickly removed my rollerblades and put on the

thongs I had brought along. Rick followed suit. I stuffed our rollerblades into the backpack and handed it to him to carry. I then led the way down the boardwalk to the next corner.

Memories flooded back like a tidal wave as we approached the door to Joe's. I hadn't been back since Stephen's death. We'd loved coming here every Friday night. As I stood outside and stared at the door I could see the interior clearly in my mind: The hand-crafted wooden tables, with bright red- and white-chequered tabled cloths, the beautiful hand-carved chairs surrounding each table like individual works of art, the simply painted walls, with their subtle undertones of yellow and orange, the light from the sky washing through the floor to ceiling windows, and the imported Mexican tiles, with its hues of gray and blue that made you feel like you were sitting on floor of the ocean.

I felt myself starting to panic. My breathing became shallow, nausea flooding in. I shouldn't have come. I was just about to turn around and flee when Rick broke the trance I was in.

"Are we going in or what? I'm starving!"

I turned slightly and gave him a half smile. It took all the strength I had in me to propel myself up the stairs and to open the door. We were quickly engulfed by the rich aromas wafting into the entrance hall from the kitchen. Although my stomach was tied up in knots, it started to rumble due to the smell in the air. As we stepped in further, I peeked around the greeting desk into the main part of the restaurant, and saw that it was completely full.

No one was manning the desk. I heard the swinging door that led to the kitchen start to open, and I turned to look. There in the doorway stood a young girl. She looked at me like she was seeing a ghost. It seemed like an eternity had passed as we stood there staring at each other. I broke the silence.

"Hello, Theresa."

She looked at me and dropped the tray of drinks she was carrying. The glasses landed on the floor with a loud crash. She started to shriek. "Oh, my God! Oh, my God! Oh, my God!"

She turned on her heel, running back into the kitchen, a stream of Italian coming out through her mouth and filling the entrance hall. As I turned to look at Rick, who had a very puzzled look on his face, I could see into the dining area. The people seated at the tables nearest the entrance hall had stopped talking to stare at Rick and I. Rick turned to see what I was looking at and he blushed with embarrassment. Loud Italian conversation between two women, coming from behind the kitchen door, broke the silence. The kitchen door then flew open and on the threshold stood Maria.

I just stared at her, taking in the beauty of her. She was dressed perfectly in a brightly coloured sundress, turquoise jewellery surrounding her neck and adorning her ears. Her long black hair was swept back into a perfect low bun at the nape of her neck. She didn't look like she was over fifty, but I knew she was.

We both stood, staring at each other. Sizing each other up. Neither one of us made a move. Finally, she broke the stalemate.

"Jackie!"

She threw up her hands and started towards me. I crossed the entrance hall. She embraced me, and, as we hugged, I took in the smell of her signature Chanel N°5. When we stopped embracing, I could see tears in her eyes. She held my face in both her hands, shaking my head. Then, without warning she promptly slapped me across the right cheek.

"That is for not coming to see Maria sooner!" she said, with only a hint of her accent noticeable. "Jackie, we have missed you. Theresa, come give Jackie a hug," she said over her shoulder.

Theresa didn't move a muscle.

"Theresa, come here."

Theresa held her ground.

Maria strode toward Theresa and the two women once again began a conversation in Italian. The conversation ended with Theresa looking at me with bright eyes and exclaiming, "Jackie!"

She ran to me and threw her arms around me, choking me in her embrace.

"Theresa! Get off him; go get your father," Maria said, as she pried Theresa's arms from my neck. "Forgive her. She was a little confused. She thought you were the one that died. We never let her come with us to the funeral. Felt she was too young. When she saw you come in, she thought you were a ghost, and thought she might be dead. Way too many horror movies that girl of mine watches."

"You know I called you several times throughout the year."

"I'm sorry," I said.

"It's still hard."

"You're here now," she said, and she patted my face gently. "And who might this handsome young man be?"

Before Rick could open his mouth to reply, the kitchen door slammed opened, the threshold filled up with none other than Joe himself. He was standing there in his kitchen apron, starched white shirt and pants, and his grey hair cut short in military style.

"Jackie!"

As he started to move towards me I could see Carlos, Simon, and Franco completing the entourage behind him. Joe held out a hand for a shake, giving me a pat on the back at the same time.

"It's good to see you back here, my friend."

"Thank you," was all I could get out before Carlos,

Simon, and Franco swarmed me in a flurry of handshakes and greetings in Italian and English.

"Who are you?" Carlos asked Rick.

Everyone turned to look at an overwhelmed Rick, myself included.

I answered for him. "This is Rick. My, um, step-nephew."

No one registered what I just said.

"He's my sister, Julie's, stepson."

"Oh, Julie, I remember her," Maria said. "Jackie's sister, Julie, from San Diego."

It did the trick. At once, everyone remembered my sister and swarmed around Rick to shake his hand.

Maria directed her attention to the dinning room, where people still stared at the scene we made.

"Have you people never seen a family reunion? Stop staring and eat your dinner!"

Everyone turned back to their dinners, embarrassed. Conversation began again.

"We must feed you! Look how skinny you are," Joe said, as he turned and went back toward the kitchen. "I will go prepare a feast for you and your young friend."

"Theresa, go seat Jackie upstairs on the deck," Maria said. "And Carlos, go get his usual drink."

"I'm sure the deck is completely full, since it's such a beautiful night. We'll sit anywhere you have room," I responded to Maria's instructions.

"You go upstairs with Theresa. I will come check on you soon," Maria said.

*   *   *

THERESA LED THE WAY UP THE CIRCULAR STAIRCASE THAT WAS located in the far left corner of the entrance hall. At the top of the stairs we passed through double glass doors leading out onto the deck. The warmth of the air hit us once again as we stepped back out into the night. The deck— which was small, only ten or twelve tables— was completely full of patrons as we weaved in and out of tables towards the front ocean side.

When we reached the front, Theresa stopped and motioned for us to sit at a premium table, with a perfect view of the boardwalk, beach, and ocean below.

This had once been my usual table. The table I shared with Stephen.

I quickly noticed the reserved sign placed on the table.

"Theresa, this table is reserved. We can't take someone's table."

"It is reserved for you," she replied.

I shot her a puzzled look.

"*Mama* doesn't let anyone sit here on Friday night. She has been keeping it open for you."

"You mean…?"

She looked at me and nodded, *yes*.

"What an ass I've been," I said under my breath.

"What?" Rick was looking at me.

"Nothing. Just talking to myself," I replied.

He saw the tears in my eyes. "You okay?"

"Totally," I said, as I looked towards the ocean.

3

"So what's the story on this place? This family and you?"

I took my attention away from the ocean. I was just about to respond when Carlos slammed an ice-filled bucket of Coronas on the table announcing, "First round is on me."

"Beer. You drink beer?"

"Of course he drinks beer," Carlos answered for me. "It's their— I mean *his* usual."

"Really?" Rick didn't seem to believe it.

I reached into the bucket, cracked open one with the bottle opener that was attached, and downed it all at once.

"Surprised?" I asked, as I reached in and took out two more. I handed him one.

"A little. You don't seem like a beer kind of guy."

"Rick, you barely know me. We've spent, what? A total of maybe one or two holidays together over the last ten years?"

"I guess I made an assumption based on knowing— and living part-time with— your sister," he replied.

"As much as my sister and I are alike, we're also two very different people," I said, looking directly into his eyes.

Rick shifted his gaze down towards the table, looking a little uncomfortable.

"Okay, so I am going to leave you two alone for now," Carlos interrupted.

"Can we get some menus?" Rick asked.

"Menus? No, no, no. Jackie, where did you find this boy?"

I shrugged.

"You do not get menus when you dine at Joe's. We decide what you will eat. My father is downstairs in the kitchen, already preparing a feast for you. I will spare his feelings and mention nothing of this request to see a menu."

With a dramatic flare, Carlos turned on his heel and headed toward the service stairs that led to the kitchen below.

"What was that about?" Rick asked, looking a little puzzled.

"When you're a regular customer of Joe's, they consider you family. When you go to your families for dinner, you don't ask to see what's on the menu, do you? Same applies here. They take very good care of you, and the food is always amazing."

Rick seemed convinced. "So tell me the story about this place."

"Well, Joe and Maria bought this place nearly thirty years ago, a few years after they arrived here from Italy. Carlos is the eldest son; I think he's close to thirty. He leads and supervises the dining room staff. The two younger boys, Simon and Franco, are following in their father's footsteps and training to become chefs. Theresa, I think, is seventeen. Last I knew, she was in high school and working here on the weekends."

Rick smiled, looking into my eyes. "Not the answer I was looking for."

I turned away knowing what he wanted to know, but avoiding it.

"Soup's on!"

Carlos was back, placing a basket of nachos and salsa in front of us.

"Enjoy, my little friend," he said to Rick as he whisked

himself away.

The nachos smelled and looked scrumptious: hot peppers, three different kinds of cheese, and pickles. I was hungrier than I thought.

I quickly dug in, dipping the nachos into the homemade "secret" salsa Joe was famous for.

"Rick, you really need to try these; you'll love them," I said.

He scooped up a few nachos, dipping them into the salsa. "So, are you going to tell me your connection to this place?"

His persistence was really starting to piss me off. Why should I tell him anything? We had just met— sort of. Why did he need to know so badly?

I finished chewing the remainder of nachos that I was working on, took a large swig from my bottle of beer and began telling him what he wanted to know.

"Stephen and I discovered this place one rainy afternoon. The L.A. area was experiencing a massive amount of rain and flooding the year we were building the house. The roof had just been completed, so Stephen wanted to make sure it was holding up. We drove out here in a torrential storm. We arrived to find the house in perfect order. Perfectly dry. On our way back out of town, the storm got really bad. Water was pooling on the road, and Stephen lost control. The car hydroplaned went into a spin, and it was stopped by a light pole. We weren't hurt and there was minimal damage to the car, but the engine wouldn't start. A cell tower had been damaged by the lightning from the storm, making a call for help impossible, so we got out and started walking looking for a phone and some refuge from the storm. The storm had caused the local businesses to close up. There was virtually no one, nothing open in the downtown section of Hermosa Beach. We ran along trying doors, looking in windows, trying to find a sign of life."

I paused, taking a sip of beer. Rick stared at me with interest.

"We finally came to the end of the street— Joe's being the last building. Praying, I tried the door. Relief and surprise came over me as it opened when I pulled on it. We quickly entered and were greeted by Joe and Maria, and their family, stranded in the restaurant, unable to make it to their home. They welcomed us out of the storm, providing us with towels to dry off. Feeding us. We spent the night with them. The storm ended early the next morning, and Joe was able to get our car in working order, but Joe or Maria wouldn't take anything in return for helping us. When we moved into the house and became permanent residences of Hermosa Beach, we started coming here every Friday night. It became our ritual, this table becoming ours. They treated us like family, and since both our biological families lived elsewhere, we relished being included in their family. After Stephen's accident, I couldn't bring myself to come back here alone."

Rick was still sitting quietly as I finished the story.

"Well, I see we brought our appetites with us tonight." Maria was standing over us.

I looked down and realised Rick ate all the nachos and salsa while I was telling my story.

"Sorry, I was starving. And you were right; these are the best nachos I have ever had," he stated.

"I was just telling Rick the story of how we met," I said, taking my eyes from Rick and looking up at Maria.

"You should have seen the two of them, looking like drowned rats, especially this one." Maria pointed to me. "Standing there in my entrance way, designer clothes wrinkled and sopping wet. Hair all dishevelled. He was a sight!"

Leaning closer to Rick, she finished by saying, "Right

then and there I knew I was meeting a real life princess."

"Hey!" I protested.

Maria started to laugh; Rick looked at me with a huge grin on his face.

"That's why we call him *Jackie*; 'cause you ain't going to find any princess named Jack."

Maria continued to laugh.

"So, Princess Jackie, where did you learn to drink beer?" Rick smiled. "I mean, they probably didn't serve beer in the ivory tower of designer holiness where you came from. Are you a princess who likes to slum it a little?"

He was obviously proud of his humour, his joke directed at me. I was just opening my mouth to give a quick comeback, when Maria started laughing uncontrollably at Rick's comments. Tears rolled down her perfectly made-up face. Rick soon joined her. I just looked at both of them. It was kind of funny. I could have fumed and been mad at both of them, or I could have embraced the comments in the spirit they were intended, and joined in.

Maybe it was the beer clouding my mind, or just the warm feeling and atmosphere of being with Maria at Joe's again. Whatever it was, I felt lighter, with a slight edge of happiness peeking into my psyche. I started to laugh. I laughed and laughed. I couldn't remember laughing like that since Stephen's death. It felt good.

"*Sssh*. All of you!" Carlos was back carrying a tray with our dinner. "You are disrupting the other diners. *Sssh, Sssh, Sssh!*"

"Don't tell me you just *ssshed* your own mother," Maria said to Carlos as she was wiping away the last of her tears, on her mascara strewn face. "I am in charge of this restaurant, and I will decide what is appropriate or not, and when to *ssh* or not. Remember, I brought you into this world, and I can take you out just like that!" Maria said with a snap of her fingers.

"Sorry, Mama," Carlos replied sheepishly.

"It looks like Carlos has brought your dinner. Eat, drink, enjoy. I will be back to have dessert and espresso with you later. Carlos, serve them their food!"

With that, Maria turned and was gone. Carlos, still quiet from the tongue-lashing he just received, began to place dishes of hot food in front of us. When he was done, he asked if we required anything more. I said *no,* but Rick asked for another bucket of beer. Carlos nodded and left.

I looked down at the feast before us. There were beautifully wrapped enchiladas, with sides of sour cream, refried beans, homemade guacamole, and a huge bowl of taco salad topped with the "secret" salsa and ranch dressing, and to complete the feast a plate of feta-stuffed jalapeno peppers. I dug in, placing a portion of everything on my plate. But Rick didn't move.

"What's the matter, not hungry anymore?"

"Just a little confused," Rick responded.

"About what?"

"Didn't you say Joe and Maria were Italian?"

"Yes," I replied, directing my full attention to him, and not my plate of food.

"Well, this looks like more of a Mexican dinner to me."

"Joe likes to prepare all kinds of food, and he's great at whatever he tries. You never know what he's going to serve you. He once served us a five-course French cuisine meal that could hold its own up against any meal you would be served in France."

"This is delicious!" he said after his first few bites, speaking with his mouth half full of food, spraying the table a little.

"Nice. Your mother never teach you not to talk with your mouth full?"

He replied by sticking his tongue out at me. I shook my head, feeling slightly aroused by his response. We devoured our meal in total silence. Carlos stopped by with the fresh bucket of beer, and asked how we were doing. Rick gave him the thumbs up and said, "Awesome, dude."

I smiled silently, devouring my meal.

Awesome dude. Yup, he is twenty-three, I thought. I couldn't stop looking at him as we ate our dinner. His chiselled face, perfectly tanned. His crystal clear blue eyes with a hint of innocence and little-boy mischief lurking beneath them. He had an air of confidence that surrounded him, or was it cockiness?

"What? You're staring. I got something on my face?" Rick asked.

"Um, no," I stammered. "I was just noticing how much you look like your father."

Nice save, I said to myself.

"Thanks, I think. Is that a compliment?" he asked.

"More of a statement than a compliment, I guess. Your father is a very handsome man, and he passed those genes down to you."

"More like an old man," Rick responded.

I laughed. "I guess someone your age would think someone the age of fifty is old."

Truth be told, my sister Julie knew how to pick them. Rick's father, Max, was one of the most handsome, distinguished men I have ever met. He was slightly taller that Rick, with a full head of salt and pepper hair that had a natural shimmer to it. He exuded confidence, and he thought he was better than everyone else due to the fact that he was a very successful divorce attorney. Max "The Rottweiler" Stevenson. That was what everyone called him; he always went for the jugular and had a talent for sniffing out his opponent's weaknesses. That's how Julie and Max met. She'd hired him to represent her in her divorce from Allan, her third husband. He did very well with Julie's divorce, getting her far more than the fifty-fifty split that the State of California regulates in no-fault divorces. When Julie's divorce from Allan was finalised, she managed to get Max so smitten with her that he whisked her away to Hawaii, proposed to her, and convinced her to marry him on the spot. That was my sister, a natural born manipulator. Over the years she had even managed to do a number on me. Bending me to her will. Although I had to admit, I believe she really is in love with Max; and they do make the perfect couple.

"My dad and I don't really get along all that well." Rick broke the silence. "He's super pissed that I chose to get BA in English and become a teacher, instead of following his lead and becoming an attorney. 'You'll never amount to anything being a teacher, make no money and be poor your whole life. Is that what you want'." Rick was doing a good job of imitating Max's voice. "'I'm not going to subsidise your income. Once you graduate, you will be totally on your own'."

A smile curled at the corners of my mouth; Rick was nailing his dad.

"The truth is, money is not that important to me. I would rather spend my life being poor helping people reach their potential, than being rich and profiting of their misery," Rick said.

"Easy to say, when you've grown up with affluence," I replied.

"I don't know how much you know about me, but I can assure you I wasn't raised in total affluence. My mother divorced my father before he became really successful. She didn't get a huge settlement. She manages a bank in Seattle. She does okay, and we have a nice lifestyle, but it's nowhere near the lifestyle my dad and Julie live. I only went to private schools at the insistence of my father. He believed I needed to get 'the best education' possible, and he was prepared to pay for it. I only came out here from

Seattle to finish my degree, since the internship at UCLA is the best in the country. It will give me the contacts and credential to work anywhere I want."

I felt about an inch high when Rick finished speaking. I had made some assumptions about him, based on his father. I thought he was a spoiled rich boy.

"I'm sorry, Rick. As much as you don't know me, I don't know you. My apologies for making assumptions. Truce?" I held up my bottle of beer. "To assuming nothing about each other."

Rick clinked my bottle with his.

4

I WOKE UP FEELING LIKE I HAD BEEN RUN OVER BY A VERY large truck. When I opened my eyes, the brightness was so painful that I buried my head in my pillow.

"Who is pounding on my walls?" I screamed, soon realising the pounding was coming from inside my head.

My mouth felt like sandpaper. I slowly uncovered my head to look at the bedside clock. Through blurred vision, I read 11:15 a.m.

"What the hell happened to me?"

I tried to get up and quickly fell back into bed, my body aching all over. I pressed the back of my hands into my eyes, trying to get relief. I rolled over onto my side, placing my back to the bright windows that were intensifying my pounding headache. I opened one eye to look around. *Okay, I am at home, in my own bed. This is a good sign.* I looked over at the nightstand and saw a bottle of water; I noticed a note attached to it. I put the note aside, opened the bottle, and downed half of it. My mouth felt better, but my stomach rebelled. I picked up the note and read:

Morning, Princess Jackie, Thought you might need this.
I left you two Tylenol and a Gravel pill that I found in your bathroom. Gone to meet my teaching group. See ya later.

Rick

Okay, so I wasn't dying, I was just very hung over. I took all three pills, downing them with the remainder of the water in the bottle. The last thing I remembered was having dessert and espresso with Maria. *Think, Jack.* My mind was a cloudy haze. I tried getting up again, then gave up.

* * *

RINGING, MORE RINGING, AND MORE RINGING. I BURIED MY head in my pillows once again. It stopped. Then it started right back up again.

"What the fuck?"

I reached out and knocked the phone to the floor.

"Hello? Hello? Jack, are you there? Hello?"

"Fuck off," I said into my pillow.

The caller finally gave up, and I soon heard the hum of the disconnected line. I fell back to sleep.

* * *

WHEN I WOKE AGAIN, I WAS HOT. I KICKED OFF THE DUVET cover. *Man, why is it so hot?* The pounding in my head seemed to be gone. I decided to take a chance and open my eyes. Bright, it was still so bright. I closed them. *I just had to design a house with floor-to-ceiling windows in the bedroom, didn't I?*

I was sweating a cold sweat. The sheets beneath me felt soaking wet. I wanted to stay here forever, but my bladder thought better of it. I sat up, half opening my eyes, trying to get my bearings. I opened my eyes completely.

Okay, not so bad.

The pounding from before had been replaced with a dull throbbing.

You're okay, Jack.

I looked around the room, adjusting to the daylight. I

glanced at the clock; it now read 1:35 p.m.

"Shit! I slept the whole day away!"

It was definitely time to get moving. I placed my feet on the soft carpet that was the floor of my bedroom, stood up, and sat right back down. I felt dreadfully dizzy. I put my head between my legs, waiting for the dizziness to pass; I contemplated crawling to the bathroom. My bladder was screaming to be released.

Once the wave of dizziness passed, I stood and wobbled my way to my bathroom. I pulled down my underwear and sat to relieve myself. As I sat there, I began searching my mind to remember what had happened to me.

Nope— nothing.

I stepped into the shower thinking it would make me feel better and hopefully improve my memory. The water felt like a million pins hitting my skin when I stepped under its gentle spray. Eventually, the warm water started feeling good, and the throbbing in my head seemed to be going down. My mind was starting to clear. I grabbed the body wash from the built-in shelf and put a generous amount on my loofah. I scrubbed my body, trying to wash away the remainder of my hangover. A hangover I still couldn't remember how I got.

"Ouch!" I screamed when the loofah touched my right side. I looked down at my arm, seeing a huge dark purplish/yellow bruise surrounded by cuts that were already starting to scab over.

"What the fuck?" I inspected the wounds more closely. "What happened to me last night?"

I was starting to worry. I immediately looked over the rest of my body. I found another smaller bruise just below my kneecap. I avoided both areas while I finished washing. I rinsed myself clean, staying under the water for what was beginning to feel like an eternity. I hoped my memory of last nights event's would come flooding back the longer I remained under the water.

Nothing.

I gave up hope as I turned the water off and stepped into the steamy haze of the bathroom. Towelling myself dry, I made my way over to the sink and immediately started brushing my teeth. As the steam evaporated from the mirror in front of me I leant in to take took a look at myself.

"Ahh!" My right eye was completely black. Purplish-black to be exact. And there was a small cut right above my eyebrow. I reached up to touch it. It was tender but actually not that sore. I tried to remember.

Okay, Rick arriving— check. Beer and dinner at Joe's— check. Dessert and espresso with Maria— check. Getting home, and bruises— no check.

I had to sit down. I turned around, leaning on the counter and sliding to the floor. The ceramic tile was cool and refreshing against my skin.

What happened after dessert?

I began searching my mind once again.

Maria; espresso; dessert. Maria, espresso, dessert. Maria; espresso; dessert. Joe!

That's it!

Joe. Joe came and joined us.

I remember now!

The restaurant was emptying out, the kitchen was closed for the night, and Joe came up to join Maria, Rick, and I on the deck, bringing with him his favourite bottle of tequila. I clearly remembered Joe pouring four shots. One for each of us. I remembered declining his offer, but he insisted. I did the shot, to appease Joe, and to quell the guilt that I was feeling. One shot lead to another, and another. *How many did I have?* I couldn't remember. I remembered visiting, and laughing at the stories Maria and Joe were telling, and then nothing. I woke up with a hangover. *What had happened to Rick? Where was he?*

Oh, the note. He was at school.

I lifted myself off the floor, feeling guilty for what I might have done last night in my drunken stupor. I tended to my cuts with an antiseptic lotion, made my way to my closet, and threw on cargo shorts and a tank top. Back in the bedroom, I stripped the bed, finding bloody bandages entangled in them.

Who bandaged me up? Rick?

I felt sick to my stomach as I put a fresh set of linens back on the bed, hung up the phone; and ignored my voicemail. Last night's clothes had been crumpled up, so I threw them in a pile with the linens. As I made my way to the stairs, I peeked into the guest room— Rick's room. The bed was made, but there were clothes strewn about. Fighting the urge to go in and straighten up, I went straight downstairs instead.

Head pounding with every step, I finally made it to the downstairs landing.

"I can't remember the last time I felt this bad," I moaned to myself as I headed into the kitchen.

I thought better of having something to eat; the continual flip-flopping of my stomach was a good indication that nothing was going to stay down. I grabbed a bottle of water from the fridge and downed it in seconds. Taking another, I decided to head outside for some fresh air.

I am sure it will make me feel better, I reassured myself. The warm air and the brilliance of the day hit me like a ton of bricks as I opened the sliding doors that led to the deck. I immediately felt sick to my stomach and raced for the downstairs washroom and threw up. I lay down in the washroom, my body drinking in the coolness of the tile floor, resting until I felt well enough to pick myself up again. Stomach aching and head throbbing, I went into the den, threw myself on the sofa, and promptly fell asleep again.

* * *

THE LIGHTS FROM THE PARAMEDIC'S TRUCK STREAKED THE *morning sky with bursts of blood red. A crowd was beginning to form behind the police warning tape that was being guarded by a young officer. The whirl from the rescue helicopter overhead was constant and unnerving. I watched helplessly from the shore as the rescuers in a Zodiac searched the ocean for any sign of life. The waves were pounding the shore with a vengeance, the overhead sky darkening as the impending storm was blowing in.*

"They're having a challenge controlling the Zodiac in those waves," the rescue captain next to me said, with his attention on the mission. "We're going to have to pull them out soon. Resume when the storm passes."

He looked at me. "Your friend's body— um, I mean, your friend— could be anywhere out there now. The undercurrent is strong."

I looked at him numbly, unable to respond. Two hours had passed since I discovered Stephen's surfboard on the beach in front of our house, with no sign of Stephen. The safety cord which was to prevent the board from being separated from the rider had ripped away from the metal clip that anchored to the board.

The first sprinkles of rain wet my face. I wiped them away as I strained to decipher what was being said on the portable police band radio that the captain was carrying. He picked up the microphone. "Everyone, pull out. We're done here. The storm is becoming too violent."

"No!" I screamed. "We can't stop! Please, oh God, no! Please don't stop!"

I fell onto my knees in the sand as I pleaded.

"We can't do anymore in this storm, Mr. Perry; it's just

too dangerous."

He knelt beside me, putting a hand on my shoulder. Tears stung my eyes as I watched the rescue team being pulled back into shore, the helicopter overhead turning away.

"We got something here," someone announced over the radio.

The captain stood, putting his binoculars up to his face. "I told you to pull out," he barked into the microphone.

"No. We are going in," the response came back crackled.

Looking out into the ocean, I saw the small Zodiac struggle to keep its balance, two of the three rescuers on board leaning down into the water. Through my tears and the rain I could just barely make out the form of what I assumed was a body as they began hauling it into the boat.

* * *

"Jack. Jack!"

My eyes flew open, trying to focus. "Stephen?"

No. As my vision began to clear I realised it was Rick sitting next to me on the sofa, hands on my shoulders, shaking me.

"Jack, you okay?"

I looked up him, and saw the concern on his face.

"*Ya.* What's going on?" I asked as I pulled myself into a half sitting position, rubbing the sleep from my eyes.

"I think you were having a nightmare. I heard you calling out for help when I came in the door. You sure you're okay?"

I looked towards him. "Perfectly okay."

I realised his hands were gripping my shoulders tightly as I answered; I looked down at them. Rick immediately loosened his grip.

"Sorry," he said, with a hint of embarrassment. "What was your nightmare about?"

"Don't remember. It's totally gone," I lied. "That's the one great thing about nightmares; as soon as you wake, the memory of them is usually gone. What time is it?"

"6:30."

"6:30! Shit, I slept the whole day away," I said as I hoisted myself into a full sitting position, realising I was feeling a whole lot better than before.

"Where have you been all day? I tried calling a couple of times."

"Here. Sleeping. Recovering."

"All day?"

"Yes." This time, it was me with the hint of embarrassment in my voice.

"Would you like to fill me in on what happened last night?" I asked as I pointed out the cuts and bruises on my arms and legs, and the black eye I was sporting.

"Dude, you were so wasted. I mean, I never have seen a dude so wasted. You were like way out there." He pointed to the ceiling, dramatically rolling his eyes and flopping into the chair opposite the sofa.

"*Dude*. Fill me in right now," I said, failing miserably at the surfer boy imitation.

"You seriously don't remember?"

I ran my hands through my hair. "Not much. It's kind of sketchy. I never drink anything harder than wine or beer. Hard alcohol doesn't agree with me."

"Well, where to start? So much to tell." He was pondering, obviously enjoying himself.

"How about starting with these," I said, pointing to my bruises once again.

"You fell."

"And?"

"And what?" He looked directly at me with those

crystal-clear blue eyes of his, making me uncomfortable.

"You're going to milk this for all it's worth, and enjoy it as much as possible, aren't you?" I said, slightly aggravated.

"Yup."

With that, he hauled himself out of the chair and headed toward the kitchen "I'm starving. Let's eat."

I stood to follow him and had to steady myself with the arm of the sofa. I felt dizzy and weak, most likely from lack of food. Once steadied, I followed him into the kitchen.

"Jeez, you don't look so good." He stopped rummaging inside the fridge and looked at me.

"I haven't eaten since last night. I guess I'm not bouncing back like I did when I was younger."

"You need the cure."

"The cure?"

"Get some shoes on. I know just where to find it."

5

I caught sight of myself in the outside mirror of Rick's Jeep as he drove down Ocean Front Avenue. The blackness of my eye was deepening, turning less yellow, and more purple, by the minute. The top was down and my rumpled hair was blowing in the air. *How attractive,* I thought as I looked at myself. I felt like I'd aged ten years since yesterday.

"Where we going?" I asked.

"To get you the cure. We'll be there soon." He kept his attention on the road in front of him as he responded to my question.

Rick took a right onto Fifth Street pointed the Jeep towards 'the strip', a road that paralleled the 405 freeway, running about one mile in length. It was made up of strip malls, grocery stores, gas stations, restaurants, and a few motels. The buildings also provided a sound barrier for the town, from the continuous noise created by the traffic on the 405.

I leant back in the seat, staring up into the twilight sky, watching the palm trees sway in the breeze as we drove.

"We're here," Rick announced as he turned into a parking lot.

I brought my gaze down from the darkening sky. "Burger Boy? *This* is the cure?" I asked as he manoeuvred into a parking space close to the door.

"Grease is the ultimate cure for a hangover. I found this

place on my way to school this morning. Fixed me right up."

"I don't eat fast food, Rick," I said, appalled.

"It's the cure. Trust me. You'll feel a million times better as soon as we get a little grease in your system." He opened his door and jumped out.

Walking in front of the Jeep, he motioned for me to follow him. I unfastened my seatbelt, but remained glued in place.

"Come on." He shot me a look. "Come on."

With reluctance, I opened the door and slowly got out, joining him on the sidewalk.

Bright white lights and walls assaulted my eyes the moment we stepped into Burger Boy.

I scanned my surroundings. Plastic tables with red Formica tops, surrounded by yellow— which I assumed to be originally white— plastic chairs. Framed pictures of smiling families enjoying their Burger Boy meals. Pots of artificial plants scattered throughout the restaurant.

As I finished my appraisal I realised Rick was already in line at the counter. I joined him.

"So, what are you going to have?" he asked, gesturing up towards the menu, which was *cleverly* displayed above the order counter.

Nothing seemed appealing. Single burger, double burger, Big Boy burger, chilli Big Boy burger, French fries, onion rings, deep fried cheese, deep fried cheese with fries— the list went on and on. I felt disgusted, but my stomach rumbled in anticipation of being fed.

"Next please."

I looked down from the menu and noticed that the couple in front of us had received their food and had moved from the counter.

"Can I take your order, please?" the pimply faced teenager was asking Rick as he moved to the counter.

The nametag on her white- and red-chequered overalls identified her as Becky. Frizzy red hair stuffed beneath a red Big Boy baseball cap made her look like she had an enormous head. Poor thing. I felt sorry for her, to have to work here.

"I'm going to have the Big Boy double burger special with fries and a coke," Rick said.

"Would you like melted cheese on your fries?" Becky asked.

"Why not? It's Saturday," Rick said, smiling and looking directly into Becky's eyes.

Flustered and a little red-faced from the Rick's attention, Becky looked down at the display of her cash register and pushed more buttons.

Poor girl; I knew how she felt. He had the same effect on me when he looked directly into my eyes.

"Anything else for you?" Becky didn't look up. Rick looked over at me. Realising I was scared by the menu, he took the initiative of ordering for me.

"My friend here is going to have a Big Boy chilli burger combo with fries, melted cheese, and a strawberry milkshake."

Rick put his hand up as I opened my mouth to protest. Becky glanced from her screen and looked up at me, releasing a quiet gasp as she did so. I instantly became self-conscious of how bad I must have looked.

"Skateboarding accident. Lost complete control of his rig and ran right into a light post," Rick told Becky.

"Oh," was all Becky said before directing her attention back to her order screen.

*   *   *

WE SAT ACROSS THE TABLE FROM EACH OTHER SILENTLY eating our dinners. I couldn't believe I was actually enjoying the meal. I couldn't believe how much better I was starting to feel. Rick was right. It was the cure. But I wasn't about to let on that I was actually enjoying my Burger Boy experience.

"So you've had your fun making me wait. What happened last night?"

Rick looked up at me from across the table.

"Spill it, now!"

"What are you going to do if I don't? Beat me up?"

"I could probably take you on," I replied.

He looked amused.

"I mean, look what I managed to do that guy," I said, pointing to my reflection in wall mirror that bordered our table. "By the looks of him, he's probably sorry he decided to mess with me. I totally kicked his ass!"

"I'll tell you everything! Just please don't hurt me!" Rick responded with mock fear in his voice.

We stared at each other in the mirror, then burst out laughing at the same time.

"Dude, you crack me up," Rick said through his laughter.

As I wiped the tears from my face, I realised we were attracting the attention of the people seated at the adjoining tables. Funny, I really didn't care. Usually it bothered me being the centre of attention. I wasn't good at it. Tonight, sitting in Burger Boy, being stared at by teenagers and families with a black eye, I thought nothing of it.

"Time to spill, mister," I said, pointing at Rick.

"You want the long or the short version?"

"The short; I don't think I could take the pain of the long one," I groaned.

"Well, I do have to say, you are quite the entertainer."

I look at him, fear beginning to form in my stomach.

"Julie never mentioned you were a singer as well as a writer," he said.

Oh, God, here we go, I said to myself.

"You and Maria make quite a pair, with a bottle of tequila and a piano."

"How bad was it?" I asked as I looked down, dreading his response.

"Not so bad. You're okay on the piano, but you really, really should rethink the singing thing. Maria, on the other hand, has a voice like an angel."

I pictured it now. Maria and I, drunk, sitting at the piano in the main dining room of Joe's, entertaining ourselves more than the others.

"What was I trying to sing?"

"You guys did a combo of things; my favourite was the, um… Who originally did it?" He looked up with a finger to his cheek, pretending to search his memory. "Oh, *ya.* I think it was Donna Summer and Tina-something."

He paused.

"*Arena*! *Enough is Enough*," I filled in.

"That's it!" He looked at me with bright eyes.

"Please tell me no one else was in the restaurant," I pleaded.

"Well, there was also this old couple hanging at a table in the corner, but I think they were both hard of hearing 'cause they seemed to like the show."

He smirked. I could feel my face flushing.

"Jack, don't be embarrassed about letting go and having a good time. You're allowed. Everyone does it. You weren't hurting anyone."

"Except maybe my image," I responded, still feeling the flush in my cheeks.

"Image is only a projection of what oneself thinks of oneself."

"Deep," I said.

"My minor is in human behaviour." He took a sip of his soda.

"Okay, so what else? How did the bruises come to be? How did we get home?"

"Not much more to tell, really. Everyone just had a good time, hanging out, enjoying each other. Maria and Joe really care about you."

"And the bruises?" I asked again.

"That's kind of funny and embarrassing, I guess," he mumbled. "Joe had Carlos drive us home. Halfway there you told Carlos to stop the car; you were going to be sick. He started to slow down and pull to the side, but you decided you couldn't wait until the car had completely stopped, so you opened the door and fell out. By the time Carlos got the car stopped a few more feet ahead and we got out, you were already pulling yourself out of the ditch and back onto the road. Scraped, bleeding, and laughing."

"Oh God, tell me it's not true," I said with horror in my voice.

"Scout's honour," he said, raising his right hand and putting his left over his heart.

"I think I'm going to be sick." I covered my face with my hands.

"Dude, it's totally okay," he said as he pulled my hands away from my face, pinning them to the tabletop.

"No, it is not okay." I looked up. "I'm thirty-eight, not nineteen! And please stop calling me 'dude'. It's not appropriate."

He let go of my hands and slid his chair away from the table.

"Sorry," he quietly responded.

"I think we should go," I managed.

Rick nodded, and we made our way out into the night and to his Jeep. We drove back to the house in silence.

6

I STOOD WATCHING, THE RAIN COMING DOWN MORE HARSHLY *now, the Zodiac being tossed in the waves as it made its way back to shore.*

"Please God, please let it not be Stephen," I repeated to myself over and over.

Paramedics stood at the water's edge, waiting for the Zodiac to come to shore, and ready for any lifesaving measures. The rescue captain left my side, heading to join them. I stood numbly. Willing my legs to move. The Zodiac getting closer and closer.

*　　*　　*

I AWOKE WITH A START, SCREAMING, FLINGING MYSELF INTO A sitting position, unable to catch my breath. My skin was clammy with a cold sweat. I took in a few deep breaths and fell back into the softness of my bed, fully awake now. I turned and looked at the pre-dawn sky.

Why am I having the dream again? I wondered to myself silently.

I glanced over at the bedside clock: It said 5:35 a.m. I closed my eyes, willing myself back to sleep. After a few minutes of tossing I concluded that more sleep was never going to happen. I got up.

After flipping on the light in the bathroom, I relieved myself, brushed my teeth, and splashed cool water on my face. I dressed in my running gear and headed for the stairs. I noticed the door to Rick's room was firmly shut. I paused outside of it. Last night, he'd only mumbled a quiet goodnight to me as he went straight upstairs to his room. I was now just realising that I'd directed some of the anger I was feeling at myself, toward him. Guilt-ridden, I made my way down the stairs, deactivated the house alarm, and went outside to the beach.

* * *

WAS THAT A SCREAM, RICK ASKED HIMSELF AS HE OPENED ONE eye.

Alarmed, he flung the bedcovers off and made his way out into the hall. There was just enough light coming in from the skylight above to illuminate his way to Jack's bedroom door. After raising his arm to knock, he thought better of it and pressed his ear to the door to listen instead. He heard Jack breathing heavily, struggling for air. He was just about to open the door when he heard Jack sigh and flop around in the bed. He kept listening. He continued to make out more tossing and turning sounds, confirming that everything was okay, but he was unable to leave the spot where he stood.

He heard Jack get out of bed, footsteps padding toward the bathroom. The soft glow from the bathroom light spilled out from beneath the bedroom door. Rick quietly opened the door a crack and peered in. He could see Jack through the reflection of the mirror that was just inside the opened bathroom door. He watched Jack as he brushed his teeth and splashed water on his face, clad only in boxer briefs, his lean muscular body glowing beneath the overhead bathroom lighting. He felt the fabric of his shorts start to strain, as blood rushed down making him instantly hard.

Man, he is hot, he said silently to himself. He watched

as Jack came out of the bathroom, flipping the light switch on in his walk-in closet. Not being able to see from his vantage point, Rick heard Jack rummage around. Assuming Jack was dressing, Rick quietly returned to his room. He stood listening at his closed door, gently stroking himself through the fabric of his shorts. Rick heard Jack's bedroom door open, and then heard his footsteps on the hall floor.

Excitement building, he released his hard-on from the fabric of his shorts and started to stroke himself full on. He heard Jack's footsteps stop, just outside his door. Rick immediately stopped stroking himself, and held his breath. After a brief pause he heard Jack bound downstairs. He opened the door a crack and heard the beeping of the alarm panel by the sliding doors. He went across the hall into Jack's room, making his way over to the windows that looked out towards the beach and ocean. Looking down he saw Jack at the bottom of the stairs that led up to the back deck, stretching the muscles of each leg. Rick's cock started screaming for attention as he watched Jack turn and start his run down the beach.

Releasing his raging hard-on from his shorts once again, he made his way to Jack's bed. He lay down on the unmade side, feeling the warmth of the sheets. He turned and buried his face into Jack's pillow. Pulling his shorts down to his knees, he increased the rhythm of his hand as he stroked the entire length of his shaft. He imagined Jack was there with him, straddling his hips, their two cocks lying together. He fantasised about kissing him, running his tongue along his full lips before parting them, his tongue entering, exploring the inside of Jack's mouth with feverish desire, Jack softly moaning.

Jack leans over, kissing Rick's neck softly, his tongue leading the way to his chest. Rick's body quivers with excitement as Jack runs his tongue over each of his nipples, gently sucking and biting each one before continuing toward his abdomen. Jack's hand is now on Rick's cock, gently stroking it as he kisses the inside of his thighs. He runs his tongue around the base of his hard-on. Rick tangles his hands in Jack's hair, guiding his mouth closer. Jack resists, flicking his tongue teasingly at his balls. A moan escapes Rick's lips, and he shivers as Jack's tongue makes its way from the base of his shaft to the head. His tongue surrounds the head, flicking it gently, taking it in, sucking it with delight. Rick looks down as Jack opens his mouth, taking in the entire length of his shaft, his mouth and tongue expertly sucking and licking as he makes his way towards the base. Rick grabs Jack's hair tighter, pulling at it as Jack continually goes up and down on him. Rick's hips lift off the bed, meeting Jack's hungry mouth. Rick feels his orgasm building, his muscles tense and twitch. Jack increases the rhythm of his sucking. Rick now has both hands entangled in his hair pushing him harder and faster up and down the length of his shaft. The warmth of Jack's mouth drives him to frenzy. Rick cries out as his orgasm releases. Jack's mouth takes in the intensity of it.

Rick opens his eyes, spent he pulls up his shorts and leaves Jack's room.

* * *

I STOPPED AT THE BOTTOM OF THE STAIRS THAT LED UP TO THE back deck of my house. I stretched my legs out, feeling the burn. Looking down at the pedometer attached to my runners, I calculated that I ran fifteen miles. Five more than my Standard Ten. I wiped the sweat from my brow as I caught my breath and made my way up the stairs.

"Ouch!" I said as my muscles protested again the sudden incline. I kicked off my sandy runners and sweaty socks at the top of the stairs and towelled off the sweat with the towel I had left on the railing.

The smell of freshly brewed coffee grabbed my senses as I opened the sliding doors and went into the house. I looked around and determined I was alone. I padded across the kitchen in my bare feet, making my way to the fridge. I took out a bottle of water and downed it within seconds. My heart was still beating rapidly. I took out a second bottle and sipped this one more slowly. I looked over at the clock on the oven: it said 7:30 a.m.

"Hour and a half. Not bad time for fifteen miles," I said to myself.

I poured myself a cup of coffee. Leaving it on the island, I went out the front door and retrieved the Sunday morning edition of *The L.A. Times*. I noticed Rick's Jeep still parked in the driveway next to my car. I took the paper in, placing it on the island next to my coffee and made myself comfortable on the barstool.

"How's the coffee?"

I jumped, spilling coffee down the front of my shirt and onto the paper. I turned around to see Rick at the bottom of the stairs, dressed in a white t-shirt and cargo pants, with a mailbag-type knapsack slung over his shoulder.

"Geez! You scared me. I didn't hear you come down," I said as I reached for the dishcloth and started wiping up my mess.

"Sorry." He started to move towards the island.

"It's perfect. The coffee, I mean. Thank you for making it. Aren't you up a little early for a Sunday morning?"

"I'm meeting with my teaching group on campus," he said as he dropped his bag on the floor and poured himself a cup of coffee. "Class starts tomorrow, and I need to be really well prepared. Do you have sugar?"

"Second shelf in the pantry." I gestured with the hand that held my cup.

Rick finished fixing his coffee and leant against the counter opposite me, not saying anything, just sipping quietly.

"Do you want breakfast before you leave?"

"Nah, I can get something on the way," he responded with aloofness.

"Rick." I paused and looked down. "I'm really sorry that I snapped at you last night. I was a jerk. I took out the anger I was feeling at myself on you. Forgive me? Can we be friends again?"

"More like an asshole."

"What?"

"You were more of an asshole, than a jerk. And 'cause we are friends I can say that to you." A smile was creeping at the corners of his mouth.

"Okay, I was an asshole. Forgive me?"

"All right, bro. But du– *Jack,* you really need to lighten up. You take yourself way too seriously." He sat next to me. "Julie was right. You need more fun in your life."

"And what else has my lovely sister been saying about me?"

"Nothing, except the obvious."

"And what is the obvious?" I picked up my coffee and took a sip.

"You're very successful, attractive, hard worker, etcetera, but lacking in the fun department. You going to make me breakfast now?" he asked.

"Nice try at changing the subject." I turned my chair towards him.

"I'm starving! And I'm really interested to see what you're going to come up with from what's inside that fridge of yours."

I opened the fridge, taking out eggs, bacon, peppers, mushrooms, and cheese. I quickly placed the bacon on a baking grill and put it in the oven. Then I chopped, combined, and finally poured my mixture into the preheated skillet on the stove, covering it with a lid. While I was doing that, Rick was reading the paper and enjoying his coffee.

I walked over to the built-in desk and retrieved a notepad and pen.

"Here. Write down the foods you like. I'm going to go shopping later," I said as I dropped the pad and pen next to him.

"Ah, gee, Mom, anything I want? Really?"

"Skating on thin ice, mister," I replied with a glance at him over my shoulder. I took out two plates and two glasses for organic orange juice, then, I fixed our plates.

"Breakfast is served," I announced as I put our plates on the counter and sat next to him.

"Smells awesome. What is it?" he asked as he was chewing his first bite.

"Frittata. Well, my version of a frittata. I'm famous for it."

"I may have to take the chick food comment back." He smiled at me.

We ate the rest of our breakfast in silence; me reading the paper, him writing out his grocery list. When we were done, Rick picked up the dishes and put them in the sink.

He refilled both our coffees before he sat back down.

"Here it is. All done," he announced.

I scanned the items he listed. Top of the list: steak— so surprising— and burgers, various fruits, mac & cheese— yuk— various snack foods, and Captain Crunch.

"I am not buying you Captain Crunch!" I exclaimed.

"But it's my favourite. *Please*."

"Not in a million years. Might as well just add milk to a bowl of sugar and eat that," I said.

He smirked. "Got ya. You are so easy."

I smiled. "And you're a little bastard."

Fake shock registered on his face. Staring at each other, we both started to laugh.

"Shit. I'm going to be late," he said as he caught a

glimpse of the time on the oven clock. Jumping from his chair, he grabbed his bag from the floor. "I'm supposed to be on campus at nine."

"You can make UCLA in about thirty minutes if you push it. Sunday morning traffic is always light," I said, as I trailed behind him to the front door.

Opening the door he paused, turned toward me, and hugged me. "I'll see you around six."

I stood there stunned as he left.

What was that about, I asked myself as I returned to the kitchen. I cleaned up our breakfast dishes, then headed upstairs to get ready for the day. Passing Rick's room, I glanced in and noticed that today there weren't clothes strewn about. But he had left his bed unmade. Fighting the urge to make it, I gently closed the door, not wanting to invade his space. As I showered I was careful not to scrub the scabs that formed over my cuts. I dried my hair and peered in the mirror at my black eye. It was nasty.

I pulled out the 'movie magic' bag given to me by Cindy, one of the make-up artists on the show. She gave it to me after I had a severe acne breakout, right before one of the award shows I was required to attend.

"If I can make a washed-up, fifty-year-old starlet look thirty-something with the contents of this here bag, then I guarantee it will hide anything that may appear on your face, Jack," she'd told me in her Southern drawl. She sat me in her chair and proceeded to apply the make-up expertly to my face. When she was finished, I could not see the acne breakout at all, and it didn't look like I was wearing make-up either. I hugged her with gratitude for the amazing job she did. She gave me the "magic bag" along with pointers on how to use the products inside.

Now, I fished out the tubes of product I thought I would need to hide my black eye. I applied three layers of different tubes to the blackened area of my eye. When I finished, I couldn't see the blackness of the eye at all. It looked exactly like the normal colour of my skin. The only thing noticeable was that it was slightly puffy, from the swelling.

Good enough to go out in public again, I told myself as I headed to the closet to get dressed. I chose a light-weight pair of jeans and a white t-shirt. Then, I slid into a pair of leather flip-flops and put the silver cross I bought in Spain last year around my neck.

As I made the bed, I noticed the voicemail light on the bedside phone screaming at me for attention. Reluctantly I sat on the bed, dialling the voicemail access number, turning on the speakerphone, to listen to yesterday's messages.

"You have six new messages," the robotic voicemail lady told me.

Wow, when did I become popular again?

First new message: *Hey Jack, its Rick. Calling to check on you. You okay? Call me on my cell.*

Second new message: *Jack, Rick again. Hope you're doing okay; man, you really did a number last night. Be home around six; see you then.*

Third new message: *Jack darling, it's your lovely sister. Call me.*

Fourth new message: *Hi Jackie, its Maria. Just calling to see how you are feeling. We sure did it up last night, didn't we? Anyway Carlos told me of the little detour you took on your way home. Let me know if you need anything.*

Fifth new message: *Hello, Jack. Vivian. Call me, we need to talk. I'm trying you on your cell as well.*

Last new message: *Jackie bear. It's Julie again, are you still mad at me about yesterday? Please forgive me. Anyway Max and I are headed to New York for a couple of days. I'll call you when we get back. Love you.* End of new messages.

I erased them all.

I picked up the handset and dialled Vivian's cell. After

three rings my call went to voicemail.

"Hello, you have reached the personal and confidential voicemail of Vivian Wentworth. I apologise I missed your call. Please leave your details and I will return your call at my earliest convenience, *ciao*. Remember to wait for the beep, darlings."

Even her voicemail message sounds seductive, I thought as I waited for the beep.

"Hey, Viv. It's Jack calling you back. Try me again when you have a second."

I hung up and then dialled her home number.

"Hi, you have reached the Wentworth's…"

I hung up before the beep, not leaving a message since Vivian was usually glued to her cell phone, checking her messages often.

Why is Vivian calling? As producer of the show, she was off on summer hiatus as well. It was unusual for her to contact members of the show during hiatus. Puzzled, I looked at the bedside clock: 10 a.m.

* * *

WHAT WAS THAT ABOUT, RICK ASKED HIMSELF AS HE DROVE from the house. *Why did I hug Jack? What did he think?* He looked a little shocked. I was a little shocked too. *Why was I compelled to do it? Why after only two days of being with him is he all I can think about? What's going on with me? I haven't had feelings for a guy since high school. Why now? Why him?*

Almost missing the exit for the freeway, Rick cranked hard on the wheel, the tires of the Jeep screaming in protest. Rick turned his attention from Jack to merging onto the freeway. Jack was right; Traffic was light on a Sunday morning. Rick looked at his watch: 8:40 a.m. He hit the accelerator. Flying down the 405, concentrating on the road, he kept his thoughts from wandering back to Jack.

*   *   *

PULLING INTO THE PARKING LOT OF THE HERMOSA BEACH community food store, I found a parking space with ease. This was my favourite time to grocery shop, because the store was quiet on Sunday mornings. I grabbed a cart. Forty-five minutes later, I was loading my purchases into the trunk of my car.

"Jack!"

I looked up.

"Jack!"

I saw Sheila and her fiancé, Michael, walking towards me from across the parking lot.

"Jack! Jack!" Sheila exclaimed as she ran into me, hugging me tightly. "I thought you might turn and bolt if I didn't get to you quick enough!"

Ouch, I thought. Sheila had made several attempts to contact me throughout the year, and like Maria and Joe, I ignored her attempts, too.

"Hello, Michael." I directed my attention to Sheila's fiancé, extending my hand.

"I think we're beyond that, Jack." He slapped my outstretched arm to the side and grabbed me into a strong embrace. "We've missed you so much. I knew if I kept the faith our paths would cross, and I could back you into a corner before you disappeared."

Double ouch!

Standing there in the parking lot, under the mid-morning sun, looking over at Sheila and Michael, my eyes began to fill with tears. The realisation of how much I hurt the people around me came crashing down on me once again. It was becoming apparent that I was so wrapped up in my own grief that I couldn't see how my actions affected the other people in my life.

"Sheila, Michael," I started, thanking God they couldn't see my tear-filled eyes behind my sunglasses. "I really owe you both a huge apolo—"

"Don't," Sheila said, squeezing my arm. "Do not apologise. You did what you needed to do to get through a very difficult time in your life. I understand that and cannot judge your actions, because I don't know what I would have done under the same circumstances. We're just really glad to see you again."

More tears filled my eyes and spilled down my cheeks. I grabbed Sheila into a hug. "Why don't you come to dinner tonight?" I asked them on impulse when I released Sheila, wiping my tear-stained cheeks.

"Tonight?" Sheila looked over at Michael. "Honey?"

Michael paused for a moment, before saying, "We'd love to!"

"Great! How about six-thirtyish?" I asked.

"Perfect. We'll bring the wine and dessert," Sheila said.

We all hugged once more and said goodbye. I stood watching them until they disappeared into the grocery store. I got into my car, took off my sunglasses, and looked into the rear-view mirror, analysing the damage my tears may have caused to my made-up eye.

"Not too bad," I said to myself.

Most of the bruising was still covered up. Praising Cindy and her little bag of magic once again, I turned the key to start the car just as my cell phone shrilled.

I looked at the caller ID. *Vivian W,* it read.

"Hello," I said into the phone.

"Jack, darling, how are you?" Vivian purred.

"Hey, Viv, great. What's up?"

"Why do you think something is up?"

"'Cause I just saw you two days ago, and you made it a policy that during hiatus, you separate yourself from the show completely. I never hear from you during that time," I replied.

"Oh, darling you do know my habits. So, I will get right to the point. The network wants to have a meeting immediately regarding the show."

"During hiatus? Isn't that a little unusual?"

"Well, yes it is. This is the first for me. Anyway, they want all the department heads to attend."

"When?"

"I think they want to schedule for next week. I need to let them know as soon as I finish tracking everyone down."

"Who are you missing?"

"Well, you. And I am just waiting for a call back from Daniel," she replied.

"Wasn't Daniel heading to Spain for the summer?" I asked. The show's director liked to vacation overseas.

"He is, but I don't think he's leaving until next week sometime. Do you know how I can track him down?"

"You are asking the wrong person, darling," I said dryly. "You as well as anyone knows that Daniel and I aren't exactly the best of friends."

"I know. I was hoping you heard something in passing."

"No idea. What's the meeting about, really?" I asked again.

"Not a clue. My guess is they want us to revamp the look of the show for the fall, a little facelift maybe? The network took a lot of heat since Ashley's run-in with the law last month. It wouldn't surprise me if they want her written out of the show."

She was talking about Ashley Sinclair, the lead teen on the show. During the last year she'd brought a tremendous amount of unwelcome attention to the show for making a spectacle out of herself, and not in a good way.

"Seems probable. Should I start rewriting the fall scripts?" I asked.

"Let's not get too ahead of ourselves. Let's wait to see what they have in mind— although, if what I suspect is right, we can all kiss our summer goodbye."

I groaned. Everyone involved with the show looked forward to the summer hiatus, especially after working a twelve-hour day through the season.

"I'll call you when I have a time firmed up. Don't leave town."

With that, she clicked off the line.

Great. Just what I needed: to rework the fall scripts.

The first five episodes had already been completed and approved, the shooting schedule all set to start mid-August. I was not going to be very popular if I had to call the writing team back in.

I took a deep breath as I put the car in gear, deciding not to think about it until absolutely necessary. I turned right towards downtown and the pier. I had a couple more stops to make since I was having guests for dinner. Another unexpected, but welcome surprise.

7

"EARTH TO RICK; COME IN, RICK."

"What?"

"Where are you, dude?"

Rick looked up, and everyone was staring at him. John, Brittney, Linda, and Freddy. His study group. They were the lucky five chosen for the internship at UCLA that thousands of students applied for. They were all now staring at Rick.

"What?"

"We've been waiting for your response to John's question for, like, ever," Brittney said, rolling her eyes.

"Sorry. What was the question?"

They all looked at Rick and rolled their eyes.

"Dude, you have been totally zoned out all day. What gives?" John asked.

"Nothing. Sorry guys. I guess I'm having trouble concentrating today. What was the question?"

"Oooooo. I bet he is having lady troubles," Freddy chirped in.

Rick wanted to smash Freddy's face into the table. He was a little weasel, acting like he was better than everyone else in the group. Like he was doing everyone a favour by gracing them with his presence.

"Is it? Is it *lady* trouble?" Freddy asked again. "Is it? Is it? Is it?"

"Drop it, Fred." Rick shot him his best "do-not-fuck-with-me" look.

"Touched a nerve; must be true. Pretty boy Rick got girl trouble. Ain't that a shame?"

Rick stood up, grabbed him by his shirt, and lifted him slightly out of his seat. "I said, drop it."

John jumped to his feet. Rick could feel John's grip closing around his forearm.

"Dude, put him down, now. He didn't mean anything by it," John said.

Rick looked down at John's arm. John could give him a run for his money if they were ever pitted against each other. John was tall, slightly shorter than Rick's six-foot-two-inch frame, and muscular. He was Iowa's amateur wrestling champion.

Rick met John last year while taking an advanced English lit class at Washington State, back home in Seattle. They became instant friends and hung out the entire summer whenever they weren't in class.

"Dude. Drop him!" John's grip was tightening on Rick's arm.

Rick released his grip, dropping Freddy back into his chair with a small thud.

"Oh my, I'm afraid all this testosterone in the air is going to make my hair frizzy," Brittney said in a fake Southern accent, fanning herself with her hand. "My, my, you boys sure do know how to impress a lady. Wouldn't you agree, Linda?"

Brittney looked over at Linda. The two women were as different as night and day. Brittney petite, blonde and blue eyed, and was dressed in a halter-top and a short skirt. Linda looked bookish, with mousey brown hair scraped back into a ponytail, ill-fitting, oversized clothes, and glasses. Linda was by far the smartest one of the group. She had completed her degree at Brown University, completely funded by scholarships. Her grades had never fallen below a

4.0. She was also in the summer class last year at Washington State with John and Rick.

Linda was looking down at her book, embarrassed by the scene in front of her. Rick now looked around the study hall and realised everyone that was previously engaged in their studies was now staring at their table.

"I think we're done for today," John announced as he shoved Rick's books against his chest. "Let's go, Rick."

"That's it? Just like that, we're done? Who made you the boss?" Brittney stood up.

"It's been a long day, and our internship starts tomorrow morning. We're ready, and besides, we're going to be together non-stop for the next six weeks. I think we can all use a night off."

"I just don't see why you get to make that decision, John. You're not God, you know," Brittney responded curtly.

"Why are you here even studying with us, Brittney? Huh? By the looks of things, you most likely slept your way into this programme, so why study when you can just go and put out?"

Jackie sat in a huff. Freddy snorted. Was that a smile Rick saw creeping at the corners of Linda's mouth?

"Let's jet, Rick." John shoved Rick towards the door.

* * *

"WHAT'S UP WITH YOU, MAN?" JOHN ASKED RICK WHEN THEY got outside and started towards the parking lot. "I haven't seen you since last summer, you bail on me last night, and now today you are totally somewhere else. What gives?"

The fact that he was thinking about Jack all day frightened Rick. He couldn't confide in John that he was daydreaming about his step-mom's brother, even though they had a pretty tight relationship.

"I think I'm just a little on edge. The internship is kinda freaking me out a little."

"Liar," John said. "Nothing about school freaks you out. You're a natural student, always calm. Remember, it was me you were talking down off ledges last summer when school was super intense— not me talking you down."

Damn it, Rick thought as they continued walking. Rick spotted his Jeep two rows down as they crossed into the parking lot.

"Well?" John questioned.

"Well," Rick said. "The truth is, it was a pretty intense time at my dad's last week. You know how he detests the idea of me becoming a teacher. We hashed it out over and over while I was there. He would do anything for me to drop this internship and head to law school. I guess it's still with me a little," Rick lied.

"Your dad needs to go fuck himself!" John spat.

This took Rick by surprise, since John had the utmost respect for parents and authority figures.

"*Ya.* You're right. He needs to go fuck himself," Rick agreed as they arrived at his Jeep.

"What we going to do now, bro?" John asked.

Rick looked at his watch; it was nearly five. He wanted to rush back to the beach and hang out with Jack, but he also needed to spend time with John. Rick had heard the hurt in John's voice when he said he bailed on him last night.

"I noticed a bar just off campus. Let's grab a beer and maybe shoot some pool?"

John's face lighted up at the mention of beer and pool.

"I'll take that as a *yes*." Rick laughed.

* * *

THE CLOCK ON THE OVEN SAID IT WAS 3:30 P.M. AS I PUT THE last of my packages on the island. The day had got away from me while I was shopping. Also, I'd stopped in to see Maria, who was working at the restaurant, in the office, even though it was technically closed.

"Jackie, come, sit with me," she'd called from the office door.

Time got away from both of us as we chatted and caught up on a year's worth of each other's lives. At last, we said our good-byes in the back parking lot and she made me promise I would see her again on Friday.

Now, as I was starting dinner, it dawned on me that this was the first time I was having dinner guests since Stephen's accident. My first dinner party without him.

I started to weep. My breath became short, fast, and more laborious. I felt dizzy. I sat on one of the stools that flanked the island, taking deep breaths trying to calm myself.

Looking around the kitchen, memories of Stephen came flooding into my mind: The two of us, preparing dinner. Stephen making me laugh as he acted out his 'joke of the day' using whatever food that was within his grasp as a prop. Both of us sharing stories from our respective days. Him interrupting my work and making me dance with him in the kitchen whenever the CD player changed to one of his favourite songs. Him hugging me from behind, kissing my neck as I chopped vegetables.

Tears streamed down my face as I stifled sobs. My mind's eye was reliving his touch, his smell, his presence. I started concentrating on my breathing, closing my eyes and calming myself.

Breathe in, breathe out, I could hear the calming voice of my Yoga instructor in my mind. *Breathe in; breathe out. Breathe in; breathe out.*

My breathing started to slow, the panic I felt started to

dissipate. Feeling stronger and less dizzy, I opened my eyes and wiped away my last tears. I made my way to the sink and splashed cold water on my face and neck. My whole body felt sticky and clammy from my panic attack. The water was cool on my skin.

The doorbell chimed just as I was on the last step coming down from upstairs. *Perfect timing,* I thought as I made my way to the front door, running my hands through my still damp hair. Sheila and Michael were at the front door.

* * *

"DUDE, I AM SO KICKING YOUR ASS," JOHN SAID, SMILING AS he sunk another ball, and then making his way to the other side of the table to line up another shot. "Six in the side pocket! Slam! Another one in; next shot is the money shot!"

Rick watched as he considered his next move, deciding which angle to shoot the eight ball from.

"Eight ball back corner pocket," John said. He traced his shot in the air with his pool cue, making it clear he was banking the ball off the side bank, and then back to the corner pocket. He squinted as he lined up his cue with the ball, then took the shot. The ball dropped into the pocket with just enough force to slam against the other balls below.

"Winner! Yah! In your face, Stevenson," John exclaimed as he jumped up, punching the air with his fist. Rick high-fived him.

"Rematch?" he asked.

"Dude, you've kicked my ass three times already. I'd say I'm done. I don't think my ass can take anymore," Rick said as he rubbed his butt.

They laughed, grabbed their beers, and made their way back to their table.

*   *   *

"WHO'S THE FOURTH?" SHELIA ASKED, REFERRING TO THE place settings on the dining room table.

I looked up from pouring the wine.

"For Rick," I replied.

"Rick?"

"Sorry. I guess I didn't tell you earlier. Rick is my sister, Julie's, stepson," I said as I handed her one of the glasses of wine.

"What did I miss? Who is Rick?" Michael asked as he made his way into the kitchen from the bathroom.

"Rick is Julie's stepson, Max's son," I said, handing him a glass, too. "He's staying with me for the summer while he completes an internship at UCLA."

"Why haven't I heard about this Rick before?" Michael asked, as he sat next to Shelia on one of the bar stools.

"He lives in Seattle with his mom, Max's first wife. Rick and Max don't get along really all that well," I said.

"Who does get along with Max? The man is an arrogant asshole," Michael said.

"Michael!" Shelia shot him a look.

It had slipped my mind that both Shelia and Michael had the pleasure of meeting Max once, during a visit to my house.

"He's right. Max is an arrogant asshole," I said. "Actually, he's a self-absorbed, arrogant asshole, to be exact," I said, smiling at both of them.

"Cheers! To arrogant assholes!" Michael held up his glass.

*   *   *

"HE SEEMS GOOD. LIKE HE IS STARTING TO MOVE ON," SHEILA said from the passenger seat.

"Are you kidding me?" Michael glanced over at Sheila. "He's still hasn't dealt with Stephen's death. I think he just buried the pain, keeping it out of sight."

"No. I saw definite signs of progress. And happiness, like the old Jack I know and love."

"Honey, you're kidding yourself if you think that; he's far from the *old Jack* we know and love."

"How can you say that? You can't deny he was happy tonight."

"I think he was happy tonight…"

"So you agree with me?"

"No. No, I don't."

"You're confusing me. Was he happy or not?"

"Not."

Sheila crossed her arms and looked out the side window, starting to get pissed.

Michael turned onto the Pacific Highway North, towards Manhattan Beach.

"Look, I'm not saying he wasn't happy." He paused for a moment. "What I am saying is that he's not happy like he was when Stephen was alive."

"Well, I think he's happier, compared to the last time I saw him," Sheila said.

"Of course he's happier since the last time you saw him. When was that?"

"I'm not sure?" Sheila stammered a little.

"I'll tell you exactly when it was. It was two weeks after Stephens's funeral, when we moved the office out of the lower level of his house. And yes, I will agree with you that he was infinitely happier tonight than he was that day, but still not the *old* Jack. Do you know he has the lower level rooms sealed off?"

"Really?"

"The lower level that used to be Stephen and your design offices. They're sealed off. There's a huge armoire in front of the door. Visually, you would never know there was anything behind it."

"How do you know?" Sheila stared at his profile as he watched the road ahead.

"I went down there when I went to the washroom."

"Michael!"

"I wasn't snooping; I just wanted to see around the house once again. I was curious as to what he did with the lower level after he made you move out so quickly. And you know another thing that is weird? There are no pictures anymore."

"What do you mean?" Sheila asked.

"Didn't you notice? There wasn't one picture of him and Stephen in the house, anywhere. Remember before Stephen's accident? There were pictures of the two of them in every room of that house."

"Yes, I do remember all the photos, but I didn't notice them missing tonight."

"In the main room of the house, he's filled the space with sculptures and pieces of art, so it looks like nothing is missing. I had to take a second look after I went into the den and saw the picture wall missing."

"You mean the wall between the den and Jack's office?"

"*Ya*, that one. It used to be filled with framed photos, almost floor to ceiling. They are all gone."

"Stephen used to call that wall their 'life in pictures' wall," Sheila remembered. "Anyone looking at it could see how much they loved each other. Stephen used to say that he was going to have to cover up either the door to the den or Jack's office to make more space for that wall."

Michael signalled right and took the off-ramp into Manhattan Beach.

"How could he take down the wall?" Sheila mused.

"It's like he erased Stephen from his life. No pictures, no memory, and another thing, we never once talked about Stephen tonight."

"I don't think he's done that, Michael."

"Think about it, hon. No pictures in the house; we haven't seen him in a year. Don't you think it's weird that today was the first time we ran into him after all that time?"

Michael turned the car onto their street and pulled into their driveway. He turned the car off then turned in his seat to face Sheila. "It's like he purposely avoided places he might see us. How many times throughout the last year did you try to contact him? A dozen? More? He never returned one call. And what about their other friends? I suspect he hasn't seen them, either. Where has he been for the last year? What has he been doing? It looks to me like he erased anything that, and anybody who, was a reminder of Stephen, to avoid dealing with the pain of losing him."

"Who are we to judge, Michael? Everyone has a different grieving process. I don't know what I would do if I ever lost you."

"I would hope you would lean on your friends and let them help you through the grieving process. Not bury it and hide yourself away," Michael said.

"You are such a chick, Michael," Sheila said, to lighten the mood. "No other guy I know— let me rephrase that— no other *straight* guy I know would have noticed, or picked up on what was happening with Jack. Hell, *I* missed half of it, and I am a chick!"

Sheila laughed and continued, "I definitely think you are the chick in this relationship. Do you want to wear the dress next week?"

Michael grabbed her hand, placed it on his crotch, and leant close to her face. "Does this feel like a part that belongs to a chick?"

She stopped laughing.

"Believe me, if anything ever happens to me, you will need all the support you can get from your friends. It's going to be a long life without sex after you take that vow of chastity," he said.

Shelia laughed.

* * *

THE OVEN CLOCK READ 10:30 P.M. AS I FINISHED UP CLEANING the kitchen and started the dishwasher.

"What a great evening, Jack," I said to myself. I took a sip of wine. I couldn't remember the last time I had such a great time, with the exception of Friday night at Joe's. It was so fun catching up with Shelia and Michael. I had promised to attend their wedding next weekend, so I needed to buy a gift.

I wondered what had happened to Rick tonight. He said he would be home at six when he left this morning, and all I got was his voicemail when I tried to call him earlier in the evening. I was looking forward to spending more time with him and having him meet Sheila and Michael.

He was really growing on me.

I took another sip of wine and made my way through the main floor of the house, blowing out candles and turning off lights.

He probably got stuck with his study group, I thought. It would have been nice if he'd called. But he didn't need to check in with me. When I was twenty-three, I never checked in with anyone.

Setting the alarm and leaving the front hall light on, I carried the remainder of my wine and made my way upstairs to soak in the tub, hoping to sooth the dull throbbing pain that was still resonating in my leg and arm.

* * *

11:30 P.M.

"Fuck," Rick said, as he pulled away from John's dorm, toward Hermosa Beach. He couldn't believe it was this late. He hadn't expected to be out all night, but one game of pool and a beer led to several, and John was in a surprisingly talkative mood, and the night flew by. He really wanted to spend the night hanging out with Jack. He should have answered his call earlier instead of letting it go to voicemail, but he didn't want John to ask any questions. He hoped Jack would still be awake when he got home.

* * *

THE HOT WATER INSTANTLY CALMED MY ACHING BODY, stimulating my senses and relaxing my soul. I sank down deeper into the tub, stretching out in the water. The soft glow of candle light complemented the night sky, which was visible through the skylight above. Staring off into the universe, I counted stars, my thoughts drifting towards Rick.

Tall, handsome, beautiful Rick.

I felt myself getting hard at the thought of him. His muscular, well-toned tanned body. I closed my eyes and reached down and started stroking my growing hard-on. I imagined touching him, running my hands along his naked body. He is kissing me now, it starts of soft, but the intensity of the kiss grows. I can feel the feverish desire and hunger he has for me. My body trembles at his touch, betraying me, exposing my lust for him. I can feel the excitement building within me as we explore each others bodies with our hands and mouths. Passion creates beads of sweat, covering our bodies. We move in unison with each other, our breath rapid and short. A desire-filled moan escapes my lips as I release my orgasm, and he, his.

I opened my eyes, my breath still rapid and short as I brought my awareness back to the bathroom. I ran my hands through my hair and looked back at the sky.

Riddled with guilt, I pulled myself up and out of the tub, engaging the water release lever. I dried off, wrapped myself in a towel, and made my way to the vanity. Wiping the steam off the mirror, I stared at myself. The dim light of the candlelit room cast a shadow on my reflection.

Tears formed in my eyes, blurring my vision, making it even harder to see myself. I wiped them away. I searched my reflection for answers to the guilt I felt.

"Why?" I asked, half expecting my reflection to answer me. "Is it because I fantasised about Rick? Twenty-three-year-old, sort-of-my-relative Rick? Is that it?"

My head started to pound.

"Or is it because I am feeling unfaithful to Stephen?"

I hadn't even thought of another man sexually, fantasy or otherwise, since before Stephen. Nausea suddenly overcame me. I covered my mouth with my hand and rushed to the toilet. Kneeling, I empted the contents of my stomach into the basin, tears streaming down my face. I closed the lid and pulled the release lever. I lay down on the tiled floor, pulling my knees to my chest; I stayed there, rocking and sobbing uncontrollably.

*   *   *

THE CLOCK IN THE JEEP READ 12:03 A.M. AS RICK PULLED into the driveway next to Jack's BMW. Excitement gripped him at the thought of seeing Jack. He let himself in with his key and silenced the beeping alarm panel. Taking a few more steps into the house, Rick realised the main floor was completely silent and dark, except for the glow from the front hall light. Disappointed and mad at himself for staying out so late, he reactivated the alarm system and then went upstairs. He paused at the door to Jack's bedroom as he passed, straining to hear any noise. But no, Jack didn't seem to be awake. He headed off to bed.

8

I WATCHED AS THE PARAMEDICS RUSHED TO THE ZODIAC AS IT *ran up onto the beach. It was raining harder now. The rescue captain ran towards the Zodiac, joining his team of rescuers, eager to help. I put one foot in front of the other, slowly making my way towards the activity. Everything was moving in slow motion. It was taking forever to reach the others, like I was wading through quicksand.*

As I made my way to the water's edge, I watched as the rescue team lifted someone out of the Zodiac and placed them on a stretcher. Someone was shouting, giving orders. I couldn't see through the circle they formed around the stretcher; they blocked my view. The captain turned and started toward me, but I still couldn't see past the rescuers. I didn't stop; I kept moving towards the rescuers. The captain was saying something to me, "Stay back!" He grabbed me by the shoulders, stopping me from moving forward.

"You must stay back, Mr. Perry. Let my team do their job."

"Who is it? Is it Stephen?" I barely recognised my own voice. "Is it?"

He looked away, then back at me. "I don't know."

I pushed past him, rushing towards the circle.

He grabbed me from behind, holding me back. "Let my team do their job. We need to stand back and let them do their job."

He was strong. I couldn't move forward. I just stood, helpless and staring.

* * *

I WOKE SUDDENLY, DISORIENTED AND CRYING. MY EYES adjusted to the darkness, as I made out the bathtub, its white porcelain shimmering in the moonlight. I'd cried myself to sleep on my bathroom floor. I picked myself up and made my way through the moonlit bathroom and out into my bedroom. Still wrapped in my bath sheet, I flung myself onto my bed and was instantly asleep.

* * *

AT AROUND 6 A.M., I WOKE. NORMALLY, THE SKY OVER THE sea was cloudy in the morning. It was as if the clouds always met to spend the night over the water. But today, Monday in early July, the sky was already clear and promising.

Groggy, I closed my eyes, hoping to go back to sleep.

"Jack, you're on holiday. Sleep in."

This was what I told myself, but the internal clock in my body refused to let me rest. I jumped up, noticing that I never made it beneath the covers last night. On my way to the bathroom, I stopped to open the window, letting the freshness of the early morning rush into the room. Hanging my head outside, I inhaled the clear warm air, filling my lungs. I did this for a few more breaths before continuing to the bathroom.

I dressed and went downstairs to make my coffee. Passing by the door to Rick's room I noticed from looking down at the space between the door and floor that his room was dark. I wondered whether I should wake him, in case he was oversleeping. Or was I just using that as an excuse to open the door and watch him sleep? I had to leave him alone. Assuring myself that he was responsible enough to get himself up, I continued past his room, set on my original intent of having coffee on the deck.

* * *

"GOOD MORNING, L.A.! WE'RE ALREADY AT A BALMY EIGHTY degrees and heading for a high of one hundred. All you surfers out there, grab your boards and hit the waves. It is going to be a perfect surf day."

Rick rolled over and hit the snooze button on the bedside clock, through blurry eyes he made out 7 a.m. in bold green numbers on the clock. He was tired from tossing and turning for most of the night.

Fuck! Why can't I get him out of my head, he asked himself as he pushed the palms of his hands into his eyes.

The radio blared. "And now we are going to go to Danni for this morning's edition of celebrity sleaze. Big news in Hollywood this morning, everyone. Ashley Sinclair, one of the stars of the hit TV drama *Chamberlain Heights,* was arrested last night for driving under the influence of alcohol. Police arrested the seventeen-year-old star after a brief chase through the Hollywood hills, after Ashley's car slammed into a parked SUV. Ashley was unharmed, but police reported that both of the two passengers in Ashley's vehicle were rushed to hospital; the severity of their injuries is not known at this time."

Rick snapped his eyes open and listened.

"Miss Sinclair was released into her parents' custody early this morning, and has not commented at this time."

A new voice came over the airwaves; Rick recognised it as the one which reported the weather. "Now, Danni, let me get this straight. We have a drunk starlet who slams her car into a parked car, injuring two of her friends, and all that happened was she was released into her parent's care?"

"That's correct, Chris. A police spokesman who reported on the incident stated that they are waiting until later today to charge Ashley, pending a decision from the L.A. County prosecutors as to whether or not they are going to charge her as an adult."

"You got to be kidding me!" the male DJ said, with spite in his voice.

"Well, Chris, under California State law, Ashley is still considered a minor."

"I get that, Danni. But here we have a teenage girl who made a very adult decision to drive drunk. The tabloids say she's out of control! It's not even a question in my mind that she should be charged as an adult. Let's find out what our listeners think. Give us a call here at the studio."

Rick turned off the radio, pulled himself out of bed and headed to the shower, wondering if Jack was awake and if he had heard the news yet. After his shower, he followed the aroma of freshly brewed coffee downstairs, where Jack was pacing in the kitchen with the phone glued to his ear.

* * *

"YES, I GET THAT," I SAID INTO THE HANDSET, AS RICK entered the kitchen area. I looked up and gave him a wave.

Rick smiled and reached into the cabinet for a cup.

Pouring himself coffee he looked over to the plasma-screen TV mounted on the wall above the fridge. The voice of the newscaster was muted, but a picture of Ashley Sinclair was displayed behind him and text of her recent actions was rolling across the bottom of the screen.

"Okay, Vivian, I'll be there; not a problem. Where should we meet? Okay, that sounds like a good idea. We can fight our way through the press that will be camped out at the police station together."

I took a sip from my cup. "I'll prepare a couple of statements for the studio lawyers and the publicity department. We'll be prepared. Vivian, do me a favour, please? Calm down a little. You need to be in total control in front of the press. Yes, okay; I'll meet you at your office at the studio at eleven. Okay, bye."

We disconnected. I didn't realise how hard I was looking at the handset until Rick spoke.

"Don't do it, man. I hear you can get life for killing a phone."

I put the phone down. "Thanks for the warning. I don't think I would do well in prison."

"So you've heard the news about your young drunken starlet?" Rick asked, imitating a newscaster tone.

I poured more coffee into my cup. "The passengers in the car with Ashley? One was Christina Hudson, a co-star from the show, and the other was Christina's fourteen-year-old sister. Christina was released from the hospital a few minutes ago with minor injuries, but her sister, Marissa, is in intensive care with life-threatening injuries."

I looked up from my cup, miserable, to find sympathy in Rick's eyes. "The police are charging Ashley this afternoon. Word from our contacts at the prosecutor's office is that she is going to be charged as an adult for DUI, reckless endangerment, resisting arrest, and destruction of private property under fifty thousand US dollars."

"Wow, that's quite a list," Rick said.

"There's more. If Marissa doesn't pull through, Ashley will most likely be charged with manslaughter."

Rick was quiet.

I went on, "This girl, I don't think gets it. Endangering and ruining your own life is one thing, but endangering and ruining the lives of two others is completely off the wall."

"Remember, she is only seventeen," Rick said.

"Are you defending her?" I snapped.

"No. Not defending her."

"Then what?' I asked, pissed.

"Just remember she is seventeen. At seventeen, your capacity for making decisions is quite a bit different from when you're twenty, or even thirty-something."

"You're defending her actions based on her age?"

"I'm not defending what she has done. What I am saying is that, at seventeen, your decision-making capabilities are quite different. Remember what it was like to be seventeen? Hopped up on hormones, trying to constantly impress your peers, to be liked by your peers? You made your decisions completely differently at that age, based on peer pressure."

"You finished with your speech?" I interrupted.

"Not quite."

I folded my arms across my chest.

"Just have some sympathy for her, is all I ask. She is a seventeen-year-old girl who has made a terrible mistake. That doesn't necessarily make her a terrible person. There, I'm done."

I was quiet for a moment. It was almost eight o'clock. "I have to get moving. Don't you have to be at school soon?" I asked, ending the conversation.

"Not yet," Rick said, focussing on finishing his cereal.

"Then I'll see you later," I said. I left and didn't look back.

* * *

I PULLED INTO THE STUDIO LOT ARMED WITH THREE DRAFTS of press releases for Vivian tucked neatly into my soft-sided briefcase.

"Good morning, Mr. Perry," Harry greeted me as I stopped my car in front of the security gate.

"Morning, Harry. How are you today?"

I liked Harry. Harry had been the daytime guard at the main gate to the studio for twenty-five years. I could only imagine the scandals and cover-ups he must have seen over the years.

"Great, just great! Thank you for asking," Harry said.

"Unusual time of the year to see you here, Mr. Perry."

"I trust you've seen the news, and have been briefed by the publicity department to make no comments if the press approaches you?"

"Yes, sir," Harry replied.

"Perfect. Has Ms. Wentworth arrived yet?"

"Been here 'bout twenty minutes."

I looked at my watch. I had time.

"Also, Mr. Goldman and Mr. Peters arrived about five minutes ago, followed closely by Miss. Jensen."

Uh oh, I thought. *This is serious. Ron Goldman, the president of the studio is here. Vivian didn't mention he would be in on this.*

"Thank you, Harry," I said as Harry punched in the code to lift the security gate.

"You have a great day, Mr. Perry."

I drove through the lot, turning toward the offices for *Chamberlain Heights*. Pulling into the parking area for the department heads, I was instantly greeted by the sight of Vivian's candy apple red Jaguar. There were no other cars in the small lot.

I made my way to the front door. Scanning my thumb print over the biometric lock, the frosted glass door immediately unlocked. I bypassed the elevator and headed for the circular staircase. I was happy to see my assistant, Evelyn, sitting at her desk as I entered my suite of offices.

"Hey, boss." Evelyn looked up from a list she was working on. I had called Evelyn early this morning after the news broke. She cut her vacation short to help deal with the crisis.

"How have you been making out?" I asked her.

"All our writers called and accounted for. No one has left for their holiday yet; they're all on standby."

"You're amazing, Evelyn!" I said as I opened my office door, quickly going behind my desk and unlocking the bottom left drawer. I pulled out my laptop and put it into my briefcase; I wanted to be prepared in case I had to do rewrites on the press statements.

"Let's go," I told Evelyn, and we headed toward Vivian's office.

Evelyn quietly closed and locked the door with her security card and was beside me in a second. We made our way to the end of the hallway toward Vivian's suite. The whole building was eerily quiet. We passed two other suites of offices to get to Vivian's: One was the suite of offices for the directors of the show, and the other was for the head of set and costume designers. Both were completely dark behind their glass doors.

I could see Vivian's offices were bright as we approached them. Pushing open the double glass doors, Evelyn and I walked into the area that served as her assistant Rose's office and a small reception area for guests. Rose was not behind her desk, but one of Vivian's office doors was opened.

Unsure if Vivian had called Rose in, I approached the opened door and knocked on it as I entered Vivian's private area.

"Hello, Vivian. I'm here," I announced.

Vivian was sitting at her desk with Rose hunched over her shoulder, both of them working on something together.

"Jack, thank God you're here!"

Vivian got up and rushed to me, hugging me very tightly.

"Goldman is here," she said.

"I know. Harry told me. What is he doing here? He

usually lets Peters handle these kinds of things."

"Peters is here, too," Vivian replied. "We're meeting with both of them in Goldman's office in thirty minutes. You have a press release for me?"

I held up my briefcase and patted the side.

"I think we're in big trouble."

I noticed that both Rose and Evelyn had left and closed the door behind them, giving Vivian and me privacy.

Vivian sat in her chair, covering her eyes with both her hands. "I think this is going to push them over the edge. They already requested a meeting with us this week, pulling us all from vacation. And now this!"

I looked at Vivian. Even in the most stressful of situations, she looked perfectly coiffed. Her dark red hair was pulled perfectly back into a low ponytail. Her face was perfectly made up. Nails shiny, perfectly painted.

"Where is Daniel?" I asked.

"On his way back from Spain. He called me in the car on my way in. Jack, I think they're going to cancel us."

"They won't do that. They can't. The network just renewed the contract for two more seasons. We're still within the top ten in the ratings, and we continually won our time slot every week last season. They might request an overhaul of the show that may require Ashley's character written out, but they will *not* cancel us," I replied with conviction.

"I guess you're right. This is only a bump in a very long road. Now let me see what you have written for the press release."

I fished out three versions of the press release from my briefcase and handed them to her. Vivian put on her glasses and read all three. When she finished, she looked up and smiled.

"Good work. We better get going. It's a ten-minute walk to Goldman's building."

Vivian put on a black hat and picked up her briefcase and handbag. Then we got Rose and Evelyn and headed for the door.

Once outside I reached into my pocket and put on my sunglasses, feeling like I was about to melt in my dark grey suit. Normally, I never have a reason to wear a suit to work, since our work environment is pretty casual, especially for the writing team.

We must have been quite a sight walking across the studio lot: Vivian dressed in black, me in dark grey, Rose and Evelyn in dark blue, all of us wearing dark sunglasses. I think we could have been dubbed the 'Lipstick Mafia'.

Vivian set a fast pace, so we reached the studio executive office tower in less than ten minutes.

How does she walk so fast in four-inch heels, I asked myself.

The tower that housed the studio executives, the legal department, and the publicity department was a small six-storey office tower located exactly in the middle of the studio lot. From the upper floors, you could pretty much see everything within the confines of the lot. Inside, a uniformed security guard ushered us to a private express elevator that led directly to the sixth floor. Once there, we entered a large reception hall, the walls covered in beautiful, expensive art, marble floors beneath our feet.

The reception hall was empty. I'd been on the sixth floor before, but only a few times. Usually, any meetings I needed to attend in the executive tower were held in the boardroom two floors down.

"Ms. Wentworth? Mr. Perry?"

Both Vivian and I turned to see Priscilla, Goldman's personal executive assistant, who appeared from one off the hallways leading of the reception area. "Right on time, I see."

"Hello, Priscilla," Vivian and I chimed in unison.

"Won't you both please follow me? Mr. Goldman has requested this to be a closed meeting; your assistants can wait here."

Rose and Evelyn shrugged their shoulders and sat, settling in for a long wait.

Priscilla led us through Goldman's reception area to his private boardroom. Already in attendance was Shauna Jensen, head of the legal department, and Barry Whitefield, head of publicity.

"Please make yourselves comfortable." Priscilla gestured for us to sit. "Coffee and water are on the sideboard. Help yourself."

She turned and was out of the boardroom in a flash.

"Hello, Barry, Shauna," Vivian greeted the two others in attendance with a warm tone in her voice. I followed suit. I liked Barry and Shauna, although Shauna could be a real bitch at times. I grabbed bottles of water for both Vivian and myself from the sideboard.

"So, it looks like your girl has found herself a whole bunch of trouble," Shauna said as I settled into the chair next to Vivian.

Before Vivian or I could respond, the heavy mahogany door at the back of the boardroom opened, and in came Goldman, followed by Peters, with Priscilla bringing up the rear.

Everyone seated at the table stood up.

"Good morning, everyone," Goldman said.

He walked directly to the head of the conference table. Peters took the chair to his immediate right, and Priscilla sat directly to his left, opening her laptop to take notes. We all sat.

I was surprised that Goldman sat without his usual "greeting gestures". No matter the circumstances, Goldman always greeted the men with a firm handshake, and the ladies with a peck to their cheeks... but, not today.

"Vivian, Jack, Shauna, Barry," Goldman acknowledged each of us, making his way around the table.

I felt like I was suddenly transported back to the fifth grade roll call.

"Vivian, I see Daniel decided not to join us this morning," Goldman said.

"He's on his way back from Spain, Ron. He'll be back in LA sometime late this evening," Vivian replied, without a hint of stress in her voice.

Even though Goldman was head of the studio, he liked to be addressed by his first name. Peters sat quietly, which was unusual for him; obviously, this was Goldman's meeting.

"Shauna. Where are we at with Ashley?" Goldman asked.

"Dale Justice is meeting with her and her parents as we speak. We'll conference him in as soon as you're ready," Shauna replied.

Dale Justice was the outside counsel from an exclusive Beverly Hills firm the studio retained.

"Barry. Damages?" Goldman asked.

"Global. The major networks are reporting on it, as well the local news channels. It will, I predict, be reported around the world by this evening."

"How did the story and the pictures get out so fast?" Peters asked.

"Paparazzi picked it up on the police band radio. Several of their 'reporters' made it to the scene within minutes, capturing Ashley's arrest and Marissa being pulled from the car," Barry said.

"Has anyone talked to Ashley yet?" Vivian asked.

"No, that's what Dale is doing at the moment. No one from the studio is to talk directly to Ashley until he gives the go ahead," Shauna said. "The studio needs to separate itself from her, until we know how it will affect our image."

"Let's get him on the phone, now," Goldman barked.

Shauna stood and leant into the centre of the table, reaching for the dial pad that controlled the speakerphone system in the boardroom.

Shauna set up the conference call. We heard a dial tone, a ring, then a voice, "Justice here."

"Dale. Shauna. I have you on speakerphone. You're familiar with all in attendance? Mr. Goldman, Mr. Peters, Ms. Wentworth, Mr. Perry, and Mr. Whitefield. Where are we at with Ashley?"

"Just finished up with her and her parents. I'm going to make this brief. This girl is guilty as hell." Dale paused, and each of us in the boardroom looked around to read each other's reactions.

"What's her story on last night's events?" Peters asked.

"Don, is that you?" Dale asked.

"Yes."

"Story is: Ashley and Christina were hanging out at Christina's house. Her parents were out. They got into the booze and decided it was a good idea to get some fast food. Still unclear why they took Marissa along. Ashley can't remember the details very clearly."

"What does the police report state?" Shauna asked.

"According to Officer Parks and Officer Johnson, they saw Ashley's car run a red light at Sunset and Wilshire, heading west, back into Beverly Hills from West Hollywood. They called it in and followed Ashley for a few blocks, witnessing erratic driving patterns. Dispatch responded with Ashley's name as the registered owner of the car, and that's when they hit the lights in effort to pull her over."

Everyone in the room remained quiet, listening.

"When Ashley didn't pull over, Officer Parks hit the siren. So, Ashley hit the gas. Officer Johnson called for back up from other cars in the area. Officer Parks and

Officer Johnson approached Ashley's car on the right, in an attempt to see what was going on inside the car."

It became quite apparent Dale was reading from a statement from the two officers. "The chase ended when Ashley lost control of the car on the windy road and crashed into a parked SUV."

"What's Ashley's take on this?" Peters asked.

"She tells me that she knew she would be in trouble if she was stopped, and thought she could outrun them in the hills and hide the car with a friend who lives up there," Dale replied.

"Stupid girl," Shauna spat. "Stupid, stupid girl!"

"Enough, Shauna," Goldman said. "Where do we stand from a legal point?" Goldman asked Dale.

"The good news is the police did a breathalyser test on Ashley without her parents' consent, which is a no-no. The evidence from the test could be dismissed. The bad news is that Ashley reeked of alcohol and the police found an open bottle of rum in the car. This evidence is completely admissible, because her car was impounded by the city of West Hollywood as evidence of the crash."

"What's your strategy?" Shauna asked.

"Well, I'll accompany Ashley and her parents to the West Hollywood Police Department this afternoon for her official charges and arrange for immediate bail. Most likely the prosecution will push this to trial quickly. I estimate we'll need to enter a plea in front of a judge early next week, with a trial date being set at that time."

"What's the plea?" Peters asked.

"I think we best make that decision after she gets formally charged. We want to examine all the evidence against her and to see how or if Marissa recovers."

"Who did you assign as counsel for Christina and her family? Where are we with them?" Shauna asked.

"The Hudson family refused our services. My guess is

that they don't want representation from a studio-affiliated firm."

"Do they have anyone?" Goldman asked.

"LA County Prosecutors will represent them if Marissa doesn't make it. If they choose to sue Ashley and her family in a civil suit, they will need to retain a firm. I don't think they have thought that far ahead yet. They made an official comment through Christina's publicist of 'no comment' about thirty minutes ago. It's in the studio's best interest to make a comment as soon as possible."

"Okay," Goldman said. "Vivian and Jack will be meeting you at the police station to be present when they charge Ashley. Vivian will be making a statement to the press after the charges are official, on behalf of the studio."

"Perfect. I'm preparing a statement to give at that time, too."

"Thank you for your time, Dale. Please keep communication a priority with Shauna," Goldman said.

"Always," Dale responded, and he disconnected the call.

The room remained quiet for what seemed like an eternity. We were all waiting for someone to speak, but no one wanted to.

"What have we got prepared for a studio statement, Barry?" Peters asked.

We all discussed which of the three press releases to use. Barry seemed a little miffed that Vivian had asked me to write them because my style is kinder and more diplomatic than his. But Goldman liked the second release I wrote, so we decided to use it. Goldman went over the logistics—who would do what, where, and when. Then we sprang into action, hoping to save our reputations and our jobs.

9

WHAT A DAY, I THOUGHT AS I NAVIGATED THE FREEWAY, making my way home. The top on my car was up, and the A/C was set to high. It was ninety-five degrees at almost 7 p.m.

Ashley was formally charged and after meeting with the press, Vivian and I went to Diego's, a quaint bistro & bar in Burbank, just around the corner from the studio.

We each had a glass of chardonnay and reflected on the day.

"I think she's going down," I said to Vivian. "The public is going to go wild if one more young Hollywood starlet gets a slap on the hand for this degree of criminal charges."

"Ashley being charged as an adult is a sure-fire sign that the prosecutors are making a point. I think she is going to pay for all the other starlets' misdeeds."

"Let's pray Marissa has a full recovery, or our dear Ashley will be looking at up to ten years in prison."

"Let us pray for her full recovery for everyone's sake. I can't imagine what her parents are going through. This has got to be their worst nightmare." Vivian's eyes glassed over.

I sometimes forget she was a mother of two beautiful boys. It was probably easy for Vivian to put herself in Marissa's parent's shoes.

"We need to come up with a game plan for Thursday, Jack. We have to assume the network is going to insist

Ashley be written out of the show, jail time or not."

"I'll rework the story lines regarding Ashley's character and put a new story board together. But I don't think we should get too far ahead of ourselves," I responded.

"I just think we should have something prepared. We need to be proactive, not reactive," Vivian said.

"I'll put some ideas together and email them to your home account. We can go over them before Thursday and make changes before the meeting."

"We should probably include Daniel. He's going to call me as soon as his plane lands tonight. Let's plan for a working lunch on Wednesday," Vivian said.

*   *   *

I PULLED INTO MY DRIVEWAY NEXT TO RICK'S JEEP, surprised and yet excited to see that he was home. The sound of Vivian's voice greeted me as I entered the house. I walked quietly into the kitchen and saw Rick standing by the sink, watching Vivian read my press release about Ashley on TV.

"You hungry?" he asked me. "I'm making dinner."

"You cook?"

"No, I barbeque."

I looked around and noticed he had all the ingredients and utensils placed on the counter to make a feast.

"Do I have time to shower and change?" I asked, pulling at my suit.

"Lots of time. I'll wait to start the steaks until you come down."

I smiled and started for the stairs.

"Hey. What happened to your eye? It's healed?"

"The magic of the movies," I said, then left.

*   *   *

AFTER MY SHOWER, I FELT LIKE A NEW PERSON. DRESSED IN cargo shorts and a t-shirt, I made my way through the kitchen and out through the sliders onto the deck. The day had cooled into a beautifully warm evening, a soft breeze blowing in from the ocean.

"Smell's great!" I said with enthusiasm. I had barely eaten anything all day.

"Thanks. How do you like your steak?" he asked, standing at the grill.

"Medium rare, please."

He turned back to the barbeque, the sound of meat sizzling on the grill soon filled the air. I went over to the outdoor table and found it to be perfectly set. The hurricane lamps at either end of the table were glowing with candlelight. A bottle of Merlot sat in the centre breathing. Beside it was an ice-filled bucket of Coronas.

"Trying to get me drunk?" I asked, one eyebrow raised.

Rick blushed slightly, looking very cute and avoiding eye contact. "Uh, um, no. I didn't know what you would be in the mood for. What would you like?"

"I think I'll have a glass of wine."

He poured a glass of the Merlot and handed it to me. He opened a bottle of Corona for himself and headed back over to the barbeque to flip the steaks. I went to the railing, taking in the beautiful evening. I heard the surf washing up onto the beach and the occasional sound of a plane descending towards Los Angles International Airport. Moonlight danced on the dark ocean.

"This is why I love living here," I announced. "The peace and quiet, away from the hustle and bustle of the Hollywood scene."

"Hey, Jack."

I looked over at Rick, who was still keeping watch on the grill.

"I think I owe you an apology," I said.

He stopped me with a raised hand. "I know I made you mad this morning with my comments on the Ashley situation. It totally was not my place. I don't know your business, I didn't know the history, and I should have kept my mouth shut. I am also sorry for not showing up last night when I said I was going to."

"So that's what this is all about— a suck-up dinner?"

"Yah, kind of," he said with a half smile. "Is it working?"

"Jury is still out. I need to sample your cooking before I make my final decision," I said, grinning.

He grinned and focussed his attention back toward the grill.

"You did make me angry this morning. But it was a good thing."

He looked back at me.

"You made me think. I was looking at the Ashley situation only from the perspective of how it was going to impact the reputation of the show and the studio. You made me remember the sweet young eleven-year-old girl she was when we first cast her on the show— not the rebellious teenager she is right now. I'm going to ensure the studio acts with kindness towards her and her family. So really, I should thank you."

I raised my glass. Rick came over and clinked his glass against mine.

*   *   *

"That was an amazing dinner," I said. The perfectly done steak, the baked potatoes, the grilled corn on the cob, all were done to perfection. "I can't grill to save my life."

"What? You have this top-of-the-line barbeque, and accessories to go with it, and you don't grill?" Rick asked.

"It was Stephen's thing," I said, looking down into my

wine.

Silence took hold of both of us.

"So what's your story?" Rick suddenly asked.

"My story?"

"*Ya*, your story. How did you end up a famous head writer on a hit TV drama series?"

"Okay, famous I am not, and I'm sure you aren't interested in my career path. You're just being polite."

"I wouldn't ask if I wasn't interested. Tell me."

I looked up at him and poured myself another glass of wine. "Okay, I'll give you the Coles Note's version. I never intended to write for a TV show. After graduating from high school in Phoenix, I headed here, to Los Angles, with a full scholarship to UCLA's journalism programme. I wanted to work for a newspaper like *The New York Times*. Fast forward to four years later. Upon graduating at the top of my class, I was offered an associate staff position at *The L.A. Tribune*, in the arts and entertainment division. Basically, I took the position to get work experience."

I looked over at Rick, searching his face for signs of boredom. He was looking at me with interest, so I went on. "My position consisted of covering events no one else in the department wanted to report on— like second-string fundraisers where B-rated celebrities would make an appearance. Or I would cover a department store opening where a washed-up celebrity was the official ribbon cutter. Finally, I got my big break. It was a Saturday; I got a call early in the morning from my editor. The head writer for the department, who covered the top Hollywood events, was deathly ill. He needed me to fill in and cover the annual sports fundraiser the daytime shows put on. It was a really good cause. All the daytime shows' casts and crews got together to raise money for the local children's hospitals. I had to meet a camera guy there within the hour, because the story was due that night. I asked him 'why me', and he replied, 'you're the first to answer your phone; now get your ass down there'. I didn't need to be told twice. Am I boring you yet?" I ask Rick.

"No, keep going," he said as he opened another Corona.

"So, about halfway through the day, I accidentally bump into this woman, causing her sports drink to splash all over the front of her shirt. That woman turned out to be Vivian."

"The lady from the news conference?" Rick asked.

"Yes. At the time, Vivian was the producer for *Deadly Sins*."

"My mom loves that show. She records it every day," Rick chimed in.

I took a drink of my wine before continuing, "Anyway, Vivian took the accident with a grain of salt, and we immediately hit it off. We lunched together on hotdogs and salad. She introduced me to all the producers of the various shows and gave me great insight into the event. I got great information for my story, and John got great pictures. Fast forward two days later: I'm sitting at my desk in the bull pen when my editor approaches me and tells me Vivian has requested my appearance for a meeting at The Four Seasons Hotel in Burbank at six o'clock. He doesn't give me any more information, just that I better show up. I thought she was upset with me for the quotes I used, or for the picture we printed of her, which I'd captioned: "Vivian Wentworth, a good sport when assaulted by a reporter." It showed her pointing at the stain on her shirt with one finger and pointing at me with another. Well, I go to the Four Seasons, expecting the worst. I was a nervous wreck, the end of my career flashing in front of my eyes. But it turned out she offered me a job as a junior writer on the show. She told me how impressed she was with my article. She slid an envelope across the table at me, with an offer-of-employment letter, outlining my starting salary— which was double what *The Tribune* was paying me. I was hesitant. I had my vision of working for *The New York Times* still in my head, but I was really intrigued by the opportunity to write for TV. Anyhow, as you probably assumed by now, I accepted her offer."

"I didn't know you worked on *Deadly Sins*," Rick broke in.

"It was my start," I said.

"How did that lead to *Chamberlain Heights*?" he asked.

"Well, after seven years writing for *Deadly Sins*, I managed to work my way up the ladder, and became one of the two assistant head writers. Vivian and I became fast friends. When the network invited her to work on *Chamberlain Heights*, she brought me along. And here we are seven years later. The end."

I was sure I'd probably bored Rick to tears with my story.

"So, do you regret not making it to *The New York Times*?" he asked.

"No. I love the show; the people I work with. I love it all. No regrets."

"Here's to no regrets!" Rick lifted his bottle, clinking my glass once again.

* * *

"WELL, IT WORKED," I ANNOUNCED, AS I HEADED INTO THE kitchen carrying the dinner plates.

Rick trailed behind me. "What did?" he asked.

I turned to face him as I set the plates on the counter. "Your suck-up dinner. I totally forgive you."

"Yes!" he said, punching the air with his fist.

I smiled. Looking at him, I forgot where I was for a moment, getting lost in his clear blue eyes. I gave him a slow once over. He caught me staring at him. He didn't say a word, but I could feel him doing the same thing to me that I was doing to him. My breath quickened a little as I started to get turned on. My growing hard-on strained the fabric of my underwear. I started to feel lightheaded, and I reached for the counter behind me. In what seemed like slow motion, Rick took the two steps toward me, closing the gap, our bodies inches apart.

He placed his hands on either side of me, resting them on the counter. His eyes were filled with hunger as he leant in and took my mouth aggressively with his. I could feel his hardness as he pushed his body into mine. I opened my mouth, letting in his probing tongue. In my mind, I knew this was wrong, but my body betrayed me, responding. We pulled at each other's clothes, stopping our kiss just long enough to get each other's shirts off. He lifted me up onto the counter, and I wrapped my legs around his hips, pulling him in tighter, thrusting our crotches together. The hair on his chest tickled my bare chest. Goosebumps ran down my spine as he moved his mouth to my neck while dry humping me through our shorts. I could feel the first beads of perspiration collecting in the small of my back. I threw my head back and a moan escaped my lips as his mouth found my nipple, first flicking at it with his warm tongue, then biting it gently.

He moved on to the other one, sending spasms of pleasure throughout my body. My hands were in his hair, guiding his mouth back up to mine. I pulled at his shorts; he stopped grinding just long enough for me to undo the buttons and push them down with my feet. He wasn't wearing underwear. His erection sprung out immediately as his shorts dropped. He resumed grinding into me, kissing me feverishly. I moved my mouth away from his and ran my tongue along his jawbone. I licked and kissed my way down to his neck. I bit his shoulder and he let out a moan, grabbed me by the hair, and kissed me hard. His chest was damp with sweat, the hair covering his pecks felt matted as I pushed him back.

He looked at me with question and fire in his eyes.

I continued to push him back, making just enough space between us so I could get my feet back on the floor. Kissing him again, I reached down and started to massage his cock. His body shivered in pleasure. With my other hand, I unbuttoned my shorts, pushing them and my underwear to the floor in one quick motion. With my hands, I pushed our two hard-ons together, massaging them into one another. Rick's breath was hot on my neck. My tongue ran over his hard abs and flat stomach, as I made my way down to his rock-hard cock. I knelt before him, taking in the sight of his manhood. I put my nose into the golden blonde hair surrounding his cock, inhaling his scent, before I ran my tongue up the side of it.

He moaned. I licked all around his cock, flicking at the head before opening my mouth and taking it in. I massaged his balls with one hand and massaged my own cock with the other. His cock made it way to the back of my throat; I relaxed and let it slide down. Rick let out a loud moan as I went to work on him. He began to thrust his hips toward my mouth. He pushed until my lips were at the base of his cock, tasting the sweetness of his sweat. He pulled back out almost completely, before thrusting in again. His cock felt like it was getting harder, and I could feel his breath quicken. He increased the speed of his thrusts; I felt his balls tighten as I continued to gently massage them. He grabbed the back of my head, pushing me forward to meet his thrusts. I tasted the saltiness of his pre-cum as the speed of his thrusts intensified and his muscles tightened. He let out a cry and spasms shot though his body as his orgasm overcame him. His seed spilt into my mouth.

I continued to suck on his cock as his thrusts slowed. I felt my own orgasm on the brink of overcoming me. I

increased the speed of my hand on my cock. I released
Rick's cock from my mouth and gently bit his inner thigh as
my orgasm built. I cried out in pleasure as I climaxed, my
cum ejecting out onto my leg and the floor. My breath was
heavy and fast, my head resting on Rick's inner thigh. I
could feel his breath slowing, returning to normal, one of his
hands still resting in my hair.

"Jack."

I couldn't respond. He reached down, placing his hands
under my arms and lifting me up. He kissed me tenderly,
then wrapped his arms tightly around me.

*   *   *

"RICK, I…" I WAS TALKING INTO HIS SHOULDER.

"*Ssh.* Don't say anything," he said as he kissed my
cheek. He released me from his embrace and led me to the
stairs, then into my bathroom. He let go of my hand only to
adjust the temperature of the water in the shower.

Looking at his magnificent body, I couldn't believe what
had just happened. He pulled me into the shower. We stood
under the spray of mist, arms wrapped around one another,
kissing slowly and gently this time. Turning me, he grabbed
the body wash from the shelf and slowly lathered my
shoulders and back, gently massaging the gel into my skin.
He continued down to my buttocks, gently massaging them.
I felt myself getting hard again. He kissed me gently and
lathered up my chest, pinching each nipple softly. He
worked his way down to my half-hard cock with the lather,
looking surprised when he felt my partial hardness.

"What do we have here?"

I felt a small blush on my cheeks; he kissed me as he
massaged my balls. He stretched down and lathered the
front of my legs, then rinsed them with water. He grabbed
my hands and put body wash into them. I rubbed the gel

into his chest, feeling the strength of it beneath the covering of hair.

I continued down to his completely hard groin. I looked at him with a raised eyebrow and he laughed. After I lathered him up completely, he rinsed us both down under the spray. We stood under the water kissing and massaging each other's cocks. Rick made his way down my neck to my nipples. I cried out in pleasure as he worked them both over, softly this time. He continued down to my hard-on, licking it, working his hand up and down the length of the shaft. He took it into his mouth, gently sucking and stroking at the same time. His mouth was wonderfully warm and I could feel myself becoming harder.

He released my cock and gently sucked my balls, one at a time, before turning me away from him. He bit my ass cheeks tenderly and ran his tongue over them. He gently pulled my cheeks apart and pushed his tongue between. I let out a small cry of pleasure, as the warmth of his tongue gently probed and pleasured me. He made his way up my body, kissing my spine.

My breath became short and rapid. He ground into me, kissing and biting my ear. His cock moved up and down on my ass cheeks.

"I want you. I want you right now," he whispered into my ear, reaching around and massaging my now rigid cock.

"*Rick.*" I couldn't even put a sentence together as pleasure overcame my body. I reached for my hair conditioner on the shelf and massaged some onto his hardness and some in between my ass cheeks. He kissed me and I braced myself again the wall.

"Go slow. It's been a while."

Rick separated my cheeks and massaged me with his fingers. I started to loosen up. He reached for the conditioner and, soon, I felt one of his fingers inside me, then another. I relaxed as he massaged the inside of me, pleasure building. He pulled his fingers out and I could feel the heat of his cock at my entrance. He pushed; his cock entered me with ease, sending ripples of pleasure throughout my body. He continued to slowly ease in until I was filled completely with him. He wrapped one arm around my waist. His tongue probed my ear, so I leant back into him, turning my face so we could kiss. We stayed like this for minutes, just kissing, him deep inside me.

"Oh fuck, Rick," I let out when he slowly pulled back and thrust forward for the first time. "Oh, gawd," I breathed out.

He began a slow, steady rhythm. My body was going crazy with pleasure. He had one arm wrapped around my waist, holding me tightly, and his other was moving up and down the length of my shaft in time to his thrusts. He constantly licked and bit at my back and shoulders. I reached around with one hand to grab his ass, trying to push it farther and faster into me. Rick sped up his thrusts, whispering into my ear, "You feel so fucking good."

His breath was hot and fast. Panting with pleasure, I felt close to my orgasm. Rick grabbed hold of my hips, increasing the speed of his thrusts, bringing us both closer to release. I reached down and continued where Rick left off, massaging myself.

"Oh man, oh Jack, I'm gonna cum."

His cries intensified with the speed of his thrusts. I sucked gently on his tongue, and he moaned into my mouth. I felt his muscles tighten, followed by the exploding heat of his orgasm as he shot inside of me. I reached my own orgasm as he finished his. Crying out, I shot my load onto the wall of the shower. Rick wrapped both his arms around my waist, holding me, staying inside me, resting his head on the back of my shoulders, both of us breathing hard.

*   *   *

I OPENED MY EYES TO A COMPLETELY DARK ROOM AND THE sound and smell of the ocean blowing in through the opened window. Stephen's arm was draped over my chest; he was snoring softly, cuddled into my back. I placed my hand on top of his and pushed closer to him. He lets out a sigh in his sleep as his body responded and pulled me tighter to him. I closed my eyes, feeling very happy.

An alarm bell suddenly went off in my head, jolting me fully awake. Wide-eyed, I tried to adjust to the darkness of the room. It wasn't Stephen's arm draped across me, not his warmth next to me— It was Rick.

What have I done, I asked myself. *I slept with my sister's stepson— oh god, how could I have done that?*

I looked at the bedside clock: 4:15 a.m.

"How did this happen? We were having dinner, then we were in the kitchen, and then he was kissing me."

I remembered drying each other off after our shower. He wouldn't let me talk about what happened: he quietened me with kisses and put me to sleep.

Now, my stomach was churning.

I needed to focus, without emotion. I gently removed Rick's arm from my chest and slowly eased my body away from his sleep. I made my way into my closet. I shut the door quietly before turning on the light. I found my running gear and quickly dressed. Turning the light out, I let my eyes readjust to the darkness before opening the door. The gentle sound of Rick's snoring assured me I hadn't woken him.

I made my way downstairs and out through the already opened sliders to the deck— We'd left the doors open last night. I hit the beach at full speed as I came off the stairs, not bothering to stretch or warm my muscles. The cool breeze coming off the water felt refreshing as I ran parallel to its edge.

With only the moonlight to guide my way, I pushed myself hard. Running always cleared my mind and helped me to focus. But no matter how hard I pushed myself, I couldn't stop thinking about Rick and last night. I never even knew he was gay. Julie didn't know either: she would never have given up an opportunity to tell me that kind of information.

My mind replayed last night's events again: his body, his touch, his kiss.

Push harder, Jack, I told myself as I picked up my pace, running with a vengeance. My mind wouldn't stop. I heard my yoga instructor's voice in my head telling me to feel instead of think.

How do I feel, I asked myself. *Guilty? Yes, most defiantly.* He was fifteen years younger than me. I felt guilty about his age, guilty about his relationship to me and my family— yes, I felt guilty.

But who seduced who? He made the first move, didn't he?

I recalled that he'd been the one to break the silence by rushing in and kissing me.

The first sign of dawn was beginning to break, the soft glow of orange trying to peek up and over the hills of the valley. Without looking at the pedometer attached to my runners I estimated that I had already run close to ten or more miles. I figured I was three beach communities away from Hermosa Beach. I never ran this far. I always did five miles one way, then returned home.

As the sky continued to lighten in the pre-dawn day, I knew it was going to be another beautifully hot day. My pace slowed as I passed the fishing pier, the landmark that told me I was one mile from home.

What am I going to say to him, I wondered. How awkward was it going to be this morning?

I considered staying out on the beach until he left for

school, to give myself the day to figure out how to react before he came home at night. I also considered packing a bag after he left and going away until school was finished and he moved out.

Real mature, Jack, I scolded myself. *You're an adult and you need to deal with this head-on.*

I slowed my pace for a cool down and decided that I would tell him it was a mistake, shouldn't have happened, I'm sorry, and we need to forget about it and move on. When I got to my house, it was completely dark. No lights on in any of the rooms. My muscles were tightening, my lower back starting to ache. I realised I most definitely over did it. I needed a really hot shower to avoid cramping and seizing up.

I quietly walked up the stairs to the deck and opened the sliders into the house. Not a sound. The house was completely silent. I set up the coffeemaker to make a pot; it wasn't even seven o'clock. I made my way into my room. Rick was still asleep, curled into a pillow. He had kicked off most of the duvet, making it easy for me to admire his beautifully toned body. I crept into the bathroom, gently closing the door behind me.

I turned the shower as hot as I could stand. I lathered up my hair and body, scrubbing away the evidence of my run. My muscles started to relax, the tightness disappearing. I was amazed at how good I felt, considering the distance I ran. When I got out, I opened the window to let out the steam.

Wiping the mirror above the sink as I brushed my teeth, I checked out my eye. The yellowing was disappearing and turning purple. I looked down at my neck and almost screamed out in horror since I saw a very faint outline of a circular bruise.

A hickey.

Great! I hadn't had a hickey since high school.

Something else to hide.

I wrapped my towel around my waist and headed out into the bedroom, knowing that I should wake Rick so he could make it to school on time, but dreading the thought of it. I went to the bed and sat next to his stretched out body. He was on his back. I reached down and brushed the hair on his forehead back a little.

"Morning." His eyes suddenly flashed open, a smile on his face. He reached for my hand and kissed it.

"Hi," I croaked out in reply, nerves suddenly overcoming me. Pulling me close, he kissed me and pulled my head onto his chest.

"You smell good," he said, talking into my hair.

I didn't respond. He pulled me closer. I was lying in the bed now, partially on top of him, listening to his heartbeat. He turned over, flipping me so he was completely on top me. He looked deeply into my eyes and smiled. When he kissed me I kissed him back. I felt his hardness through the towel that separated our bodies. He slid his legs under mine, lifting them, allowing our bodies to get closer. I turned away from him, trying to stop his kisses, but he was persistent.

"Hey, we can't do this. What about school?" I managed to get out between his kisses.

He responded by kissing me more deeply, more passionately. He pulled away my towel, exposing me completely, then rubbing his cock again mine.

"Rick, um, we should stop."

My mind was trying to stop my body from responding to his biting at my neck, but it was no good. His hands made their way down to my legs, lifting them in one quick motion. He reached over me and took the bottle of body lotion from the nightstand and massages some first on to him and then onto me. He entered me slowly and with ease, my body responding to him in a way I couldn't remember it responding to anyone before.

He lifted my legs more, putting them on his shoulders. I sucked on his tongue. His body was powerful; the strength of it intensified my building orgasm. He stopped kissing me and looked directly into my eyes. I reached around and massaged his balls; I could feel his body tightening, getting close to climaxing. I massaged myself, not believing I was about to climax without hardly touching myself. A moan built inside of me, my head tossed from side to side and I jerked up and felt my orgasm gush out. I grabbed Rick's face in my hands, wanting, needing to see his expression as he came. He turned and bit into the palm of my hand, increasing his speed, his eyes half closed; a moan escaped his lips as his body shuddered in the final stages of his pleasure. Rick collapsed on top of me, his heart racing, his breath fast and shallow. I ran my hands down his back in gentle strokes as I caught my own breath, knowing I should break the silence. He lifted his head and brought his lips to my mouth once more, kissing me gently. Then, he was looking at me so intently, I felt like he was trying to get a glimpse of my soul.

"I got to go," he said after catching sight of the clock. "I'm going to be late."

"We should talk," I said.

"I really need to get moving," he said as he got out of bed.

I watched him disappear through the bedroom door, out into the hallway towards his room. Seconds later, I could faintly hear the sound of water spraying in his bathroom. I got up and headed for the shower myself, avoiding analysing our situation. After a quick five-minute rinse, I dried myself, grabbed my running clothes from the floor and headed into my closet to get dressed. I made my way downstairs to the kitchen. As I passed Rick's open bedroom door, I heard the rustling sounds of him rushing to get ready for his day.

* * *

THE SMELL OF FRESHLY BREWED COFFEE GRABBED MY SENSES as I hit the bottom of the stairs. I poured myself coffee and made a travel mug for Rick.

"That for me?"

Startled, I looked up. "*Ya*, thought you might need this to go."

"Thanks."

Sparks ignited inside of me as brushed past me on his way to the fridge. I watched as he grabbed an apple and orange from inside, then opened the pantry and took out a couple of the breakfast bars to put in his bag.

"You're amazing. Last night was amazing. This morning was amazing," he whispered into my ear as he wrapped his arms around me from behind, almost spilling my coffee in the process.

I turned my head to meet his kiss.

"I really got to go," he said as he released me from his grip. "I'll see you tonight? Dinner?"

I nodded, as I seemed to have once again lost all capability of talking. He kissed me once again, turned, picked up his coffee mug, and headed for the front door. I watched him. He gave me a little wave as he closed the front door behind him.

"Get a grip, Jack," I said to myself as I headed out the sliders onto the deck to finish my coffee.

"What am I going to do about him?" I asked the cloudless sky. "What? Why now? Why him?"

The sky remained silent.

"Julie is going to murder me if she finds out. I can't believe I let this happen. What is wrong with me?"

Still no response.

I decided it would be better to do some work, instead of

talking to myself.

Once in my office I opened up my laptop and started creating a new story line for the fall season of *Chamberlain Heights*. My creative process soon took over, pushing all thoughts of Rick from my mind.

10

"FUCK! I AM GOING TO BE LATE!" RICK SAID TO HIMSELF.

He sped down the freeway, hoping to avoid cops. He couldn't shake thoughts of Jack from his mind as he navigated the freeway towards school. Seeing him, feeling, touching him. He reached down and adjusted himself as his erection stretched at the fabric of his pants. He licked his lips, still able to taste traces of Jack. He smiled.

*　*　*

"SO NICE OF YOU TO JOIN US THIS MORNING, MR. Stephenson," Professor Gellar announced as Rick snuck in and took a seat next to John.

"I'm sorry—"

The professor cut Rick off with the raise of his hand as he turns to face the room. "Need I remind you that this is a very exclusive internship? That you few were chosen from thousands of applicants for the privilege of acceptance into this programme? Do I?"

"No, sir. Please accept my apology for disrespecting your time and the time of my peers, sir," Rick said.

"Well then, let's continue." He turned back towards the chalkboard.

Brittney immediately turned and gave Rick a dirty look. He gave her the finger, but he wasn't really mad. He was the one who was late, after all. And yet, he didn't regret it.

It was worth it.

The intensity of the morning lecture made the time fly by, and soon it was lunch. The group's day was split into two sections. From 9:30 to 11:30 a.m. they attended a lecture. 11:30 to 12:30 p.m. was lunch, and from 12:30 to 2:30 p.m., they gave a lecture, taking turns each day. It was the responsibility of the group members to critique the lecture and provide constructive feedback at a post-lecture meeting. They were then advised to prepare for the next day's events as a group for the remainder of the day, up to 5 p.m., assuming that none of the group members were struggling and didn't require extra time.

*   *   *

"DUDE, WHAT HAPPENED TO YOU THIS MORNING?" JOHN WAS on Rick as soon as they were dismissed by Professor Gellar and heading towards the cafeteria.

"Slept in," Rick replied.

"Dude, I called you like five times. Didn't you hear your phone?"

"*Shit*, my phone," Rick said as he looked in his bag for it. "I must have forgotten it in my room."

"It's in your room and you didn't hear my calls?" John lifted one eyebrow.

"I mean, *downstairs*. In the living room."

"You can't be late again. You'll jeopardise the internship for us all," John added.

"Dude, I know. I'm really sorry. It won't happen again," Rick responded.

They walk the rest of the way to the cafeteria in silence, falling in behind Brittney, Linda, and Freddy.

"So, what's wrong with you?"

Rick looked away from his food toward Brittney, who was questioning him.

"What?" he muttered.

She waved her finger at him. "You're too quiet and it's not like you to be late. You usually have more to say."

"I still think he is having lady troubles," Freddy chimed in.

"Drop it, Freddy," John interjected.

The others took the hint and got back to work. John and Freddy bent their heads over their notes. Rick's mind drifted back to thoughts of Jack. He didn't realise Brittney was staring at him.

"You had sex!" Brittney suddenly announced.

Rick looked up.

"That's why you were late. And that's why you're all silent and brooding. You had sex. I'm right, aren't I? Who is she? She must have been really good to put you into the state you're in."

"What?" Rick asked, playing dumb.

"I can smell it on you. Sex. Sex. Sex." She was smiling at Rick in triumph.

John and Freddy stopped conversing. Even Linda looked up from her lunch with interest, everyone waiting to see where Brittney and Rick's conversation was headed.

"Not that it is any of your business, Brittney, but I did not have sex last night."

"Liar," she fired back, with a smug look on her face.

Rick took a breath. "Brittney, just because you're a slut without any moral fibre, who'd fuck anyone to get ahead, doesn't make you an expert on the subject. Nor does it give you some kind of special power to be able to tell when other people have sex. And, for the record, given that we aren't 'sorority sisters' or 'BFFs', you are the last person I would share any details of my life with."

"Woo hoo, we have a catfight," Freddy chirped excitedly.

Rick looked his way and gave him a glare that stopped

him in his tracks.

"I hit a nerve," Brittney looked directly into Rick's eyes, without even a hint of reaction on her face.

"It's time to head to the lecture hall," John broke the silence, as he got up gathering his books together.

Linda and Freddy quickly followed suit. Britney and Rick continued to stare at each other in silence.

"Best we get going. We couldn't have our little Ricky here be late for classes twice in one day, now can we? P.S., I thought guys *liked* to brag about their conquests," Britney said sarcastically in her fake Southern accent.

"Dude, let's go." John hit Rick lightly on the shoulder.

He got up, fuming at Brittney, grabbed his bag, and followed behind the group making their way to the lecture hall.

*   *   *

RICK COULDN'T CONCENTRATE DURING FREDDY'S LECTURE. HE couldn't stop his thoughts from drifting towards Jack. Beautiful Jack. He smiled at the thought of him. He was counting down the minutes until he could get back to the beach to see him. He felt someone staring at him, and he looked over to Britney. She had a huge smirk on her face. Rick smirked right back at her, trying not to let her get to him. He turned to focus on Freddy's lecture, struggling to digest the information he was teaching to the students in the class. *He's not bad*, Rick thought to himself. *A little corny, but a pretty good teacher.* He started to take notes since he knew he would have to contribute to the meeting with Professor Gellar that followed immediately after Freddy's lecture.

*   *   *

FILE SENT, MY COMPUTER ANNOUNCED TO ME ON ITS SCREEN in bold letters.

"There, done," I said to myself with delight.

Three different storyboards outlining a new direction for the fall season, all sent off to Vivian for her review. I looked at the antique clock on my desk: 1:30 p.m. My stomach growled. No wonder I was famished, I realised. I hadn't eaten all day. Shutting down my computer, I got up and headed toward the kitchen. I had been so wrapped up in my work that I lost all track of time.

I opened the fridge and took out ingredients to make a sandwich for lunch. Pouring myself a glass of milk, I headed through the sliders to have my lunch on the deck. The weather was perfect, not too hot, a light breeze coming in off the water. The sun was high and bright.

Finishing my lunch, I peeled off my t-shirt and settled into one of the loungers that faced the beach and water, soaking in the beauty of the day. Suddenly exhausted, I feel into a deep sleep.

*   *   *

"YOU WANT GRAB A BURGER OR SOMETHING?" JOHN ASKED Rick as they finished up their group meeting. "Maybe a couple of beers?"

"Rain cheque, okay?" Rick replied.

"*Ya*, sure." John looked disappointed.

"I'm still wiped today, for some reason. I think I should head back to the beach, hit the books for a while, and get to bed early."

"No problem, man," John said as they walked out of the lecture hall into the sunshine.

"You want to work out tomorrow morning? We could meet at 7:30," Rick asked, trying to appease the guilt inside him for blowing John off.

"Cool. That works. Chest and arms?"

"Chest and arms it is," Rick agreed.

"See ya tomorrow," John said, as they went in their different directions.

Rick checked his watch: 5:14 p.m. He estimated he could make it to the beach by six, depending on traffic.

* * *

THE FLURRY OF ACTIVITY AROUND THE ZODIAC CAME TO A *sudden halt. The shouts of the paramedics ceased. The beach became quiet. Only the sounds of the approaching storm broke the silence.*

I watched as the paramedics lifted themselves from their knees into a standing position and moved away from the body lying on the sand. I couldn't push forward because the captain was still restraining me. Finally, he released me from his grip. The paramedics were starting to scatter, picking up equipment. The body was now partially in view.

As I made my way closer, I started to make out the dark blond hair on the body that was definitely a man. One paramedic turned and blocked my approach, but the captain waved him away. I was within a few feet of the body. I recognised the dark blue wetsuit pulled back, exposing the lightly-haired chest. I knelt down. I touched his face which was bloated and badly bruised. Tears started to pour down my face. I placed my ear over his heart, convincing myself it was still beating and that the paramedics had made a mistake. I didn't realise until afterward that I was shouting, "Stephen is alive!"

I shook him.

"Wake up, Stephen, wake up," I screamed at his face. "Wake up, wake up, damn you! You can't leave me! You can't!"

I collapsed on top of him, screaming hysterically into his chest. My tears had become so furious that I couldn't see anymore. Someone was talking to me; I couldn't make out what they were saying. Someone was grabbing my shoulders, trying to lift me away, away from Stephen. I screamed out, No, and I pushed them away. I would not leave him. I would not leave him here alone on the cold sand. I wouldn't.

I tightened my grip on him. More hands were on my shoulders, pulling me, saying things to me I still couldn't comprehend. I screamed, "No, you can't do this! I can't leave him! No! Get off me!"

More hands joined in with the others. I kicked, I screamed. Someone was shouting.

"What are they shouting about?" I felt the wetness of the sand against my back as I was forced onto it. Hands, lots of hands were holding me down. Hands on my shoulders, hands on my arms, hands on my legs, pinning me to the ground. I continued to scream. I continued to struggle. I had get free, to get back to Stephen. Panic was overwhelming me. I felt a gentle prick in my right arm. I looked over; my vision was still completely blurred. I couldn't see a thing. My body stopped fighting and started to relax. Someone placed my head in their hands, as darkness engulfed me.

*   *   *

I WOKE WITH A START. PANICKED, I STRUGGLED TO CATCH MY breath. I wiped away the tears that clouded my vision, desperately trying to get my bearings. The bright sunshine brought me out of my darkness. I soon realised that I was safe at home on my deck.

Another nightmare.

I rushed inside to the kitchen sink and splashed cool water on my face and neck. I needed to get out, to go somewhere. I grabbed my car keys and headed for the driveway. My car was stifling hot as I got in. I turned the key in the ignition. As the engine roared to life I hit the button that automatically put the top down and opened all four windows. Without checking for traffic, I put the car in reverse, quickly backing into the street. Slamming the gear selector into "D", I hit the gas hard and peeled away from my house.

* * *

SITTING ON THE SOFT GRASS, I STARED AT THE BLACK GRANITE headstone. *ROSS* in large capital letters in the centre. *Stephen James* in smaller letters directly beneath it. And a small glass circle encasing a picture of Stephen directly beneath that. *Beloved son, brother, partner, and friend who is missed by all who knew him. A gentle soul that has gone home to rest.*

"I was just about to give up on you coming today."

I looked up. Stephen was sitting atop his headstone, dressed smartly in his favourite Boss suit.

"Traffic was heavy," I replied sarcastically.

"Just like you to blame your lateness on traffic." He smiled his beautiful smile. "So, first time here? What took you so long?"

Tears streamed down my face. I couldn't speak

"*Ssh*, don't cry. It's okay." He was beside me now, crouching next to me.

"Am I crazy?" I asked. "Am I?"

"You're not crazy; you're perfect," he said. He always said that, that I was perfect.

"I'm not. Stephen, you're dead. You've been dead for over a year. I'm sitting here at the foot of your grave talking to you, seeing you, and you think I'm perfect, and not crazy?"

"Okay, you're perfectly crazy." He wiped the tears

from my cheeks.

I decided I was experiencing a grief-induced hallucination brought on by my recent nightmares about his accident.

"So, you never answered me."

"Answered you on what?" I asked.

"What took you so long to pay your first visit to me?"

"Second," I corrected him.

"First time doesn't count. You were so strung out on Valium I don't think you remember being here."

"I remember. How could I forget one of the worst days of my life? I buried you, Stephen, you think I forgot that? That day I had to say goodbye to you, the only man I loved."

He was sitting cross-legged in front of me now, watching me as I picked one blade of grass after another from the ground.

"Why'd you leave me, Stephen, why?"

He cupped my hands in his, then looked up abruptly. "Someone's coming."

"Jackie?"

I turned and saw Maria a few feet away from me, carrying a bouquet of white calla lilies. When I turned back to Stephen, he was gone.

*   *   *

MARIA PLACED THE CALLA LILIES AT THE BASE OF STEPHENS'S headstone, executing the sign of The Father, The Son, and The Holy Ghost as she did so.

"Who were you talking to?" she asked as she kicked off her open-toed high heels and sat next to me in the grass.

"No one. Myself, I guess," I responded, embarrassed that she had overheard me. "What are you doing here, Maria?"

"I stopped by your house this afternoon to check on you, to make sure you were okay given what day it is today. When I found you gone, I assumed you would be here."

"You know what day it is today?"

"You and Stephen were a big part of our lives, Jackie. How could I not remember your anniversary? Ten years ago, today."

"You're right. I forgot. I actually forgot."

"You didn't forget. You knew. You made it here," Maria answered softly.

Tears began filling my eyes again, and Maria reached over and put her arm around my shoulders, stroking my hair. "It's hard, Jackie. All the firsts. First holiday without him, his birthday, your birthday, and now first anniversary without him. The good news is all the firsts are over now. You can move forward, remembering him with love in your heart, not heartache in your heart."

"I miss him so much. I feel lost without him," I sobbed into her shoulder.

"I know you do. Part of you always will and should. It is an honour to his memory, and the love you had for each other. You need to move past this, though, remembering him with happiness, not sadness."

All I could do was continue to cry into her shoulder.

"He was a beautiful soul. I loved him like I love my own sons. The thing I remember most of all was his big beautiful smile. When he smiled, his whole face lighted up."

There was a smile in Maria's voice. My sobs started to slow.

"He had a kind heart, and he would do anything for anybody. That was who he was."

I pulled away from Maria, my tears finally stopping. "I just wish— I wanted more time with him. I want to go back to that day, insist he not go surfing. Then he could be safe with me now." My voice was cracking. "I had a feeling that morning. A sick feeling in my stomach. I should have stopped him from going out."

"Jackie." Maria wiped my tear-stained cheeks. "Nothing you could have said or done could have stopped him from surfing that morning. Stephen's leaving was his fate, his destiny. It was his time to go. He completed what he needed to do in his life, and our Creator called him home. He left this planet doing one of the things he loved most, and the last person he got to see and say goodbye to was the person on this Earth who he loved most."

Unable to cry anymore, my tears ducts completely dried up, I sat quietly.

"You have a long life still ahead of you, Jackie. Take the experience you shared with Stephen and move forward with life. Don't sit idle and don't move backwards. Share your life. It's what he would want you to do."

I looked up and gave Maria a weak smile.

"You can do better that that, my friend," she said.

I gave her one of my great big Hollywood smiles, the kind I usually pulled out when I was at studio functions.

"You can't fool me with that smile, but I am going to let you get away with it. Just for today, though," she said, tapping my nose.

I felt the corners of my mouth creeping upward.

"I have to go," she said as she stood and put her shoes back on. "Have to get back to the restaurant. I pray Joe and the boys haven't destroyed it while I was gone."

I got up to walk her to her car.

"Why don't you come with me?" she asked. "I will have Joe fix you an amazing dinner for tonight."

"Thank you. Thank you for everything today." I held both her hands in mine. "But I think I am going to stay here for a while more."

I opened the door to her pearl white SUV.

"Maybe you'll stop by later?"

"Maybe. No promises, though."

She hugged me goodbye and climbed up into her vehicle. "Don't stay too late. Look after yourself," she said through the open window.

"I won't, and I will," I responded.

"You will be at the restaurant on Friday?"

"I promise." I raised my right hand and gave her the 'scout's honour' sign.

"You'll bring Rick again, won't you? We all enjoyed him."

I smiled and nodded as she pulled away, leaving me in silence.

*   *   *

THE SKY WAS ILLUMINATED IN A SOFT ORANGE GLOW, signalling the day's transformation into evening. Looking up into the sky I could see the faint shadow of the moon coming slowly to life. I didn't know how long I had been at the cemetery; the day went by in a flash and a blur. I waited patiently for Stephen to return after Maria left, wanting to see him again. But he never came back.

Getting up off the ground I walked the couple steps to his headstone, crouched down, and ran my hand over the words carved into it. I leant over and kissed his picture.

"I love you, Stephen."

I stood straight up and looked at the headstone one more time before turning and walking towards my car. The early evening was still filled with the day's heat. As I drove out of the cemetery, the granite headstones sparkled in the headlights.

"This place is so peaceful," I said.

Then, I came to the closed gates.

What?

I approached the gates at a snail's pace, thinking they must open automatically as a car got close.

Nothing.

I put the car in park, got out, and walked towards them. They were locked. I pulled, but they wouldn't budge. I got back in the car and steered toward the secondary exit. It was closed too.

What is going on, I asked myself as I got out of my car and once again approached the gates on foot. Looking through the bars of the gates I could read the softly illuminated sign that outlined the hours the cemetery was opened for visiting.

7 a.m. to 6 p.m. daily

I walked back to the car, leaning in to read the dashboard clock. 7:15 p.m.

They wouldn't have locked me in? Someone would have checked the grounds before locking the gates? Wouldn't they?

I took a run at the gates again, pulling at them to no avail.

"This is what jail must feel like," I said as I hung my arms through the iron bars. I looked once again at the sign that displayed the cemetery hours.

Perfect!

There was a twenty-four-hour, in-case-of-emergency number listed at the bottom.

With a smile on my face, I rushed back to my car for my cell phone. It wasn't in its usual place in the centre console I searched the passenger seat: nothing. Back seat: same thing.

I soon remembered the truth: when I ran out of the house earlier I didn't grab my cell phone or wallet.

It was almost completely dark as I sat in the car, staring at the gates which shone in the headlights of the car.

"I write about stuff like this. Stuff like this doesn't

happen to me," I said to myself.

I was out of options. I drove my car back to the visitor's parking lot, put up the top, and locked it remotely, the alarm beeping.

Then I headed back to the gates. I had to climb out. There was no other way. The walls around the cemetery were ten feet tall.

Thinking I had a better chance of scaling the gates in bare feet, I pushed my thongs through the bars, out onto the other side. Then I wiped my hands on my shorts and I jumped up onto the first horizontal crossbar.

Stretching completely up, I grasped the second crossbar in my hands. I struggled as my upper body took my full body weight and pulled it up towards the second crossbar. It took a couple swings of my leg for my one foot to connect with the crossbar. Once there I easily pushed my body up, bringing my other foot onto the crossbar, putting myself into a standing position.

I could now lift my legs one at a time over the top of the spiked gate, to a resting position on the cross bar on the outside of the gate.

Now to get down, Jack.

I reached down and grasped the crossbar in my hands then slowly pulled one foot off at a time. Gravity quickly took over and my body plummeted down, coming to a painful stop as my arm and shoulder took the brunt of the sudden weight. I almost lost my grip. I stretched downward, my feet seeking out the lower crossbar. Feeling it with my toes I slowly eased my grip off the upper bar.

Only a few feet more to go, I told myself. I slowly lowered myself from the lower crossbar, one foot at a time; I jumped down the last few feet to the ground.

"Ouch!" I cried out in pain as my bare feet made contact with the hard pavement. I cursed silently at myself for having stupidly pushed my shoes through ahead of me,

not foreseeing the barefoot jump to the ground. As I
reached for my thongs I was suddenly awash in white light.
A combination of red and blue light circled the air above me.
I shielded my eyes with my hand.

"Is there a problem here?" a uniformed police officer
asked, one hand on the holster containing his gun.

11

WHERE THE FUCK IS HE, RICK WONDERED AS HE LOOKED AT HIS watch. *He said he was going to be home tonight. Where did he go? And why was the front door unlocked?*

Rick couldn't stop his mind from considering the worst. He knew it was unlike Jack to leave the house open when no one was home. It was apparent that he'd left in a hurry, since his cell phone and wallet were still here. Rick had found them earlier on the side table next to the front door when he'd called Jack's cell phone and its ringing echoed in the house.

Was there some kind of accident? Is someone hurt?

The ringing of Jack's landline broke his thoughts. He picked it up without looking at the call display.

"Hello?"

"Hi, sweetie."

He immediately recognised Julie's voice. "Hiya."

"What? No excitement for your mean old step-mom?"

"Sorry."

"What's wrong sweetie? What's going on? Bad day at school?"

"Well, I'm a little worried about Jack."

"What's going on?" Julie asked forcefully.

"I'm not sure. It's just when I came home this afternoon, I found him gone, but he said this morning that he would be home tonight."

"And?" she asked.

"And the whole house was left open. All the doors, including the front door, which is always locked. His car is gone, but he left behind his wallet and cell phone— it's like he left in a very big hurry."

"I was afraid of this. I called several times earlier with no answer on either of his lines, trying to see how he was doing. I didn't remember what day it was until this afternoon."

"What are you talking about, Julie?"

"Today would have been Jack and Stephen's anniversary. They would have been together ten years today if Stephen hadn't died. I don't know if you noticed or not, Rick, but I don't think Jack has entirely dealt with his death. You know what I mean?"

Rick's thoughts drifted back to last night and this morning. Silently, he realised why Jack might have run off. His anniversary, combined with what had happened between the two of them, could have pushed him over the edge.

"Rick?" The sound of Julie's voice jarred him back into the present.

"*Ya*, I'm still here. What did you say?"

"I asked you if you noticed anything different about Jack?"

"No. He seemed completely fine this morning." His thoughts drifted back to the memory of their lovemaking.

"I'm more than a little worried, Rick. I never told you this, but…."

"But what?"

"After Stephen's accident, Jack attempted suicide."

"What? That's crazy? That's not Jack."

Even in the short time that Rick had been with Jack, he couldn't believe he would do such a thing.

"It's true. He was a complete mess after Stephen died. His doctor prescribed Valium and a mild sedative, at the insistence of mother and me. We couldn't help him find peace. He was completely irrational when he was awake, and when he was finally calm enough to sleep, he couldn't. We thought it would be the best for him. To help get him through the nightmare."

Julie paused.

"Go on," Rick said.

"Well, it was about a week after Stephen's funeral. Stephen's family had gone back to Texas by then, and our dad had returned to Phoenix the day before. The house was completely still and quiet— just Jack, Mom, and me. Mom had actually been successful in making him eat an almost-complete meal, not just picking at food. We thought he was doing better. Mom was exhausted and had gone to bed early. I sat with Jack in the den, watching old movies on some obscure cable channel. He was just kind of blank, no expression on his face or in his eyes. He got up, almost robotically, and announced he was going to bed. I thought this was a good sign, since the only sleep he'd had was falling asleep to late-night infomercials. I gave him his sedative because Mom and I were controlling what he took. He kissed me on the cheek and said goodnight."

Julie went silent again.

"*Please.* Go on," Rick begged.

"I heard him rustling around in the kitchen before heading upstairs. I thought nothing of it. I was soon fast asleep in front of the TV. I awoke a couple of hours later. I went into the kitchen for a bottle of water before heading up to the guest room. I found a freshly opened bottle of wine on the counter; again, I thought nothing of it. It looked like it had maybe only a glass poured from it. I knew the mildness of the sedative would not hurt him with just one glass of wine, and I hoped it would help him get a full night sleep. I looked in on him before going to my own room. He was fast asleep, looking very peaceful in the soft glow of his bedside lamp. The glass of wine he'd poured earlier looked half-full. Nothing to worry about. I was looking forward to having my first night of uninterrupted sleep. As I was getting ready for bed, I noticed that the sedatives my doctor prescribed for me were missing from my makeup case. I was sure I had brought them with me, since I sometimes have trouble sleeping when I travel."

Julie paused again. Throughout her story Rick could hear quivering in her voice.

"I then checked the dresser drawer where I was hiding Jack's Valium and sedatives. They were also gone. I rushed into Jack's room. I found all three bottles of prescription on the floor next to his bed, completely empty. I screamed for Mom. I tried waking Jack up, but I couldn't. I dialled 911 on the bedside phone as Mom came rushing into the room."

Julie stopped. Rick felt sick to his stomach. He didn't need to hear any more details about the story. He had to find Jack.

"Where might he go?" he asked Julie.

"I don't know."

"I'm going to go search for him. I need a place to start."

"Try his friend, what's her name? She and her husband own a restaurant down on the boardwalk."

"Maria."

"Yes, Maria. That's it. Check with her."

"I'm out of here," Rick said.

"Call me when you find him," Julie said as Rick hung up the phone.

Grabbing his keys and cell phone off the counter, he ran out the door.

* * *

"*MAMA. THAT BLOND MAN WHO WAS WITH JACKIE THE OTHER* night is up front asking for you," Theresa quietly told

Maria, who was checking on a birthday celebration at the back of the dining room.

"Rick?"

"He says he needs to speak to you right away."

"Please excuse me. There is something I need to attend to," Maria excused herself from the table of partygoers, already worried that something was wrong. Smiling and warmly touching her regular customers, she made her way through the maze of tables to the front entrance hall.

Rick was standing at the door, looking out to the side street.

"Rick?"

He turned at the sound of her voice. "Maria. Thank God."

Panic was starting to fill her body at the sound of urgency in Rick's voice. "What is it?" she asked calmly.

"Jack's missing. Do you know where he might be?"

"What do you mean?"

"I came home to an empty house. He said he was going to be home tonight, then Julie called and told me what day it was and about the incident when he almost killed himself."

"Slow down, Rick," Maria said, putting her hand on his arm. "You're working yourself up." She watched as he took a couple of deep breaths. "Better?"

"Yes."

"Okay. I have seen Jackie today, and he is fine."

"Where, where is he?"

"I am not sure where he is now; I assumed he would be at home."

"When did you see him?" Rick asked.

"I saw him earlier today at the cemetery, at Stephen's grave."

"When? When was that?"

"Around three, maybe four o'clock."

"Maria that was *hours* ago. I need to find him."

"I know Jackie. He is fine," Maria tried to reassure him.

"You know what day it is, right? You know what he did to himself close to this time last year, right?"

"He wouldn't do that again."

"How can you be sure?"

"I spent quite a bit of time with him there today. We cried, we talked, and we laughed. He was in a good place when I left him. Peaceful."

Rick wasn't so sure. "I need to find him. Where is the cemetery? I'll start there."

"I will show you. Let me tell Joe and the boys I am leaving." Maria turned on her heel and walked briskly into the kitchen.

The few minutes it took her to return seemed like an hour to Rick.

"Let us go," she said as she brushed past Rick and opened the door to the warm night.

"My car's just around the corner," Rick said as they walked quickly up the sidewalk away from the restaurant.

Rick opened the passenger door to the Jeep for Maria when they approached it, closing it tightly once she settled in. As he was putting the key into the ignition, the vibration of his cell phone from inside of his shorts pocket startled him, causing him to drop his keys down to the floor.

"What is it?" Maria looked at him.

He fished his phone out of his pocket, looking at the call display before flipping it open. *Private number,* it read.

"Hello?"

"Hi, Rick."

"Jack! It's Jack!" he said as he looked over at Maria.

A smile formed on her lips.

"*Ya,* it's me."

"Where are you? We've been worried about you."

"Who is 'we'?"

"Julie, me, and now Maria. She's with me."

"You're with Maria?" I asked.

"I was looking for you. You weren't home when I got there this afternoon. Then Julie called and told me what day it was, and…"

"Let me guess, she told you about my incident last year and got you all caught up in her drama?"

"She's worried about you," Rick replied.

"No need. I am perfectly fine," I said.

However, Rick knew me well enough to know that I was pissed off, probably upset that everyone was making such a big deal out of the whole thing.

"Where are you?" Rick asked again.

A pause. "Well, that's why I'm calling. I need a favour."

"Anything," Rick said.

"I need a ride."

"No problem. Where are you?"

"At the police station."

"The police station!" Rick said. That was the kind of answer he expected from John or one of his other college buddies— but not from Jack!

"*Ya*. Funny story. Can you come get me? It's on Second Avenue just on the east side of Pacific Coast Highway. Oh, and could you please swing back home and pick up my wallet before you come? It's seems like I need to prove my identity before they'll release me."

Rick didn't know whether to feel grateful that Jack was okay or to feel upset that he was at the jail.

"I'll see you soon," he said.

"Oh, and Rick. Please tell Maria not to worry. Everything is fine. I'll call her tomorrow."

"Done, "I'm on the way."

*   *   *

"Well, Mr. Perry. You're free to go," Officer Talbot said as he handed me my wallet and walked me toward the security door that led out to the lobby.

"Thank you, Officer Talbot."

He opened the door for me and led me into the lobby. Rick was sitting along the far wall, on a wooden bench that looked extremely uncomfortable. He stood as soon as we entered the room. I noticed his face brighten.

"I believe that's your ride," Officer Talbot said, gesturing to Rick.

"Thanks again."

"Good luck with your show. I can't wait to get home tonight to tell my wife I met you. She loves your show."

I smiled again.

"Oh, one more thing, Mr. Perry." He paused at the security door. "Be careful not to get yourself locked in a cemetery again. Save it for your show."

"Promise," I replied, crossing my heart with my fingers.

Rick rushed to me and hugged me tightly the second Officer Talbot disappeared through the door. Not saying a word, I half hugged him back, feeling slightly awkward in the middle of the police station lobby.

"Where's Maria?" I asked.

"She gave me directions. I think she knew I wanted to see you alone."

I was quiet, but touched.

"So, locked in a cemetery?"

"Funny, huh?" I said as we walked toward the exit.

"How did you end up here?" Rick asks.

"Well, apparently, as I was attempting my escape, a nearby resident saw me and called the police, informing them that someone was breaking into the cemetery. Little did they know I was trying to break out!" I opened the door to the passenger side of Rick's Jeep and climbed in.

"They didn't believe you?"

Rick pulled the Jeep out of the parking lot, heading in the direction of my house.

"No, after telling him my story he believed me. It helped that my car was in visible sight, on the inside of the gate. He was just following protocol. Who knew that the police could detain you indefinitely when you don't have ID on you? He was a very nice man."

"Did he cuff you?" Rick smiled at me.

"No. I asked, though. Thought I should have had the whole experience. I think I got ripped off," I said with a chuckle.

He smiled again. We rode the rest of the short drive to the house in silence. I could only wonder what he was thinking but didn't know how to say.

"I suppose I should call Julie," I said bitterly as we walked into the house, breaking our silence.

"No need. I called her on the way to the police station. She's going to call you tomorrow. They're still in New York. She's probably asleep by now."

I looked at the oven clock as I walked into the kitchen and quickly calculated that it was 1:30 a.m. in New York. Still feeling totally pissed at her for telling Rick about my suicide attempt, I opened the fridge and pulled out a bottle of water.

"You hungry?" Rick asked.

"Nah. Officer Talbot shared his vending machine dinner with me," I said, taking a drink from the bottle. There was a slight awkwardness between us, the kind of awkwardness that two people have after sharing a night of passion, not knowing how the other feels about it, not sure how to talk about it. He came over to me, pulled my face to his and kissed me tenderly.

"Rick, I… can't," I said as I pulled away from him, moving to the other side of the island.

I searched my mind, trying to figure out how to say

what I felt.

He was staring at me.

"I can't deal with this right now," I said.

"Deal with what?"

"You. I can't deal with you and what happened between us."

He turned to walk out of the room.

"Rick, wait. Please wait."

He stopped and turned back toward me, crossing his arms over his chest.

"This day," I began. "This day was, *is* a very difficult day for me. I want to talk to you. I *need* to talk to you, but I can't. I'm embarrassed that I found myself locked in a cemetery tonight. I'm embarrassed that I found myself detained at a police station. I'm embarrassed that Julie told you about my suicide attempt. Actually, I'm really pissed Julie told you about that. I'm sorry that she made you worry about me."

"She was just concerned," Rick interrupted.

"That, and Julie is a completely different conversation. Please let me finish."

I fought the tears welling up in my eyes. "I like you. I really like you, and that's very confusing to me. Today— well, what's left of it— I need to get through alone. I don't think I can handle any pressure about our situation, or pressure about anything else, for that matter, right now. I really need to focus whatever energy I have left in me, on me. Can you understand that?"

I was trying to read his face for comprehension. He uncrossed his arms and came towards me. He kissed me lightly on the forehead.

"Do you want me to leave?"

"Gosh, no. That's not what I meant. I don't want you to leave. What I need is to go up to my room and finish out the day, and figure out how I feel about the day, without having to think about us."

"Okay. I get it." He stroked my arms.

"You do? 'Cause I'm not sure if I even get it," I replied.

"This was yours and Stephen's day; I get that. You need to be alone. Can we have dinner tomorrow night?" He looked directly into my eyes.

"Yes, of course," I said, my voice cracking.

"Good. I'll see you then." He kissed me once more on the forehead, turned, and walked towards the stairs, giving me the peace sign as he climbed.

I stood there, watching him until he disappeared at the turn on the landing. I heard his bedroom door close. Just when I thought I was all cried out, more tears slid down my cheeks. I wiped them away and looked around the main floor of my house.

Stephen's and my house.

No, just my house.

I went to the far pantry in the kitchen, the one that had a wine rack hidden behind its doors. I searched the rack until I found what I was looking for: a 1998 French Reserve Burgundy Stephen and I picked up on our trip to France three years ago. He insisted we buy it. When I balked at the price of it, his argument was that it would be ten years old on our ten-year anniversary. He wanted to save it and open it on this very day.

Setting it on the counter, I reached into the drawer for the corkscrew. I struggled to open the bottle because my hands were slightly tender from my gate-climbing escapade. I reached into an upper cupboard for a wine glass and poured the rich contents of the bottle into it. I lifted the glass up to the light, noticing its rich burgundy colour. I raised the glass to my nose, inhaling its wonderful sweet aroma. On impulse I pulled an additional glass from the cupboard and filled it half full with the Burgundy.

"Ten years, Stephen. Ten years," I said, looking up at

the ceiling, clinking the two glasses together.

The first sip of the Burgundy stimulated my taste buds as it washed over them. A perfect full-bodied blend with just the right amount of boldness and hint of sweetness. The taste immediately took me back to the winery in the South of France where it was born. I closed my eyes and pictured its grand beauty, surrounded by row and rows of perfectly manicured vines, sparkling in the morning sunlight.

I could feel my eyes getting moist again.

"Ten years," I mumbled again. I drank my glass of wine quickly; I needed to calm myself. I refilled it, past the half full line, for once. Corking the bottle I left it and the second glass of wine in the centre of the island. Then, I turned out the lights and headed upstairs to my bedroom.

*   *   *

AS I STOOD BENEATH THE SPRAY OF THE SHOWER I FELT grateful for its warmth. Images of Stephen flashed in my mind like a slide show on fast forward. I saw glimpses of him, coming at me from deep within my memory. When I was just on the verge of recognising the image, it blurred into another. It was giving me a headache. I turned the water off and stepped onto the bathmat, reaching for a towel from the hook beside the shower. I towelled myself dry. After wrapping the towel around my waist, I made my way to the vanity and took a long sip from the glass of wine I had left there.

In front of the steamy mirror, I ran my hands through my hair. My eyes were bloodshot and puffy. My skin looked pale and lifeless, my eye still mangled.

Quite a sight, Jack. You are quite a sight.

I pressed my fists into my temples to try and stop the pounding. I reached up and opened the medicine cabinet.

My fingers bypassed the bottle of Tylenol and pulled out two prescription bottles. The first label read: *Patient— Perry, Jack D. Physician—Jones, M.L.*

The pounding in my head made it impossible for me to make out the scientific name that I recognised as Valium. *Take one pill when feeling anxiety. Do not take more than four doses in a twenty-four-hour period.*

The second bottle roughly said the same thing with the exception of *Take one pill thirty minutes before bedtime. Do not take more than two doses in a twenty-four-hour period.*

I stared at the bottles in my hands. I rolled them from side to side in my palm, feeling their weight. I took another long sip of wine as I made my decision on what I was about to do. The pounding in my head was dulling to a throb as I took the lids off both bottles. I spilled the contents of both bottles into my right hand. I gently fingered the hospital ID bracelet from my brief hospital stay and the ID bracelet from my fourteen-day stay at the private psychiatric hospital/sanitarium in Malibu.

Knowing I didn't need these items anymore, as reminders of what a stupid thing I attempted to do, I turned my hand over and let them fall into the garbage. I threw the bottles away too.

Taking the last remaining drink of wine from the glass, I made my way to my bed. The emotional exhaustion of the day finally took its toll on me, and I was quickly sound asleep.

12

THE SUNLIGHT'S GENTLE WARMTH STIRRED ME AWAKE, millions of sunbeams dancing along my face and neck. I stretched, as my body woke. I squeezed my eyes more tightly closed hoping my mind will be fooled into going back to sleep. It was no use. I blinked my eyes repeatedly, trying to adjust to the brightness of the day. 8:15 a.m., the bedside clock told me. Starving I threw on a pair of sweatpants and t-shirt and headed downstairs.

Confusion hit me as I entered the kitchen. There, perched on one of the stools that flanked the island, was Maria, with the morning paper spread out before her and a cup of coffee by her right hand.

"Good morning, sunshine," she greeted me with a smile.

"Uh, morning," I said as I rubbed my eyes, trying to make sense of the moment.

"Fresh coffee in the pot." She gestured for me to pour myself a cup. "Breakfast is in the warming oven."

"You made me breakfast?" I asked as I opened the warming oven and took out the stainless steel pan.

"Oh, no, Jackie," she said with a laugh in her voice, "Joe hasn't let me near a kitchen since our first year of marriage. He prepared it. I'm just the messenger."

My senses were immediately stimulated with the delightful smell of eggs Benedict and spicy hash browns when I lifted the lid off the pan— my favourite breakfast.

I quickly transferred the contents of the pan to a plate

and took a seat across from Maria.

"Not that I'm unhappy to see you, Maria, but what brings you by this morning?" I asked after my appetite was assuaged from the first couple of bites of my breakfast.

"I wanted to see you this morning."

I looked at the oven clock. "How long have you been here?"

"Oh, I would say about an hour, maybe an hour and a half. Rick let me in. I caught him just as he was leaving. I was so surprised to learn you were still asleep, since you are up before the birds usually," she said, looking at me.

"I know. I haven't a clue as to the last time I actually slept this late," I responded.

"You had a draining day yesterday. How did you sleep?"

"Like a rock. I barely remember getting into bed."

"How do you feel today?"

I thought about this for a moment before answering. "Peaceful. I think I feel peaceful."

Maria smiled at me.

"I assume Rick filled you in on my adventures of last night?" I asked.

"He did, indeed." She chuckled.

"It's not funny!"

"Oh, but my dear Jackie, it is! Stephen would have found it very amusing," she added.

"Yes. He would have." My smile faded from my face as I took a sip of coffee. "Maria, I'm really sorry that you got caught up in the drama my sister created yesterday. It was totally unnecessary."

"She was just worried about you," she replied.

"No. The only thing Julie was concerned about was how she would look if something had happened and it looked like she didn't do anything to prevent it."

"You are being too hard on her," Maria softly said.

"I just think if she had been really concerned, she would have made a point of being here yesterday. God knows I held her hand through her three divorces, letting her lean completely on me."

"And she has held your hand," Maria fired back.

"Whose side are you on?" I asked, stunned that Maria was defending Julie.

"There are no sides here. Say what you will about Julie. But the fact is she took care of you when you fell apart after Stephen's accident. She *did* hold your hand, Jackie. She held it very tightly. You shouldn't be so hard on her. She loves you."

I sat stunned as Maria ended her speech. It surprised me, since it was no secret that Maria did not like Julie, and vice versa.

"Well, I guess if *you* are defending Julie, I must be a real ass," I said after a couple minutes of silence.

"No, Jackie, you're not an ass. You just haven't been able to be present in the moment for a while," she said patting my arm as she spoke.

I could hear a touch of underlying hurt in her voice, resulting from me abandoning our friendship over the last year. I didn't know how to tell her, *sorry.* The only thing I could do now was recommit to being her friend.

"So what is going on between you and Rick?"

I nearly choked on the food in my mouth. "I'm not sure I understand your question." I stalled, trying to collect my thoughts.

"I think you do." She took a sip from her cup, looking at me suspiciously.

"I saw his fear last night when he thought you were missing and possibly in trouble. It was not the kind of fear someone has when they are just friends, or even just roommates. The fear in his eyes was that of a lover, or partner, or someone in love— almost like his life depended on finding you." Maria paused again, waiting for me to react. I didn't. "If nothing is going on here, I would be very surprised. And if nothing is going on, you definitely have a young man in your house who is on the brink of falling in love with you, whether you realise it or not."

"He's not in love with me," I managed to get out.

Damn Maria and her sixth sense, I thought. The one thing I loved most about her was that she could pick up on almost anything. It was also the only thing I probably disliked about her. There was no hiding anything from her.

I decided to come clean, since I knew it was useless to lie to her. "We slept together a couple of nights ago."

"I knew it!" She exclaimed. "Like I said, *fear*, like a lover."

"It was just the once. Well, twice. Okay, well, actually, it was three times. But all in one night." I was stumbling over my words.

"So what does this mean?" she asked.

"I don't know. What I do know is I have a tremendous amount of guilt over it."

She lifted one eyebrow but remained silent, waiting for me to continue.

"First off, he is my sister's stepson. Second, he is fifteen years younger than me. Third, I feel like I am cheating on Stephen. And fourth— well, maybe I don't have a fourth. But I know this is wrong. I don't even know what he thinks about what happened between us, since we haven't discussed it. I don't know if he is gay, or just bi, or just using me to experiment—"

I stopped to catch my breath.

"Jackie," she said as she got up and refilled both our cups with steaming coffee. "Please remember that whatever happened between you and Rick is strictly between you and Rick, not you and Stephen and Rick. You are both grown individuals, very capable of making your own decisions. Don't let the threat of what others might think take away the beauty of the experience. Let yourself feel. Let yourself enjoy. Don't analyse. Don't get caught up in 'what ifs'."

"But—"

"No buts. Take it one step at a time, one day at a time. If it was meant to be just that one night, then that's all it will be. If it is meant to be more, it will be more. Whatever it is, both of you are going to better people for having the experience. Don't crush something that might just be a defining moment in your life."

"He is almost family," I quickly interjected.

"Who's family? Not *your* family, my friend."

I thought about this for a moment. Maybe Maria had a point. Rick really was only related to Julie, not me.

"But what about the age difference? We're both in two different places in our lives," I said.

"What? Are you already picking out your wedding gown?" she laughed. "I wish I could trade my Joe in for someone fifteen years younger than me! Please don't tell him I said that."

Her comment put a smile on my face.

"Who cares about the age difference? Celebrate it! I like Rick. I like what I have seen him bring out in you," she said as she patted my arm.

I smiled and nodded in agreement. "I guess I like what he has brought out in me, too. I haven't felt alive since Stephen. He has definitely challenged me."

"Good. Then keep him for a while," she said with a smile. "Now you go upstairs and fix yourself up. When you're ready, I will take you to your car."

She dismissed me with a wave of her hand and turned her attention back to the morning paper.

* * *

AFTER MARIA DROPPED ME OFF AT MY CAR, I HEADED OUT TO the 405, heading for Beverly Hills. I estimated I would have about an hour to quickly shop before I had to be at Vivian's for our lunch meeting with Daniel. I needed to pick up a wedding gift for Shelia and Michael's wedding this weekend. One of Shelia's favourite stores was just off Rodeo Drive: It was a tiny little boutique with imported treasures from Asia. Since I neglected to ask where they registered I was taking the risk that they did in fact register at the boutique, or that I would find something incredible to give them.

I found a parking spot easily in front of Armani Exchange, a short two-block walk from the boutique. I was greeted immediately by a friendly woman who looked to be in her early forties when I enter the boutique. Judging from her stylish, expensive suit, I made the assumption she was probably the owner.

"Welcome," she said with a genuine smile.

"Good morning," I replied.

"Shopping for yourself today?" she asked.

"No. I was wondering if Shelia Smith and Michael O'Brien might be registered here?"

Her face lighted in recognition. "Yes, they are. But I'm afraid there isn't much left on their list. I'm Marion, one of the owners." She held out her manicured hand as she introduced herself.

"Jack. Very nice to meet you Marion."

"You too. Sheila is one of my favourite clients. She buys everything!" Marion said with a soft laugh. "Let me bring up her list on the computer."

I browsed the items in the boutique as Marion busied herself at a desk at the back of the store.

"Have you been in our store before, Jack?" She was suddenly beside me as I was admiring a classic-looking Ming Dynasty vase.

"Just once, a couple years ago," I replied.

"Our items constantly change. My business partner travels Asia extensively, searching out treasures. Now, let's see what we have on Sheila's list," she said, referring to a printout in her right hand. Marion took me through the boutique, pointing out the five remaining items on Sheila's list. The last item took my breath away. It was a beautiful, red silk wall hanging with a gold chain. The silk was adorned with black stitching and gold beads outlined an image of a traditional Japanese wedding ceremony.

"It's very beautiful, isn't it?"

I nodded.

"Very traditional. This type of wall hanging, in Japanese culture, is given to the bride and groom on their wedding day from the groom's family. The women in the groom's family design and create it. Then they place it in the new married couple's bedroom before they spend their first night together."

"It's stunning. This is it," I replied, not even inquiring about the price.

"Excellent. This is one of the first items Shelia picked, but the price has scared away most of her family and friends. Please come with me to my desk and I will write it up."

She gestured to me to follow and talked as we crossed the boutique. "I've arranged with Sheila and Michael to have gifts delivered directly to their house the day after the wedding, with a card attached from the purchaser. Is that okay with you, Jack?"

"Yes, please. I wouldn't want to risk ruining something so beautiful. I'll leave it in your hands."

"Perfect. Now I just need to get a little information from you. Your last name and address."

I recited the information for Marion.

"That's funny," she said while looking at the screen.

"Problem?"

"No. No, problem. It's just we have another client in our database listed with your address."

"Stephen Ross?" I asked.

"Why, yes, that's it. The computer is flagging the file as he has an item on hold. It took a while for us to import this particular item. We just received it about four months ago." Marion was studying her computer screen. "It was paid for in full, but we haven't been able to reach Stephen to let him know it has arrived. The number we have on file is listed as disconnected."

"Stephen passed away a little over a year ago."

"Oh, my goodness, I am so sorry. I had no idea." She put a hand over her mouth as she replied.

"There's no way you could have," I replied, completely composed.

"You're Jack. You're Jack. Jack and Stephen. Stephen, Shelia's former boss. My gosh. I'm sorry. I didn't put it together sooner. Shelia told me so much about both of you; she adores you both so much. Please accept my deepest regret and condolences." She placed her hand on top of mine.

"Thank you."

"I'm just going to print this bill up for you to look over, and then I'll get you a gift card."

I looked over the invoice: the total came to three thousand eight hundred dollars. I pulled out my American Express card and handed it to Marion, keeping the shock of the cost to myself. Marion handed me a silver inlaid ivory card to sign as she processed my credit card.

After handing me the printout to sign, she excused herself once more and told me she would be right back. She returned with her arms full. "I believe this belongs to you," she said as she placed a medium-sized box on the desk in front of me. "This is what Stephen ordered, and judging from what's inside, I'm sure it was bought for you."

I stared at the box as Marion folded the purchase invoice of Shelia and Michael's gift into an envelope and placed it before me.

"If you have any questions about the item, please feel free to call me any time." She handed me her personal business card.

In a fog, I picked up the box and made my way through the store, Marion at my heels.

"It was really nice meeting you, and I'm deeply sorry for your loss," she said as she opened the door for me.

"Thank you." I nodded as I left the boutique. Then I walked the two short blocks back to my car. Opening the trunk remotely, I placed the box inside and secured it with the safety net.

* * *

PULLING INTO VIVIAN'S CIRCULAR DRIVEWAY, I STOPPED short behind Daniel's black Porsche, almost hitting it. My mind was still in a fog, thinking about the box in the trunk of my car. Opening the vanity mirror on the sun visor, I quickly took stock of myself. I looked composed. I took several deep breaths before getting out of the car, building up my strength, putting up my shield. Daniel had a gift for picking up on emotions, sensing people's fears, and pouncing on them. I always put my guard up around him. I got out of the car and reached into the trunk, past the box to retrieve my briefcase. Closing the trunk, I pushed thoughts of the box far back into a deep compartment of my mind.

* * *

"HELLO, JACK, DARLING!" VIVIAN GREETED ME WITH A KISS ON both cheeks as she opened the front door. She was clad casually in an orange tank top and white linen Capri pants, and she seemed to be in a good mood. "Please come in. Daniel is by the pool. Go join him. I'm just going to check on lunch."

Without waiting for my response, she turned and disappeared through a door off the entrance hallway.

"Hello, Daniel," I greeted him once in the pool area behind the house.

He looked up from the papers that were spread out before him on the glass top table. "Jack," he responded, peering over the tops of his glasses. His six-foot frame was dressed perfectly in an Armani sport coat, white shirt, and jeans.

"How was Italy?" I asked as I sat across from him, knowing it would get a rise out of him.

"*Spain*. And it was short. Thank you for asking," he responded sarcastically.

I looked down at the papers before him: *The LA Times*, a couple of gossip magazines with Ashley's picture splashed on the front, and copies of the story board and script ideas I had sent to Vivian yesterday.

"Our little girl is in quite a bit of trouble, isn't she?" Daniel said, more as a statement than a question. On the cover of a tabloid were the words *Ashley's Going to Jail.*

Before I could respond, the glass door from the house opened and Vivian came out.

"Lunch is almost ready. What are you two boys discussing?"

I could tell she was worried that we were going to get into it. She knew I never liked him.

"I was just commending Jack on such an eloquent press release. I was very impressed. He managed to make it look like the studio was compassionate about the incident, supportive, and totally not taking an official stance in regards to Ashley. Yet, you didn't say anything much beside 'no comment'. A beautifully orchestrated 'no comment', at that."

Daniel rarely gave out compliments, so I was sceptical, but I said, "Thank you."

"Well, our Jack is the best!" Vivian exclaimed, patting my arm.

"Daniel, pour him a glass of wine and top ours off, won't you? Thanks. Lunch is going to be about thirty minutes. Let's do a preliminary overview of the ideas Jack has for the show, shall we?" Vivian asked.

I pulled out the copy of the various story boards and possible scripts from my briefcase. Vivian was looking at her copies when she spoke, "I like your first idea, Jack. Working with Ashley's character dying during summer vacation. I like how you wrote the opening scene as her funeral. I also like the fact we could mirror what actually happened to Ashley in real life, sending a message to our younger audience about the repercussions of drinking and driving."

"We have to keep in mind that we may lose Christina's character, too," Daniel added.

"If we lose Christina, I think we should recast her role with a new actress." Daniel and Vivian both looked at me.

"We can't afford to lose two out of the six main characters of the show. It will be suicide." Vivian exclaimed.

"Jack's right," Daniel spoke up.

"And Christina can't quit the show. The studio won't allow it. They'll sue her," Vivian said.

"No, I don't think they will. I think they'll let her out of her contract quietly if needed. The studio won't want the negative publicity, especially if things don't work out for her sister," Daniel responded.

"How do we recast without knowing what she'll do?" Vivian asked.

"We put out an open casting call under the pretence of

casting a new character for the show. If Christina stays with the show, we'll create a new character for the new actress, since either way we're going to lose Ashley," I answered.

"That will work. I think it's our best bet," Daniel said.

"What do you think, Viv?" I asked, turning to her.

"I think if the two of you agree on an idea, it must be a brilliant one. Let's go with your instincts, boys. Let's develop this. After tomorrow's meeting, let's light a fire under casting to arrange opened casting calls in LA and New York."

*   *   *

DRIVING HOME FROM VIVIAN'S, I FELT ALIVE WITH excitement and anticipation. The storyboard we created was good. I no longer feared the scheduled meeting tomorrow with the network. *Chamberlain Heights* was a good show. The direction we came up with for the new season would make it a great show.

I made a quick stop at the grocery store and headed home. Pulling into the empty driveway, I figured I had about thirty to forty-five minutes before Rick arrived. Dropping the grocery bags on the island in the kitchen, I pulled out a bowl and mixed a red wine marinade for the steaks I had just picked up. Next, I cleaned and sliced the vegetables, then arranged them in foil packets with olive oil, fresh rosemary, and dill. Deciding to wait until dinner was under way to make the salad, I quickly put away the remaining groceries and headed upstairs to change into shorts and a tank top.

13

"JACK?" RICK CALLED OUT AS HE ENTERED THE HOUSE. HE
dropped his bag at the base of the stairs. "Jack?" He
noticed what looked like the preparation of dinner spread
out on the island. "Hello?"

The soft sounds of jazz filled the rooms as he walked
towards the open sliding doors that led out to the deck.

Jack was standing with his back to the house, looking
out to the ocean. Taking in the sight of him, his long legs,
his perfectly toned body, immediately sent blood to his
groin. Rick had looked forward to this evening all day. But
now that he was actually with Jack again, the memory of
what happened yesterday made him uneasy. He knew he
couldn't compete with a love that lasted ten years and the
thought of Jack rejecting him put fear in his blood.

He stood, his feet rooted to the floor, unable to move.

* * *

THE WARM BREEZE FROM THE OCEAN MADE THE
approaching sunset hour magical. A perfect ending to a
perfect day. I stared out into the ocean, awed by it vastness
and strength. For the first time in a long time the feeling of
fear, loathing, and anguish were nowhere to be found in my
thoughts. I lost myself as the evening sun danced upon the
blue water.

Sensing I was not alone, I slowly turned around to face

the house. There he was, standing in the doorway. He looked a little uncomfortable. I smiled at him and he smiled back, but he made no attempt to cross the threshold to come outside.

I walked toward him. He made no attempt to meet me. I ran my hands around his waist, linking them in the small of his back as I leant in and kissed him. I felt him respond immediately at the touch of my lips.

"Hey," I said as I pulled away slightly, looking into his eyes.

"Hey, yourself," he said as he wrapped his arms around me, crushing me into his body. He kissed my neck; I inhaled the warm smell of him.

Rick loosened his grip on me just enough to bring our lips together once again. His kiss was passionate. I could feel the beginnings of passion within me. I pulled away.

"Okay, mister. Let's take a breather," I said huskily.

He released his hold and laced his fingers with mine, staring into my eyes. I felt a slight blush coming on and so I turned my head away. He responded by kissing my hair.

"So, what do you have going on in there?" he asked, pulling up our hands and pointing into the kitchen behind him with his thumbs.

"I prepped dinner while waiting for the gourmet barbeque chef to arrive," I said.

"Great. I come home from a long day at the office, and now I have to cook? Where is the justice in that?" Rick was teasing.

"Well, if I recall, you were the one who said I eat like a chick, so you, *sir,* are now in charge of dinners."

His kissed my forehead. "I'm going to go change. Be right back."

I followed him as far as the kitchen, then started the preparation of the salad. He was back in what seemed like seconds, dressed in cargo shorts and a loose fitting white t-

shirt, which given its ill fit, still showcased his muscular
chest beneath the loose fabric. I watched him as he opened
the fridge and retrieved a beer from inside.

"Beer?" he asked as he held one up.

I nodded. He opened two bottles and passed one to me.

"What's in the box?" he asked as he gestured to the box
from the boutique, which was sitting at the end of the
island. I had forgotten about it entirely until he pulled my
attention back to it.

"I don't know."

"Is it a gift?" he asked.

I took a deep breath. "Sort of."

"Sort of a gift, huh? Interesting. From who?"

"It's from Stephen."

"I don't understand."

I explained how I had ended up with the box.

"Open it," he said when I finished.

"Maybe later," I stuttered.

"No, right now. Open the box right now."

I was surprised by the forcefulness in his voice. "I said
no."

"And I said open it. Now," he picked up the box and
placed it directly in front of me.

I felt the first hint of anger starting to boil in my blood.

"Open the box, Jack. You need to open the box, now."

I bit my lip, holding back anything I might say.

He pulled at my hands, placing them on the lid of the
box. I tried to pull away, but he was stronger than me; his
grip was tight.

"Look. I am not going to tippy toe around this house,
pretending that Stephen never existed. And I am not going
to let *you* do it any longer, either."

I struggled to break free of his grip.

Rick went on, "He bought this for you. Open it. Find
out what he wanted you to have. The timing is amazing.

Open it, Jack. I am not going to let you hide from this."

My hands trembled as he released them from his grip. Shaking, I opened the cabinet drawer to my left and took out a knife. Carefully, I ran the serrated edge of it along the tape that secured the lid. It cut easily. The top of the box popped open when the tape released.

I placed the knife on the counter and paused before reaching inside to retrieve the contents. The plastic of the bubble wrap felt soft in my hands as I gripped the object inside.

I couldn't tell if the object was heavy or I was weak from emotion, but I struggled to get it out. I placed the object on the counter. Rick put the box on the floor.

With shaking hands, I slowly unwrapped the bubble wrap protecting the object, to reveal a bowl. A crystal bowl.

I looked at it in confusion. It looked old, but the crystal was still completely clear. I took in the Japanese writing along the bowl's rim. I couldn't take my eyes from it. It was stunning.

"It's an anniversary bowl." I heard Rick's voice, not taking my eyes from the bowl and the magical prisms of colour reflecting in it. "It's given as a blessing to the couple who has completed their first decade together, to welcome them into the second decade of their love and commitment to each other."

"How do you know that?" I turned to look at Rick.

He held up a single white sheet of paper. "It was in the box."

He handed it to me. My eyes clouded over with tears and the words on the page blurred. Rick hugged me from behind.

"What a gift," was all he said.

I didn't let my tears last for long; I wiped them away. Rick released me and picked up the bowl. He placed it on the fireplace mantel, which visually separated the living room from the kitchen, perfectly in the centre.

"The paper says the bowl is to be placed in the most prominent place in the home, so all who enter can honour its presence. I think this is perfect." He paused and then walked back toward me. He kissed my cheek gently, picked up the bowl containing our steaks and headed out to the deck.

*   *   *

THE BEDSIDE CLOCK READ 5:45 A.M. WHEN I OPENED MY eyes. The morning light was just starting to peek into the room. Rick was snoring softly beside me, curled against my back. I gently lifted his arm off my hip and got out of bed. He remained undisturbed, sleeping peacefully. I dressed in my running gear and headed out to the beach.

Taking the time to stretch first, I started my run off slowly, absorbing my surroundings. I felt like a shift had been taking place within me. The morning colours seemed brighter and more vibrant. The smell of the air, fresh with life, stimulated all my senses. I continued at a slower pace, feeling the earth beneath me, feeling the pull from it grounding me. I felt as if a weight had been lifted from my shoulders. For the first time in a long time, I was looking forward to the future.

Rick? Is Rick my future, I asked myself as I turned around and headed back in the direction of my house. I wasn't sure. But I decided to take Maria's advice and let it be what it was going to be— one day, one month, one year— whatever it was suppose to be.

I let myself into the house through the sliders. Rick was sitting at the island, dressed and drinking coffee.

"Morning," he said with a smile.

I walked over and kissed him lightly on the lips.

"I thought you would still be asleep. I was looking forward to getting back into bed with you."

He pulled me close.

"Don't. I'm all sweaty," I said.

"Don't care." He pulled me onto his lap, kissing me.

"Why are you dressed so early? It's not even seven o'clock," I said.

"I promised John I would workout with him again this morning. Need to meet him at 7:30," he said as he nuzzled my neck.

"Who's John?" As I asked the question, I realised how little I knew about Rick's life. All our conversations had revolved around me and my life.

"We're in the internship together. But I would much rather stay here with you." He kissed my neck. "What are you doing today?"

"We have our meeting with the network today." I was starting to feel dizzy with pleasure from his kisses.

"That's right. I forgot. You nervous?" He pulled back.

"No. I feel really good. We came up with a great game plan for the show. I think the meeting will be a breeze." Reluctantly, I pulled myself out of his lap, knowing he had to leave for campus.

Standing, he grabbed me from behind and locked his arms around my waist, pulling me into him. Flashes of last night's lovemaking instantly flooded my mind. I turned my head and he kissed me intensely. He released me and grabbed my hand, leading me to the front door.

"See you tonight? I should be home by six."

"Yes, you will see me tonight. I'm not sure how this meeting is going to go. I may have to work afterwards on the new scripts, depending on what kind of timeline the network gives us. I might be late."

"I'll wait," he said. He picked up his bag from the floor and slung it over his shoulder. Then he kissed me quickly once more and headed out the door. I stood in the doorway, waving at him as he pulled out onto the street. I didn't close the door until his Jeep was completely out of my sight.

14

"YOU SEEM VERY *UP* THIS MORNING. WHAT GIVES?" JOHN asked Rick between sets of leg extensions.

"Nothing out of the ordinary. Just in a good mood," he answered between breaths.

"It seems like a more than that," John said as they started the last set of exercises.

Rick ignored his last comment and changed the subject, "You ready for your turn at leading the afternoon lectures?"

"*Ya.* I had lots of time to prepare last night," he responded, breathless as he finished the last of his set.

Rick didn't miss the shot John took at him for abandoning him once again last night. He pretended that it went over his head. John was a good friend. But how could Rick tell him he was ditching him day after day to spend time with Jack? Would he understand?

Hell, Rick could hardly understand it himself. It was new for him. He has never felt this kind of pull towards another person, ever. He had never felt so connected or happy from just being with someone. He couldn't tell John. He could only hope that John didn't see completely though his lame excuses. He didn't want to hurt John's feelings.

* * *

"JACK!"

"What?" My awareness was quickly brought back into

151

the present. I turned my head to look at Vivian, who was sitting next to me in the sixth floor waiting room.

"Where were you?"

"Sorry. I just drifted out for a moment," I replied.

"I just asked you if you have all your notes. I'm a nervous wreck about it."

I tapped the side of my briefcase. "Everything is outlined. It's going to present beautifully. There is nothing to worry about."

"Jack's right. There's nothing to worry about, Vivian," Daniel chimed in from his chair directly across from us, looking very at ease in his Armani suit.

"We've been waiting for thirty minutes already. What's up?" Vivian asked.

It surprised me that she was so nervous. She never appeared nervous about anything.

"Good morning, everyone," Pricilla greeted us as she entered the waiting area.

We all stood– Vivian, Daniel, Rose, Evelyn, myself, and Debra, Daniel's assistant who had joined our group for this morning's meetings.

"They're ready for you now. Everyone, please follow me."

We fell into single file behind Pricilla, Vivian leading Daniel and I, our assistants following behind. Inside Goldman's office, Pricilla instructed Rose, Evelyn, and Debra to sit in the chairs away from the board table, directly behind us against the wall.

Vivian looked over at me and whispered, "I expected everyone to be here already. I assumed we were being invited in last."

Pricilla disappeared through the heavy door into Goldman's private office. I could hear her announce through the partially opened door we were all settled and ready. I quickly pulled out my notes and laptop, confident that I would be successful in selling the new *Chamberlain Heights.*

"Something's wrong," Vivian said under her breath.

I looked up just as Goldman, Peters, Shauna, and Shauna's legal assistant Shelley came into the room.

"Good morning, everyone. Thank you for coming," Goldman greeted us as he entered, gesturing that we should stay seated. The rest of his group remained completely silent.

"Nice to see you, Daniel," Goldman said as he took his seat at the head of the table.

Daniel nodded.

"Ron, am I misunderstanding the protocol here? Are we meeting before the network people arrive?" Vivian asked, confused.

Goldman paused and sat back in his chair. "The network representatives aren't coming."

Vivian, Daniel, and I all looked at each other, confused.

"Don and I met with them earlier," Goldman said.

"I'm a little confused here, Ron. Why weren't we notified about the change?" Vivian asked.

"It was at their request and discretion. Look, I'm not going to draw this out or sugar coat it for you three," he gestured to Vivian, Daniel, and me. "The network has cancelled the *Chamberlain Heights* contract. They're not going to pick it up for the fall season."

The room went silent for a moment.

"How can they do that? They signed for two more seasons," Vivian responded.

"They can, and they did. They still have to pay the studio for the show to uphold their contract, but it is at their discretion if they want it on their fall line up," Goldman said.

"Then we sell the show to another network." Daniel was speaking now. "We finished last season in the top ten.

After seven seasons, that's a phenomenal achievement for any show. Any of the other three major networks will jump at the chance to sign *Chamberlain Heights.*"

I was beginning to smell a set-up.

"The studio has decided not to actively pursue that route, Daniel. I say, with deep regret, we are cancelling the production of *Chamberlain Heights,*" Goldman replied, his voice completely flat. "Given Ashley's situation, the show might not be easily sold to another network. We're going to cut our losses before we have any."

Vivian pounded her hand on the table. "We can't do this. We can't cancel the show without winding it down. We owe it to the fans of the show. We need to wrap it up properly. With a proper ending. We need to have endings and the shadow of new beginnings for the characters after the show. The fans will demand it. I demand it."

"The decision is done. Production has officially stopped," Goldman said.

"But the fans! We can't end with the show in limbo," Vivian repeated herself.

"The fans will move on to another show. They'll find a new show and forget all about *Chamberlain Heights,*" Goldman answered, looking directly at Vivian.

"But what about the new story boards, the new script, the new ideas you had us work on? You need to look at them. It's going to make the show greater than it ever was. Jack... Jack set up the presentation. You need to show them." Vivian was tugging at my arm with panic.

"He doesn't care, Vivian," I said. "This was all a set up, wasn't it?" I asked, looking directly at Goldman. "You had this planned all along, didn't you? You'd already made this decision when you met with us on Monday, didn't you?"

"The network made the decision. Not me," Goldman replied.

"But you knew about it. You knew you were cancelling

us. The decision had already been made." I stood up. "You self-righteous, arrogant asshole."

Goldman glared at me. "Vivian, I suggest you tell your boy here to sit down, and mind his manners."

"But why? Why would you lead us on like that? Why would you make us go to all the work of re-doing the story board and coming up with new script ideas?" I felt like I was having an out of body experience. I could hear myself talking, but it felt like I was a bystander in the room. "I got it. You used us. When the Ashley situation occurred, you realised you need us to smooth it over, making the studio look good." I felt something snap inside of me. "You fucking prick!"

"That's enough! Sit the fuck down Jack!" Goldman screamed, leaning on the table and trying to get closer to me.

"No! You sit the fuck down!" I pointed at him. "You are going to sit in that fucking chair and listen to what I have to say. You owe that to us, at the very least, after you bent us over this very table, without so much as a kiss or a call in the morning."

Goldman remained standing, his eyes burning with fury.

"You screwed us, sold us out. What was the kickback?"

I could see from Goldman's face that I was beginning to figure it out.

"I got it." I snapped my fingers. "You needed a new show picked up, didn't you? You needed a favour from the network. You used *Chamberlain Heights* as a bargaining chip. But for what?"

A new calmness overcame me. I knew I was on the right track. The anger I was feeling earlier was leaving me.

"The new show is for Troy Silverman, isn't it?"

The vein on Goldman's forehead was visibly throbbing, looking like it was about to pop.

"We all know you're fucking him behind your wife's back," I said.

"Shut the fuck up, Jack. You are way out of line here," Peter said, standing.

I went on. "He's what? Twenty-six? Twenty-seven? Aren't your daughters older than that, Ron?"

Goldman was trying to stare me down. "This meeting is finished," he said, releasing his grip from the table and standing completely upright.

I wasn't done, though. "Don't be mad, I know your little secret, Ron. You should have been a little more discreet than screwing him at the Hollywood Hilton."

Goldman looked like he was going to come over the table at me. I could tell he wanted to hit me, and hit me hard. "You're finished in this town, Jack. By the time I get through with you, you won't be able to get a job writing want ads."

I could hear the fury in his voice as he turned towards the door to his office. I kicked out my chair and crossed the few steps that separated us.

"Am I, Ron? Am I really finished in this town? Or can I just follow you into your office and let you fuck my brains out? You know, I am really quite good. I should be able get *my* very own show. Hell, I could probably get two shows. What do you think?"

He turned slowly to face me. "Goodbye, Jack," he said, smiling angrily at me.

Peter and Pricilla followed him quickly into his office then shut the door.

"I guess I will take that as a definite maybe!" I shouted at the closed door.

When I turned around, I was met with shocked faces from everyone remaining in the boardroom— everyone except Vivian, who looked like she was in a coma.

"I just have a couple of things I wish to discuss, if that's okay with you?" Shauna broke the silence.

I sat back down in my chair without saying a word.

"My department will be sending you copies of letters formally cancelling your contracts with the studio, effective immediately. Along with it, a cheque for the total cost of the remaining monies owed to you on your two-year contract term. Similar packages for your creative staff will be delivered, as well. This will not include your administrative staff and show crew staff, since they are employed directly by the studio. They will be re-assigned to another position within the studio. The studio would appreciate this be done as quickly as possible and requests that your production offices be cleared of any personal items. All studio property must be inventoried and returned to the studio by the end of next week. This includes items such as laptops, cell phones, keys, etcetera. Questions?"

"What about the actors?" Daniel asked.

"They'll be informed of the cancellation through their agents as per studio policy. None of you are to contact any of the actors directly. It would be a breach of your contract, which could result in legal action against you from the studio. Anything else?"

Daniel and I both muttered a 'no'. Vivian was still completely silent.

"Good. Goodbye then." Shauna got up and headed out through the glass doors, Shelley close on her heels.

"Let us take our leave now," Vivian said after a few moments, her face stricken and white.

* * *

"NO! YOU SIT THE FUCK DOWN!" DANIEL SAID, POINTING AT me, recreating my earlier outburst. "I got to hand it to you, Jack. I never thought you had a set that big."

We were sitting in my office drinking beer that Daniel had retrieved from his office mini fridge. Vivian disappeared into her office the second we got back to the production offices, making it very clear that neither of us should have followed her.

Evelyn and Debra were at their desks, making calls and arranging meetings for both Daniel and my respective teams as soon as possible. I assumed Rose was doing the same for Vivian.

"And calling him a 'fucking prick'. That was my favourite!"

He was amusing himself more than he was amusing me. Even though the prospect of my career in Hollywood was completely over, I had no regrets about what I had just done.

"Here's to writing want ads." I lifted my bottle in toast.

"I really admire you, Jack."

"What?" Daniels statement caught me off guard.

"You called one of the most powerful men in the industry on his shit. You stood up for not only yourself, but for Vivian, and me, and for everyone connected to *Chamberlain Heights*. I wish it was me who had stood up and said those things to Goldman. Here's to you, my friend, here's to you." He raised his bottle and toasted me.

I raised mine in response, taking a very long drink from my bottle. I was starting to look at Daniel in a new light. Over the years I had lost track of the fact that we were both on the same team, both trying to reach the same goal of putting out a great show. We spent so much time over the last seven years challenging each other that I forgot how much we had in common. How much we were alike. I missed seeing the softer side of him.

"Well, I guess it's time to call my agent and get the word out that I need a new gig," Daniel said as he put his feet up on my desk, stretching his long legs.

"And I guess its 'call the *Hollywood Reporter*' for me. I hope they have an opening for a junior copywriter," I said, smiling.

Smiling.

My career was about to take a drastic step backwards and I was smiling. This was what a nervous breakdown must feel like.

"More like you better hope they have an opening for a receptionist, 'cause no one's going to hire you to write shit in this town, except maybe telephone messages," Daniel responded.

We both looked at each other and burst into a fit of laughter. I was laughing so hard tears were streaming down my face, and I could barely breathe.

"Hey, Jack. You should apply at a phone sex line. You can call men fucking pricks all day and get paid for it!" Daniel was wheezing, he was laughing so hard.

"Stop it! I can't take anymore." I was pounding my fist on my desk, trying to regain composure. My stomach was crying out in pain.

"Hey, what about writing a children's book? You could call it *Jack and the Prick*."

Daniel's last joke pushed him over the edge, making him lose his balance and fall onto the floor. This sent me into a whole new fit of laughter. Through blurry eyes I watched Daniel as he rolled from side to side, clutching his stomach on the floor of my office, laughing hysterically.

"I'm glad you boys find our situation so amusing," Vivian said sombrely on the threshold to my office.

Neither of us had heard her come in.

"It's just so funny. *Jack and the Prick*," Daniel said between laughs.

Vivian looked at him like he had two heads as she stepped over him to get close to my desk. She waited patiently as both of us struggled to regain our composure.

"We were just discussing my career options," I said, wiping the tears from my eyes. "Daniel here thinks I should write children's books."

Daniel was trying to stifle his laughter as he struggled back into his chair.

"Well, Jack, darling, I'm not sure you would be the best influence for children, given your steamy, soap opera experience. But I do have a contact at *Penthouse*. I'll put a good word in for you," Vivian said, smiling.

This broke Daniel up once again, and soon Vivian and I were both laughing with him. After several minutes, we all managed to completely regain our composure.

"What's with the bottle, Viv?" I asked as soon as my eyes cleared. I didn't remember seeing her carry it in with her.

"This, my friends, is a bottle of 1986 Dom Perpignan," she said, holding it up for us to see. "By far, 1986 was its most successful year. I bought this bottle seven years ago, right after we shot the very first episode of *Chamberlain Heights*. I bought it for this very moment. To be opened when it was time to say goodbye to *Chamberlain Heights*. I wanted to open it at a cast and crew farewell party, but since we're going to be robbed of that, this seems like the most appropriate timing. Rose, come in now," Vivian turned and said.

Rose walked in carrying a silver tray with six crystal champagne flutes upon it. Evelyn and Debra were on her heels.

"Daniel. Please do the honours and open this for me," she said, handing him the bottle.

The bottle opened with a pop and a little spill. Rose quickly moved towards Daniel and he filled the six glasses. Vivian handed each of us one of the beautifully etched glasses.

"A toast," she said, raising her glass. "To a memorable seven years together. To creating a show that challenged the confines of conventional television. To each and every person involved with its production, whose energies bonded together to create a second home and family for us all. And to my boys." She turned to Daniel and I. "Jack. Daniel. I couldn't have done it without either of you. You're my strength. You're my passion. You're my rock. Thank you."

Tears were starting to form at the corner of her eyes. "To *Chamberlain Heights*," she finished.

We all raised our glasses, clinking them together, repeating, "To *Chamberlain Heights*."

All of us had tears in our eyes, including Daniel. Vivian downed her glass completely in one quick swallow and made her way to the sofa after Daniel refilled her glass. Our assistants took their glasses and walked out into Evelyn's outer office, closing the door behind them.

Evelyn informed us we would have to tell our teams the bad news tomorrow. I was scheduled for 11 a.m. My stomach churned with anxiety. Tomorrow was not a day to look forward to.

The three of us gradually became silent, drinking our champagne, lost in our own thoughts, our own grief, finding comfort just being with each other.

"I feel like I just lost a part of me," Vivian broke our long silence. "I put my heart and soul into this show. It's part of me." She started crying.

Daniel and I moved in on either side of her to comfort her.

In the decade plus I'd known Vivian, not once had I ever see her cry. Not once did I ever see her breakdown. She started sobbing uncontrollably, head down, facing her lap. Tears began forming in my eyes as I pulled her against my shoulder. Daniel moved in closer, wrapping his arms around both her and I, tucking his head into the back of Vivian's.

* * *

"YOU NAILED THAT LECTURE, DUDE," RICK SAID TO JOHN. "You're a natural. Every student in that class loved you," he finished.

"Thanks. It felt really good. I mean, it was so much different that student teaching for middle school kids. These are college students. Not much younger than us. It was very cool to watch them 'get it'. You know what I mean?" John asked, looking over at Rick.

"Totally. I hope I can have as much impact as you did on my lecture day. You even had Professor Gellar singing your praises."

John smiled as they make their way through campus.

"You got time to hang? Or do you have to rush home to the beach?" John asked suspiciously.

Rick's immediate reaction was to say he had to jet, but what excuse was he going to give John today? He thought, *maybe I could spend a couple hours hanging with him; I could still be home between eight and eight-thirty; lots of time to see Jack.*

"Sure. What do you want to do?" John looked over at Rick, obviously surprised at his response.

"Um. Beer and pool at that place we found last week?"

"Sounds good. I have to hit the can before we go. Jeep's in the second row, towards the end. I'll meet you there," Rick said, handing John the keys. Rick walked towards the men's room, then waited until John was out of sight before ducking around to the back of the building that housed the washroom.

After fishing his cell phone out of his mailbag, he quickly dialled the number to the beach.

"Hi, you've reached Jack at home. Leave me a message if you want a call back," the voicemail message sang out after four rings.

"Hey. It's Rick. Something came up. I'm going to be later than usual. Probably between eight and eight-thirty.

See you then."

Remembering Jack had his meeting at the studio and could possibly still be there, or on his way home, he decided to try his cell.

"You've reached the personal and confidential voicemail of Jack Perry. Please leave a detailed message at the tone. I will return your call as soon as possible."

Leaving a similar message on his cell phone voicemail, Rick tucked his phone back into his bag and headed back around to the front of the building and out to the parking lot to join John.

15

"WHAT TIME IS IT?" I ASKED THE TAXI DRIVER AS HE signalled his intention to exit onto the ramp leading into Hermosa Beach.

"7:35," he responded curtly.

The movement of the car was making my head spin.

How much did we drink, I asked myself. Vivian was on a roll. I could remember arriving at The Four Seasons Hotel at 1 p.m. It was now 7:30 p.m. That couldn't be right. Did Vivian, Daniel, and I really sit in the lounge and drink for six and a half hours?

Vivian had been intent on getting drunk, drowning her sorrows. She was funny, insisting on paying with her studio credit card.

How many bottles of chardonnay did we have? I'd lost track at six. I pushed the power button for the window, letting it go down as far as it could go and letting in the freshness of the beach air. The afternoon went by in a blur. Vivian, Daniel, and I, crying, laughing, and reminiscing over the last seven years together. Telling each other our favourite stories. Our challenges. Our highs. Our lows.

"I'm so happy to finally see my boys get along," Vivian slurred out at one point, pulling both Daniel and I close to her.

Funny. *Daniel.* We'd bonded this afternoon. Shared with each other on a professional, and personal, level. I hated to admit it after hating the guy for the last seven

164

years, but I really kind of liked him. I regretted not seeing the real Daniel until now.

Surprisingly, I was really going to miss him. He was a real class act. He put both Vivian and I in taxis home, pre-paying them with his credit card and ensuring the driver knew exactly how to get to our houses.

"We're here," the taxi driver announced, as he halted the car in front of my house.

"Here, give this to your friend." He shoved the receipt at me for the ride home.

"Thank you," I slurred, and stumbled out of the back seat.

My house was completely dark. The driveway was empty. Rick was not home. I was relieved, because I had meant to be home earlier.

I let myself in the front door and made my way to the kitchen, turning on lights along my way. I pulled out a bottle of water from the fridge and downed it in seconds. I repeated this two more times until I felt my head clearing. I pulled out an additional bottle and sipped on this one more slowly.

The voicemail indicator light on the kitchen phone was blinking at me. I hit the speakerphone key and dialled the access number.

My mother had called "just to touch base". They had just spent the month touring Europe and I was eager to hear about their trip. Later— when I was sober.

The second message was from Rick, saying, "Something came up."

Perfect, I thought as I read the oven clock display: 7:52 p.m. I picked up my water and headed upstairs, intent on having a shower and changing my clothes before he got home. I walked into my closet and stripped out of my suit, leaving it in a crumpled mess on the floor. I didn't have the coordination or desire to put it back on its hanger. I hit the shower. I stayed under its gentle spray, changing the water to a cooler temperature, thinking it would sober me up a little. Slipping as I got out made me realise my attempt was futile. I brushed my teeth and combed my hair with my fingers, assuring myself it made a huge difference in my drunken appearance.

My intention was to get dressed and go back downstairs to wait for Rick, but my bed looked so comfortable. I convinced myself I could just lay down for a few quick moments. It would help me regain my composure. I pulled back the duvet cover and dropped the towel wrapped around my waist to the floor. Climbing into the softness of my bed, I passed out within seconds.

*　　*　　*

I WOKE TO WARM HANDS ON MY BODY, GENTLE KISSES ON my neck and ears.

"Mmm," I released a small sigh. I let go and let myself fall further into the dream. Someone pulling me close. I could feel his hardness against me. Moving me, turning my head to meet his. Passionate kisses met my mouth.

"You smell like a bar," the voice whispered in my ear.

"Rick?"

"Who did you think it was?" he asked, and continued down, kissing my neck. I struggled to open my eyes. My body gave into the passion that was overcoming it.

Rick rolled over, his body on top of mine. *This is the best dream ever*, I thought. He took possession of my body like he owned it, moving it to accommodate him, fuelling the passion within me.

He started slowly, but soon was overcome with his own desire and increased the speed of his movements. My body responded by lifting up to meet his. His breath was hot as he leant in and kissed me hard. My eyes flew open at the explosion of my orgasm, bringing me into the moment, making me realise that this was real and not a dream.

I watched Rick's face as he succumbed to his own orgasm. I felt the intensity of it inside me. Breathless, he fell on top of me, burying his face into my hair. After several minutes, he rolled on to his side, wrapping his arms around me from behind and pulling me against him very tightly.

"Wow. That was great," he said when his breathing returned to normal.

"That it was," I replied.

"So what happened to you?"

"Mmm. What do you mean?" I asked, feeling exhausted.

"I come home. Your car's not here, but every light in the house is burning. I find you naked in bed— and, might I add, quite happily. You smell like a bar. Or like you drank a bar. What happened today?"

I pulled his arm surrounding my chest, more tightly to me. "I'm so sleepy."

He kissed my head. "Please tell me."

"I got fired today," I said lazily.

"You what?"

I tried to open my eyes to stay focussed on him, but it was so hard. "They cancelled *Chamberlain Heights*. Vivian, Daniel, and I accidentally got really drunk."

"Are you okay?" The concern in his voice was deepening.

"*Ya*. I'm good. I called the president to the studio a prick and told him to go fuck himself."

"You did not," Rick said, stifling a laugh.

"Yup. I did. Scout's honour. Probably won't ever get hired in this town again. Going to go apply at Wal-Mart in the morning. Or maybe at a sex hotline. Daniel thinks I would be good at that."

Rick laughed. I was obviously amusing him. "Seriously,

are you okay?" he asked again.

"I'm good. Can I sleep now?"

"*Ya.* Go to sleep, babe." He pulled me in closer, kissing my head once again. I drifted back to sleep within seconds.

* * *

"GO DO YOUR WALK OF SHAME, MISTER," RICK SAID WITH A smile. It was early. 8 a.m. We were outside of The Four Seasons in his Jeep and I was feeling slightly embarrassed by the fact that I had to retrieve my car from the valet. I was unsure as to what extent I'd made a spectacle of myself here yesterday. The sun was so bright behind my dark glasses I squinted as I looked at Rick.

"Off with you. I want to see the show before I have to jet off to school." He waved his arm.

"I'm not feeling well. Can't you just take me to the studio? Please?"

"Nope. We're here now. And you are going to have to get your car sometime. You can't just leave it here."

I made my best pout face for him.

"Not going to work. Out with you."

Knowing I wasn't going to sway him, I opened the door and got out.

"Don't forget your breakfast," he said, leaning over the passenger seat and handing me a bag filled with greasy fast food.

The movement of the Jeep on the ride in made me queasy and kept me from eating on the way. He grabbed my arm and pulled me halfway back into the Jeep when I reach for the bag. He leant down to meet me and kissed me full on the lips. Right there, outside the main entrance to The Four Seasons Hotel. I could feel myself blushing.

"See ya later," he said, as he released my arm.

I closed the door and turned to walk over to the valet.

"Can I help you, sir?" I knew he'd witnessed Rick kiss me. I handed him my ticket.

"My car, please."

He looked down at the ticket. "Right away, sir." He was gone in a flash. Rick sat in his Jeep, watching, waiting. The valet was back within a few minutes with my car. I handed him a twenty as he held the door open for me as I got in.

"Thank you very much, sir. And may I say, sir, your boyfriend over there is very cute," he gestured with nod towards Rick.

"I'll let him know you think so," I responded, grabbing the door handle, pulling the door closed as the valet drooled over Rick.

*   *   *

"MY BOYFRIEND. MY *BOYFRIEND* IS VERY CUTE. WHO SAYS he's my boyfriend?" I was talking out loud in my car, not believing what just happened. I was a little freaked out that someone referred to Rick and me as *boyfriends.*

But what are we then, a voice in the back of my head asked. I blocked the voice and concentrated on the short drive to the studio lot.

*   *   *

"EVERYONE HAS ARRIVED. THEY'RE WAITING FOR YOU," Evelyn said as she entered my office.

I looked up from the paperwork I was going over.

"Give me two minutes."

"Ready when you are," she replied.

I looked once again down to the papers I was concentrating on before she came in: This was my own personal severance package, which included a copy of my original contract with the studio. I looked once again at the cheque that was attached to the dismissal letter. Lots of zeros behind that first number. I would have to call my lawyer and thank him again for hammering out such a great contract for me, making it very expensive for the studio to get rid of me.

Putting the paperwork and cheque back into the envelope, I placed it in the side compartment of my briefcase. I picked up six similar envelopes and headed to the outer office.

"Ready?" I asked Evelyn.

"Right behind you," she said, gathering up her supplies for the meeting.

We walked in silence down the staircase to the first floor. As we crossed the lobby to the boardroom I smiled at the newly installed security guard behind the reception desk. He was there to protect the interests of the studio, making sure no one took studio property when they left. I paused at the frosted glass door that led into the boardroom. I didn't want to pull it open.

"You okay?" Evelyn asked.

"*Ya*. Yes. I just really hate what I am about to do," I replied.

I pulled the door open and walked in. My team of writers was sitting at one end of the twelve-seat table. Jodi, Amy, Dave, Juanita, Stewart, and Bobby. They all stood when I came in, but they remained silent.

"Please, everyone, sit. Thank you for coming on such short notice." I turned to make my way to the head of the table, and thought better of it. This was my team, I was part of them, and they were part of me. I was not going to separate myself from them. That was not our relationship, studio rules or not.

I pulled out the next available seat at the end of the table where everyone had gathered together. Evelyn sat to the left of me.

"Okay. I know we're a team," I started. "As leader of this team, this amazing team..." I looked directly at each one of them. "I..."

"Rip the bandage off quickly, Jack, please. We're cancelled, aren't we? Just say it," Bobby said.

I swallowed the lump that had formed in my throat. "Yes. We've been cancelled. I'm sorry."

"Why? Why are they cancelling us?" Jodi asked with a tremor in her voice. "Was it the Ashley thing?"

"Between you and me, no. It wasn't the Ashley thing," I replied.

"They're going to let us shoot a proper final episode, aren't they? We can't end the series on the last episode we shot," Stewart said.

"Production is cancelled effective immediately." I fought back tears.

"What about the characters? We can't do this. We just can't!" Juanita cried out.

How much everyone loved the characters and show was apparent. As writers, we breathed life into the characters we created. We related to them as actual living beings. Not being able to write an ending for them made it feel like a sudden, unexpected death.

"Jack. You can't let this happen," Dave screamed at me.

I noticed Amy was crying. Amy was the fist member of the team to be hired. She was a junior writer on *Deadly Sins* and I brought her with me when I left the show to develop *Chamberlain Heights*.

"There's nothing more I can do."

"Did you do anything at all? Did you?" Dave stood, clearly blaming me.

"Dave," I began.

"May I interject?" Evelyn asked. She was in a very uncomfortable position right now. She had been my assistant for the seven year run, but here in this meeting she was a representative of the studio, not my assistant. She had been empowered by the studio to ensure I acted appropriately.

"I would like to make clear that this man did everything he could to avoid this very moment," she said.

"*Ya* right," Dave spat.

Evelyn stared him down. He sat back into his chair.

"Like I was saying, Jack did everything he could to save *Chamberlain Heights*. He spent the last few days rewriting the fall storyboard and preliminary script. You are all going to leave this room today and hear gossip about what happened in the meetings with the studio executives. I would like to tell you what I saw in that meeting, since I was present in it."

"Evelyn. Don't." I turned and touched her arm. As a permanent employee of the studio, she was about to break the confidentiality clause in her contract, by revealing details of yesterday's meeting.

She continued, "He fought very hard for the show. In fact, he fought so hard it has probably cost him his career in Hollywood."

Everyone was at full attention now.

"He took it very personally. In case anyone has forgotten, he co-created *Chamberlain Heights*. I know you're all hurting and in shock over the cancellation, but you all will get past it. You're all extremely talented writers and you're going to be picked up for other shows. Maybe even within the walls of this studio. For seven years, I watched, supported, and helped nurture this show. I'm going to miss *Chamberlain Heights* and all of you terribly."

She finished and sat in her place beside me. The room was completely silent.

Clearing my throat, I suppressed my emotions and got into my role as leader. Standing, I touched Evelyn's shoulder. "Thank you, Evelyn."

I handed out the envelopes containing everyone's personal severance packages. I explained what the studio would need them to do and what they could expect. No one opened their envelopes. Even after I'd explained everything, they were silent.

"On a personal note," I said. "I wish to thank each and every one of you for your time with me on the show. I can't believe how lucky I was to have found each of you. I'm so grateful for the team we created, and proud of the work we did. I'm a better person and a better writer for knowing you."

I walked around the room, lightly touching each one of their shoulders as I spoke. "I consider each and every one of you part of my family. In fact, given all we've been through, we may have even become closer than our real families. I am really going to miss you guys." Tears were starting to fill the corners of my eyes as I finished.

No one moved. No one said anything. Everyone kept his eyes down. Amy was the first to get out of her seat. Picking up her envelope she made her way around the table to me. Eyes filled with tears, she grabbed on to me tightly.

"Thank you for giving me my chance. My break. I love you." She went over to Evelyn, signed the required studio paperwork and left quietly. Jodi was next.

"I'll miss being here. Thank you." She gave me a light hug, signed her name, then she was gone.

Juanita went next, followed by Stewart, and Bobby. Juanita hugged me, the boys gave me firm handshakes and slaps on the back before they left.

Only Dave, Evelyn and I were left. Dave got up and approached me. His eyes were glassy.

"Thanks for everything, Jack. You hired me off the street. Giving me my first chance. I won't forget that. You say you are in awe of me? It is I who am in awe of you."

I couldn't hold back anymore, tears flowed freely from my eyes. Dave gave me a huge bear hug.

"Who would have thought it would be you that would push me over the edge today," I said to him, as I brushed away the tears.

He smiled, brushing past me to sign his paperwork with Evelyn.

"Oh, and Jack?"

I turned to look at him.

"I don't care how badly you jeopardised your reputation in the industry. When I am head writer on my own show, there will always a place reserved for you on my team." He smiled, winked, and was gone.

*   *   *

"YOU DID GOOD, JACK," EVELYN BROKE MY SOLITUDE.

We were back upstairs in my office.

"Thank you. What I said in the boardroom was meant for you, too."

"I know," she replied.

"I couldn't have done it without you. Your support made me and the show a success. I am really going to miss you."

She came over and hugged me.

"Okay. Time for official business," I said as I broke our embrace. "My building access cards, ID badge, cell phone, laptop, PDA, keys, and studio credit card. All here and accounted for."

After I arrived early at the studio this morning, I'd packed up my personal belongings before the meeting. Three boxes sat on the credenza by the door.

"I'm just going to go down to see Vivian before I go."

"Rose left instructions on behalf of Vivian this morning. She doesn't want to see you today."

"What?"

I was shocked and hurt that Vivian didn't want to see me. "She said to tell you she'll be in touch." Evelyn could obviously read the hurt on my face. Seven years together on this show and Vivian wouldn't see me off. "Think about it, Jack. She has to tell her team today, too. You co-created the show with her. I don't think she can handle saying goodbye to you, as well."

"I suppose you're right."

"You guys are great friends. This isn't the end for you two," Evelyn added.

"I guess it is time to go then." I swung my briefcase onto my shoulder, noticing how light it was without the laptop inside.

"I'll walk you down," Evelyn said as she picked up one of my boxes.

"I can manage."

"I want to walk you down," she said.

I nodded. I took one last look around my office before picking up the remaining two boxes from the credenza. We took the elevator down since my legs felt like they were made of rubber. As we walked through the main lobby, I saw one of Daniel's assistant directors come out of the boardroom, head down. She didn't even notice Evelyn or me.

Daniel was in the process of doing what I had done earlier. The security guard jumped from behind his post at the desk and rushed ahead to open the doors for us. I mumbled *thank you*, and we made our way to my car. We closed the boxes and my briefcase in the trunk.

Then, I turned to Evelyn for our final goodbye.

She grabbed my hand in hers. "Off the record, Jack? I am so proud of you for standing up to Mr. Goldman yesterday. Your passion is what makes you so great at what you do. It probably wasn't the smartest thing, but probably one of the best things you have done."

She let go of my hands, turned, and walked briskly back into the building. I looked up to the third floor of the production offices, which was my home away from home for seven years. Vivian was standing by her window looking down at me. She blew me a kiss. I pretended to catch her kiss and put it on my heart. She smiled, turned, and was gone from my sight.

As I approached the main gate of the studio lot, Harry came out of his booth and made his way over to my car.

"Mr. Perry. I heard the news. Let me tell you we are going to miss seeing you on the lot."

"Thank you, Harry. Thank you for always having a smile for me every morning. I'm going to miss that."

He reached into the car and shook my hand. "We'll be seeing you again on this lot, Mr. Perry. I'm sure of it."

I smiled and drove off the studio lot for the last time.

16

"Earth to Jack. Hello. You in there?" Rick tapped my forehead, bringing me back to the present moment. We were on the upper deck at Joe's.

After the day I had, I really didn't want to go anywhere, but earlier in the week I had promised Maria, and I didn't want to let her down.

"Where did ya go?" Rick asked.

"Nowhere far." I smiled. "I just drifted back to my thoughts of what am I going to do now, or rather, *next.*"

"Why worry about it? Sit back and relax for a while. You have lots of time to work things out," he said as he took a drink of his beer.

My thoughts drifted back to my afternoon after I left the studio lot. I called my mom. I listened to her for a good hour about their trip to Europe and all the things they experienced. When I told her about *Chamberlain Heights* she asked me if I was going to be okay. I assured her I was. She invited me to come home, to spend some time in Phoenix with them. I told her I would plan a visit soon.

I also called Julie, knowing she would be furious if I didn't tell her about the cancellation of the show before someone else did. I left a message on her cell phone voicemail. Knowing she and Max were still in New York, I wasn't going to hold my breath for a quick return call.

"I got it!" Rick's voice broke my thoughts. "You should become a writer!" He snapped his fingers and pointed at me with enthusiasm.

"I *am* a writer, Einstein. Have you listened to me at all over the last day? Once Goldman gets through with me, no one is going to hire me."

"You can write something else," he said.

"Like what?"

"Like for a magazine or something. You should write a book!"

"A book? What kind of book could I write?" I asked.

"Any kind of book. I don't know. Pick a topic and write about it."

"All I know is writing for the show. All I want to do is write for the show."

"Well you can't. So pick something new," Rick said a little harshly.

Like I could do something new just like that. Writing dialogue, writing scripts, and developing scenes and characters was what I had trained myself to be good at over the years. What did he think? I could just go to supermarket and pick a new career?

"What are you boys talking about?" Maria pulled out a chair and sat with us.

"Career options," I said, breaking my stare from Rick and putting my attention to Maria.

"What's on the table?" she asked.

"Couple of things," I responded.

"Let's hear them," she replied.

"Well, the lists starts at receptionist, followed by phone sex operator; after that, we have writing for *Penthouse*, and, finally, Rick here thinks I should write a book," I finished.

"What kind of book?" she asked Rick.

"Don't know," he said. "Any kind of book. He's a very talented writer; I think he could write anything he sets his mind to."

"He's right, Jackie." Maria turned to me.

"He is?" I asked, surprised. I noticed the grin on Rick's face immediately. He felt proud of the fact that Maria was siding with him.

"My friend," Maria said, patting my arm. "You would make a terrible receptionist. You're used to giving orders, not receiving them. You might do okay as a sex operator, but do you really want that on your resume? And *Penthouse*? How did you come up with that idea? Who is going to read erotica written by a gay man, in that pig's magazine? I think Rick is right. You are destined to write a book," she finished.

"Again. My question is: write a book about what?" I asked.

"Write what you know, with your heart, and it will be spectacular," she said, patting my cheek as she got up and left us.

"Wipe that smirk off your face right now, mister," I said to Rick.

"What?"

"Just because you got her to agree with you does *not* make you all superior and such."

"Don't think I am. I'm just enjoying the evening." He looked out towards the water.

"So we have a whole day together tomorrow. What are we going to do?" he asked.

"About that. I kind of have plans tomorrow."

"You do?" he asked, surprised.

"It's my friends', Shelia and Michael's, wedding tomorrow. I have to go."

"Oh," he said with a touch of hurt in his voice.

"I thought of asking you to come. Actually, I struggled with it."

"You don't have to explain." He turned away.

"Rick. Look at me."

He turned back to face me.

"The reason I struggled with it is that Sheila was Stephen's friend. She worked with Stephen. I just think it wouldn't be appropriate for me to take someone else to her wedding. Some of Stephen's friends and former clients will be there."

"What you are actually saying, Jack, is that you don't want to answer any questions about me."

"That's not what I'm saying."

"Really? Are you sure about that? Let me ask you this: would you take Maria as your guest?" His eyes were burning.

"It's not the same thing," I said.

"Just answer me. Would you take Maria with you?"

"Yes. I would take Maria with me. But that would be a totally different situation."

"How is it different? Maria's your friend. I'm your friend. Friends act as friend's dates when needed." His voice had an edge of anger to it.

"We're more than just friends, Rick."

"No one knows that."

"I know that. You know that." I reached for his hand, but he pulled it away.

"Okay. You're right. I don't want to have to answer questions about you. Especially since I don't have the answers."

He looked away.

"If I can't answer the questions about who you are in my life for myself, how am I to answer them for someone else?"

"You don't know who I am in your life?" He turned toward me.

"No. Do you know who I am in your life?"

Silence.

"I thought not. You've been here a week, and we have

just kind of fell into this relationship."

"Fell into a relationship?" He raised one eyebrow.

"You know what I mean. Us. This. It just happened," I said, pointing back and forth between us. "We haven't talked about it. I don't know where you're coming from."

"What do you mean, you don't know where I am coming from?" he asked.

"Where you're coming from. Are you gay? Are you bi? Am I an experiment for you?" I started rambling.

"An *experiment*? You think you're an *experiment*?" He was giving me his full attention now.

"Well. I don't know. I don't know anything about you, or your past relationships."

"Jack. Do you really think that if you were an experiment we would be spending this much time together? Intimate time. I would have fucked you and then left if you were an experiment," he said, his voice full of anger now.

I stayed quiet.

"I'm not going to label myself gay, bi, or straight, so you can feel better about who we are."

I had hit a nerve. He turned back to the water. I could feel his anger.

"I'm sorry. This is all very confusing for me."

"And it's not for me?" He turned back.

"I'm sorry. I haven't thought about it from your side," I said.

"That's right, you haven't. How could you have? You are so self-absorbed in your own life, your own crises, you can't see anything else."

"How dare you!" I said loudly.

"How dare I what? Call it as it is?"

I could feel something about to snap inside of me. I took a deep breath, then another, and then another. "I guess if you think I am self-absorbed, then I am self-absorbed," I said calmly, fighting the anger that wanted to lash out at him.

"I'm going to go now," I said as I stood.

"You're going to walk out?" he asked.

"I'm going, before this leads to something I'll regret. Before you judge me for being 'so self-absorbed' you may want to consider that you're twenty-three, and I'm thirty-eight. *You* haven't just lost your job, ruined your career, and you haven't been an adult long enough to have experienced the loss of a partner of almost a decade."

I turned and made my way through the patio, down the stairs to the reception area. I paid the bill, gathered my rollerblades from the coat closet, and left the restaurant without saying goodbye to either Maria, Joe, or the boys.

Furious with Rick, I saw nothing of the night-time scenery on the boardwalk. Deep in my anger I pushed myself hard, to my limits, trying to release the rage that was consuming me. I could feel the burn in my legs as I continually pushed off on my rollerblades, increasing the speed with each push. The breeze from my speeding cooled me in the warm night.

Me? Self-centred? He's crazy. Stupid little boy. He doesn't even know me. My inner dialogue fed my increasing anger.

The path changed from the brightly lighted, very active boardwalk, to a more subdued feel. I knew I had just crossed the invisible line that separated the boardwalk area, with its restaurants and shops, from the residential area of Hermosa Beach. With the sudden change of energy, I slowed my pace down, to become more in tune with my surroundings. My thoughts and inner dialogue slowed as well. I breathed in the night, and calm started to replace the anger.

Am I really even angry at Rick, I asked myself. *Or am I still hurt and angry over the cancellation of Chamberlain Heights?*

I pondered these thoughts for a few moments.

Am I self-centred? I don't think so.

As I thought about this, I realised that someone new to my life might assume I cared for little but myself. I thought about the last year of my life, and how I had withdrawn from anyone close to me. Feelings of guilt overwhelmed me.

Why should I feel guilty for processing Stephen's death the only way I could? Or knew how?

The inner dialogue started back up again as I reached my house. After taking off the rollerblades, I walked up the stairs to the back deck and let myself into the house. I tried to shake off the last of my anger and guilt as I poured myself a glass of wine. I headed back outside and settled in on one of the deck chairs to wait for Rick. I knew I owed him an apology. As I sat waiting I decided I would take him to Shelia and Michael's wedding tomorrow. Maybe it really wasn't important what anyone would think.

* * *

"JACK. WAKE UP."

I ignored the distant voice that was trying to disturb me.

"Come on, wake up. You need to go to bed."

Again, I ignored it, wanting to go deeper into my sleep. I could feel my body being lifted up. My eyes fluttered as my mind tried to figure out what was happening.

"Put your arms around my neck."

My body obeyed the voice without hesitation.

"Rick?"

"*Ya*," he said.

"What are you doing?" I asked, my eyes trying to open unsuccessfully.

"Taking you to bed. You can't sleep out on the deck."

I felt the forward movement of my body and realised he was carrying me. I couldn't seem to completely wake up. I felt a sudden change in his movements and determined that he was walking up the stairs.

"You can't carry me; I'm heavy," I mumbled and nuzzled into his neck.

"I seem to be managing. I'm a big strong boy, and you're not that heavy," he replied. "Okay, almost there."

A few more steps and I felt myself being lowered onto my bed. He pulled my arms from around his neck.

"Okay, lift up a bit."

I could feel my shirt being pulled over my head. Next my cargo shorts were pulled down, and I suddenly felt cold. I instinctively hugged my chest and rolled onto my side. He rolled me back and forth and lifted me.

"You're going to be no help at all, are you?" he asked me as he manoeuvred me under the duvet.

I could sense the change in weight on the bed as he got off of it.

"Rick, don't go."

"Not going anywhere."

I heard rustling and soon I felt the warmth of his body next to mine, pulling in close.

"Rick?"

"Yes."

"I'm sorry."

"Me too."

I quickly fell back into my deep sleep.

* * *

WHEN I WOKE MY HEAD WAS POUNDING. I LOOKED OVER AT Rick; he was sprawled out, sleeping on his stomach. I kissed his shoulder, got out of bed, and made my way to the bathroom. Filling a glass with water from the tap, I washed down four Tylenols. After splashing cool water on my face, I went back to bed. The clock read 8 a.m.

Rick woke as I got back into bed.

"Where you going?" he asked.

"Nowhere," I replied.

He rolled onto his back, and I curled into his arm, putting my head on his chest.

"Rick?"

"I know. I'm sorry, too. I shouldn't have said those things to you," he said into my hair.

"You're probably right. I probably am self-centred," I replied.

"No. You're allowed. You've had a lot happen in a short period of time." He kissed my head. "I was thinking. Why do we need to put a name on us? Can't we just enjoy the experience, and go with it?" he asked.

"You've been talking to Maria," I said.

"No. Well, maybe. How did you know?"

"She gave me a variation of that same line a couple of days ago," I replied. "What else did you two talk about?" I asked, as I ran my finger through his chest hair.

"Nothing much. Just life stuff."

"She's a very wise woman," I added.

"Yeah, she is," he agreed.

"I thought about it and I would like you to come to the wedding with me today. "

Silence.

"Did you hear me?" I asked again.

"I heard you."

"Well?" I persisted.

"Are you asking me out of guilt, or you asking me because you want me to be there?" He stroked my hair.

"Because I want you to be there," I responded without any hesitation.

More silence.

"Thank you. But my answer is no," he replied.

"No?" I tried to lift my head to look at him, but he held

it down on his chest.

"Yes, *no*. I know, in this moment, you believe you want me to go, but, in reality, we both know it isn't a good idea."

"Explain yourself," I stated.

"Me going will put unnecessary pressure on you. You'll have to explain me, and I think that it's unfair to you to have to do that, especially to a room filled with Stephen's friends. You won't have a good time if I go. I want you to go and have a good time. You need to reconnect with some of those people. You need to do that on your own."

"More Maria?" I asked at the end of his speech.

"More Maria," he responded in agreement.

17

Rick knew what he is doing was wrong, but he couldn't stop himself. He was searching through the drawers in Jack's study, searching for the key to the room downstairs.

He had already moved the armoire, which hid the door at the bottom of the stairs. He was surprised to find a double deadbolt on it, not just a regular interior door lock, which he could have picked quite easily.

Where would he put the key, he asked himself.

Curiosity as to what was behind the door beat out his guilt about rifling through Jack's personal stuff.

It's got to be in here somewhere.

He had already searched Jack's bedroom to no avail. He sat on the desk chair. The room was darkening with the impending evening. He reached over and turned on the desk lamp. He spun in the chair, looking up as he did so. On the wall near the ceiling he saw a shadow. Staring at it, he made out what looked to be part of a key. Following the shadow from the ceiling down, he scanned the items on the desk, trying to figure out the origins of the shadow. He turned the light on and off. There was not much on the desk. A clock, pen, and pencil holder. A small filing rack and the phone. He lifted and turned each item, looking for the source the shadow.

"Bingo!" he said, as he lifted and turned the clock.

Taped neatly on the backside of the clock with clear

tape was a silver key. He pulled the tape off gently and retrieved the key. He was out of the room in seconds, taking the stairs to the basement two at a time.

The key fit easily into the lock on the door. It turned the same as well, giving a soft 'click' as the lock disengaged. Rick took a breath in as he turned the handle. The door opened with a slight groan. The room was pitch-black. He felt the wall, searching for the light switch. Flicking it, he shielded his eyes as the room was brought out of darkness.

He stood on the threshold and took in the room. One very large room. Harwood floors just like on the upper level of the house. The floor was very dusty. He walked around the room. The floor to ceiling windows were covered in heavy black paper. There were locked double glass doors on one side, covered as well. There were also two interior doors, one leading into a small bathroom, leading into what might have been a fully functioning darkroom at one time.

He gave his attention to the random items in the room. Several boxes were stacked neatly against the only full solid wall. A mountain bike and two brightly coloured surfboards also leant there. He ran his fingers over the bike and surfboards. His finger turned black from what looked like months of dust. He looked at the stack of boxes. They were all labelled as neatly as they were stacked.

"Clothes, clothes, clothes, shoes, shoes, personal papers, work files, etcetera, etcetera," Rick read out loud.

He stopped at a box labelled 'pictures'. He pulled it down off the stack onto the floor. The tape pulled off easily. He took out a layer of bubble wrap. He spread out the different shaped and sized frames and arranged them on the floor into a story. Most of the pictures were of Jack and Stephen. Or just Jack. Or just Stephen. Different backdrops filled the pictures and told the story of the travelling they must have done. He found a couple pictures with Julie and his dad in them, as well as some with Maria and Joe. A few others were with people he didn't know. A pang of jealously hit him in the heart.

"Jack was right. I haven't lived long enough to experience this part of life," he said, his voice softly echoing in the empty room.

Needing to know more, he pulled down the box marked 'personal papers' next. Again, the tape sealing the box pulled off easily. The first item in the box was an unmarked oversized manila envelope. It was sealed.

"I've gone this far," he said to himself as he tore open the envelope and dumped its contents onto the floor. A California driver's licence grabbed his attention first.

Ross, Stephen James
DOB: 17/03/1968
Hair: Blond
Eyes: Blue
Height: 6'1"
Weight: 190 lbs
Expires: 17/03/2009

He stared at Stephen's picture on the licence, trying to imagine his presence in life. He focussed on the remaining items on the floor in front of him. He reached and opened his passport. Flipping to the identification page, the only thing he learnt new about Stephen that his driver's licence didn't tell him was that he had been born in Dallas. He continued flipping through the pages, which were filled with the stamps of the foreign countries he had visited. Norway, Italy, Egypt, England, France, Ireland, Spain, Germany, Canada, Mexico; there were so many. Some stamps were repeated.

"The guy got around," he said to himself.

The remaining items from the envelope consisted of his birth certificate, his official death certificate. A simple, yet heavy silver ring. An American Express Platinum Card. Bank One Gold Visa. An ATM card, from Bank One as well. And the registration and insurance cards for a 2004 Porsche Boxster. Silver.

"Nice ride, Stephen," Rick said, and wondered what had happened to the car.

The last item he found was a neatly folded newspaper article. *Prominent Hermosa Beach resident killed in surfing accident.* Rick read the article out loud.

Prominent Hermosa Beach resident and business owner Stephen Ross was killed in a freak surfing accident yesterday morning. Police and rescue teams blame the sudden storm that unexpectedly blew into the coastal area yesterday morning. Mr. Ross was believed to be an expert surfer and strong swimmer. The coroner has not released the official 'cause of death at this time. Mr. Ross, a well-known landscape architect, was responsible for designing some of the most stunning landscapes along the coastal region of Los Angles, including the grounds of the Hermosa Beach City Hall. Mr. Ross's family could not be reached for comment at this time.

Rick sat in silence for a moment. He reached into the box and removed more items. He poured through the papers: business licence, university diploma, high school diploma, and bank statements— business and personal. He learnt that, the month Stephen had died, he had bank balances of a hundred and two thousand U.S. dollars in his business account, and twenty-three thousand U.S. dollars in his personal account.

He knew he should stop looking through the box. This was totally none of his business, but he couldn't stop himself. He found an envelope containing Stephen's will. A quick scan revealed to him that Jack was named the sole beneficiary of his estate. He also found the original deed to the land they built the house on. The last papers he found were life insurance papers, again naming Jack sole beneficiary. He read the cover letter attached to the policy.

Dear Mr. Perry:

Upon conclusion of our investigation, with the cooperation of the Hermosa Beach City Police, as well as the local branch of The California State Coroner's Office we have determined that Mr. Stephen James Ross's death was due to an accidental incident.

As outlined in the original insurance agreement signed by Mr. Ross we are now authorised to transfer funds for the complete insured amount to you.

Please find enclosed a cheque in the amount of $1,000,000.

As you hold a similar policy with our company listing Mr. Ross as sole beneficiary, you will need to contact our office at your earliest convenience to update your policy, outlining a new beneficiary.

If you have any concerns or questions, please do not hesitate to contact the undersigned.

Please accept our deepest condolences on your recent loss.

Regards,
Pamela Massey
Agent for Caldon Personal & Business Insurance, Limited

Rick put the document down. Looking at all the items before him, the pictures, the certificates, bank statements, etcetera, he knew he had crossed the line. He was way past the line. He felt sick to his stomach for what he had done.

* * *

"FIND WHAT YOU WERE LOOKING FOR?" I ASKED AS I disrupted Rick.

He looked up at me from his place on the floor.

"Or is there a particular item I can help you find?" I asked, my voice beginning to tremble with anger.

"Uh, Jack," Rick said, turning red.

"Expecting someone else?" I asked sarcastically.

"You're home early," he said.

"Yes," I said as I walked into the room. A room I hadn't been in a year. "I left the wedding early, so we could hang out." I looked down at the floor. I saw the pictures that used to make up the picture wall from upstairs. I scanned the other items.

"I'm sorry. It just kinda happened," he said as he slowly stood up and faced me.

"Just kinda happened? Really? How does this, just 'kinda' happen, Rick?" I asked as I motioned to the items on the floor.

"I didn't mean to go this far," he replied, his voice sullen.

"Didn't mean it to go this far? Really? So I should be okay with what you have done?"

He looked down and remained quiet.

"Do you even know what you've done? Do you? This isn't like you're twelve years old and you search your house when your parents are out looking for your Christmas presents. This is my personal life! You went through my personal items!"

My voice was dripping with venom. "You had no right to do what you did. What didn't you get when I told you this floor was off limits? Huh? And wasn't the locked door a huge sign that maybe you shouldn't come in here? How did you get in, anyway?"

I looked back toward the open door and saw the key still tucked neatly into the lock.

"Searched my office, did you? Nice. Where else did you search?" I paused to take a breath. "What do you have to say for yourself? Anything?" Anger was ripping through me.

"I'm sorry," he said.

"You went through my stuff. Personal stuff. And all you have to say for yourself is *I'm sorry*? Interesting." I walked past him and faced the wall of windows, staring at the black paper covering them and trying to get a hold of my anger.

"I really am sorry," he said.

"That's comforting. Thank you very much." I couldn't keep the anger out of my voice. "Please get out," I said, not turning to look at him.

I heard his feet shuffle on the floor as he made his way to the door.

"Jack. I really am sorry."

"Get out," I said flatly.

"This room is kind of weird," he said.

I didn't acknowledge his statement.

"It's like you're trying to hide the fact that Stephen ever existed, and like you're waiting for him to return."

I snapped. "Get the hell out of here!" I screamed.

Surprise filled his expression as I moved towards him, screaming over and over, "Get the hell out of here!"

He stepped backwards into the hallway, tripping he fell to the floor. I looked at him, filled with hatred. I reached the door. Angrily and forcefully I slammed it shut. Rick pulled his feet back from the threshold just in time as the door connected with the frame.

I stared at the closed door, breathing heavy; I could feel the anger pulsing through me, filling every fibre of my body. I turned and faced the room. My breathing slowly started to return to a more normal state, slowing my racing heart. I walked over to the items Rick was going through. Picking up the paper documents, I put them back into the box they came from. I replaced Stephen's credit cards, licence, and passport into the opened manila envelope.

I picked up the silver ring. Holding it in my palm, I fingered it. His wedding band. Well, not actually. We called them our wedding bands, but actually they were unofficial symbols of our life and commitment to each other. I read the inscription on the inside of it: *my love promised to you forever.* The letter J finished off the inscription. I lost my matching ring to his on the morning of his accident, somewhere on the beach. I scoured the beach after I came out of my fog and realised where I must have lost it. My search proved to be fruitless.

I gently placed the ring, his ring on the third finger of my right hand. I placed the manila envelope back into the box, closed it, and returned it to its place on the stack. I sat on the dusty floor. I looked at the pictures that Rick had neatly arranged on the floor. He had done a pretty good job of putting them in chronological order. I searched through them, touching each one with a smile on my face as my memory brought forward the details of each picture. The place. The time. The experience. Beautiful memories of our life together. I picked up my favourite one: a picture of us asleep in a hammock during our cruise through the Greek Isles. A staff photographer captured the image. My head nestled into Stephen's shoulder, his arms wrapped around me. The brilliant blue of the ocean as the backdrop. Both of us, looking peaceful and happy.

I placed this picture beside me. Scanning the remaining pictures I next pulled out a picture of Stephen on the beach, surfboard in one hand and a trophy in another. He had just won the Manhattan Beach Amateur Surfing Competition. His expression was beaming with pride. He had beat out all competitors to achieve first place, most of them ten to fifteen years younger than him.

I placed this one next to the one of us in the hammock. I picked up and piled all the other pictures and gently replaced them in their box, which returned to the stack against the wall.

Looking down I realised I was covered in dust. I'd made a complete mess of my suit. I didn't care. I touched his surfboard. The one he was riding the day of the accident, bringing the memory of that day back into focus. I looked at the memory in a different light. Panic and sadness didn't overwhelm me. I thought, maybe what Maria had said to me was right. Maybe it was time to move forward without him, keeping the memory of Stephen with love in my heart, not heartache in my heart. I wiped the few tears that had filled my eyes away with the back of my hand. After picking up the two pictures I set aside, I gently opened the door, turned out the light, and made my way into the outer hallway. The door stood open as I climbed the stairs to the main level of the house.

The main floor was empty. Various lights were a blaze filling the kitchen and living room. I recognised the sound of *Matchbox Twenty* filtering through the speaker in the ceiling, which Rick must have been listening to. I placed the picture of Stephen and me on top of the fireplace mantel, next to the anniversary bowl.

I felt perfectly calm. I went into the kitchen and poured a glass of wine, the last glass from the bottle of the ten-year Merlot from France. Turning off lights, I headed upstairs. The door to Rick's room was firmly closed, light spilling out from beneath it, so I presumed he was awake. A small amount of anger and hurt still resonated inside of me for what he had done. I was not ready to talk to him yet, I decided as I made my way into my room, closing and locking the door behind me. I placed the picture of Stephen on the beach on the bedside table. After dropping my dusty suit on the floor of my closet, I made my way into the bathroom and filled the tub with warm water.

18

I SAT COMFORTABLY IN ONE OF THE LOUNGE CHAIRS ON THE back deck, coffee in one hand and the Sunday edition of the *L.A. Times* in my lap. The morning was beautiful, the mid-morning temperature already hovering at eighty-five degrees. I looked out to the water and watched as a father was teaching his son how to surf. The dad was knee-deep in water with his son laying flat on the surfboard practicing his paddling skills. The boy looked to be about six or seven. The pathway that led into the centre of town was already alive with activity, populated by runners, bikers, and a few couples going for a morning walk.

"Is it safe to come out here?"

I turned and looked at Rick, who was standing on the inside of the threshold to the deck.

"It's safe," I said as I put my coffee and paper down on the table next to me.

He slowly walked out. He approached the lounger, keeping a few feet between us.

"Rick."

He raised his hand for me to stop. "Please, let me start," he said. "I barely slept last night. I know what I did was so wrong. I have no excuse. My curiosity got the better of me. I know saying sorry over and over is not going to make it better. But, I am very, very sorry. You never talk about Stephen. I feel like I am in competition with your memory of him. That you are comparing me to him. When I saw his

196

things in the room, I couldn't help myself from going through them. I wanted to know who he was. Who *you* were with him. Again, I know it was wrong. If you want me to leave, I'll leave. I really like you, Jack, and I really want to spend time getting to know you better, but if you're done, I will respect that." He sighed as he finished his speech.

Pulling my legs up into a cross-legged position, I patted the vacant part of the lounger for him to come and sit. He hesitated.

"Promise I won't lunge at you."

He slowly came over and sat, not facing me, head down, like a puppy that about to be spanked.

"I don't want you to leave. So if you're already packed you can go back upstairs and unpack," I said with a small smile.

He didn't look up.

"I was, and maybe still am, a little mad at you for last night. No, let me rephrase that. I think I'm a little hurt. I feel disappointed that you violated my trust." I paused. "That said, you did me a favour last night."

He looked up.

"You're right. I never talked about Stephen. I cleared the room downstairs that was once his business and locked away the remaining items that I had of his down there. I realised last night, looking at his things, that it's time for me to move forward. Your presence has got me to that point. Whether you know this or not, you've given me the push I've needed. And for that I thank you." I touched his arm as I finished.

He leant towards me and kissed me.

"So I'm off the hook?" he asked holding my head close to his.

Knowing he needed to lighten the conversation, I replied, "Not entirely," with a smile.

He kissed me again.

*   *   *

"EXCUSE ME," JULIE SAID, CLEARING HER THROAT loudly.

I opened my eyes, instantly awake. Rick and I had fallen asleep on the lounger. His arms were still wrapped around me. I nudged him and struggled to sit up.

"Julie. What are you doing here?" I asked. "What a surprise."

"You bet it is," she replied sarcastically.

Rick, who had woken now, jumped off the lounger, putting distance between us.

"Julie. Hey." He lifted his hand in a wave. "What are you doing here?" he asked.

"Your dad and I came to take you two to lunch."

"Dad's here?" Rick asked, panicked.

"Yes. He is. He's in the car on the phone. Why don't you go join him? I'll be right there."

"Hello? Where the hell is everyone?"

I recognised the distinct drawl of Max coming from inside my house.

"Julie, where are you?"

"On the back deck, darling," Julie called out toward the open doors of the house.

"Here you all are," Max said as he stepped onto the deck. He was dressed in a dark grey suit. I didn't think I could remember a time when he wasn't dressed in a suit.

"Rick," Max said and nodded at him.

"Hey, Dad," Rick replied, but made no effort to greet him with a hug or any sign of affection.

"Jack, how are you?"

Max reached down and shook my hand. We were

cordial to each other only for Julie's sake, and we both knew it.

"Sorry to hear about your show, Jack," Max said.

"Thank you. I appreciate that," I said politely as I stood.

"We going to lunch or what? I'm starved," Max said.

"Yes, darling. I was just telling Rick to join you in the car when you came in," Julie replied, not taking her eyes off me.

Max turned to go back into the house.

"You coming, Jack?" Max asked me.

"No, darling. He can't. He's not feeling well," Julie said before I could open my mouth.

"Hope it's nothing contagious," Max responded as he headed into the house.

"No, darling, I am sure it's not. You and Rick go to the car. I will be right there. I just want to make sure Jack is comfortable and has everything he needs before we go," Julie said as she nodded to Rick to follow Max.

Rick looked panicked, but obeyed.

"Julie," I started.

"Wait," she said, listening for the sound of the front door closing. Once she was satisfied we were alone, she turned on me.

"How could you, Jack? How could you do this to me?"

"Do what to you?" I interrupted.

"Can you imagine what would have happened if Max came into the house with me and witnessed how I found the two of you? You would be pounded black and blue by now. I convinced him to drive up here the minute our plane arrived in San Diego from New York, and this is what I find?"

"It's not what you think."

"Really, it's not? I'm not stupid, Jack. How could you? How could you do this to me?"

"Do this to *you*?" I asked, puzzled.

Yes. To *me*. I trusted you to look after Rick for the summer," she said.

"You're not seeing the whole picture," I replied, getting agitated.

"Really? The whole picture? Well, I'll tell you the picture I see," she said, pointing at me. "I see in front of me my brother who I love, and who has betrayed me by enticing my young stepson into his bed."

"I guess that is the picture you *would* see," I replied.

"What's the matter? Can't find someone your own age?" she asked angrily.

"You're one to talk," I replied. Max was much older than she was.

She slapped me hard across my right cheek. I was surprised by her strength.

"You listen to me, and you listen to me good." She was holding me by the face with her right hand. "You stop this right now. Today. Don't make me do something I may regret. That all of us might regret. You, me, or Rick. I cannot tell you how disappointed I am in you right this very moment."

I stared right back at her, not letting her see the pain from the slap or the pain from her nails digging into my cheek.

"I don't know how far it has gone. But it's done as of this moment. Are we clear?"

I didn't say a word. She released my face.

"Mom called me, all worried about you. I'll tell her you're fine. Obviously, she shouldn't have been worried," she said as she turned to go.

I held my position. I listened as her shoes clicked loudly on the floor of the house, the sound heading to the front door. Only after I knew she'd gone did I relax and touch my face. The warmth of blood greeted my fingertips.

* * *

BLOCKING THE INCIDENT WITH JULIE FROM MY MIND, I found myself cleaning out the downstairs room. I pulled the black paper sheets from the windows and doors, letting the light flow into the room. I dusted off the boxes. The bike. The surfboards. I decided to give all of Stephen's clothes to the homeless shelter. The bike and surfboards would go to the local kid's recreation centre.

Placing the items in the garage for easier pick up, I was greeted by Stephen on my second trip back. He was standing by the remaining boxes.

"What are you doing? This is my stuff?" he said angrily.

"It's time for it to go," I replied and started stacking another pile to take up to the garage.

"You can't do this. This is my stuff. I need this stuff!"

"No, you don't. Stephen, it's time for someone else to make use of it," I replied calmly.

"I can't believe you let that kid you're fucking talk you into getting rid of my stuff."

"It's time to move on," I said.

"You think you can replace me with that boy?" He paced the room.

"Nobody is replacing anybody. It's time for me to move on. Move forward. You are becoming part of my past now. You need to let me go into my future." I took a breath.

"You can't just forget me like this." He was fighting to hang on.

"Trust me. I will never be able to forget you. You helped shape me into the person I am today. You'll always be part of me. I've never loved someone as much as I have loved you."

He turned his back on me. I picked up the next load of

boxes for the garage and left the room. When I returned he was gone.

*   *   *

WITH THE BASEMENT EMPTIED OF ITS CONTENTS, THE WALLS, floor, and windows scrubbed to a gleaming shine, I sat at my desk with the only two remaining boxes I had kept out. I went through the pictures first, separating the ones that contained images of Stephen only. I wrapped them carefully in bubble wrap and I placed them inside a new empty shipping box. I next went through the box filled with his personal items. I selected Stephen's birth certificate, passport, college diploma, and high school diploma. I placed these items into a new large manila envelope, and then I placed it on top of the pictures. I cut up his driver's licence, credit cards, and ATM card, letting the pieces fall into the garbage. I tucked the papers for his car into the top drawer of my desk as I pulled out a writing tablet and wrote:

Dear Mr. & Mrs. Ross:

Please find enclosed items I know Stephen would have liked you to have. I know you didn't completely agree with his lifestyle and the choices he made. I want you to know you son was amazing, loving, kind, and wonderful— qualities I know you are both responsible for. He loved you both very deeply.

I personally am a better person for him being part of my life. He taught me how to love unconditionally and freely with my heart. He showed me how to enjoy and participate in life, not just to be a bystander.

I thank you for bringing into this world such a beautiful soul. I thank you for raising such an amazing man.

You both occupy a place in my heart and thoughts.

Jack Perry

I labelled and placed the box by the front door, planning to UPS it to them in the morning. After returning to the study I placed the boxes with the remaining items into the storage closet. The antique clock on my desk read 6:05 p.m. Unsure as to when Rick was going to be back I prepared a light salad for my dinner, taking it and a glass of wine out to the deck. As I ate I made a mental note of what I needed to do tomorrow. Go to UPS. That was it. It felt strange to me not to have a purpose. My whole adult life I had either worked or gone to school. Or both. *What was I going to do with my life?*

"Hey," Rick's voice broke my thoughts.

"Hey yourself," I replied as he sat next to me. "How was your lunch?"

"Long. We had to drive into Beverly Hills, since my dad didn't want to eat anywhere at the beach. Needed to go to the Wilshire. What happened to your face?"

I reached up and touch the newly formed scabs on my cheeks.

"Julie. She got a little rough," I said jokingly. "She say anything to you?"

"No, nothing. My dad never left us alone. I was on edge all day thinking she would blurt something out at any moment."

"She won't. She'll keep this from your dad," I said.

"How can you be sure?" he asked.

"I know my sister. And she has instructed me to stop whatever is happening between us."

"Screw her. She has no say in this," he replied quickly. "Let's go for a walk on the beach."

He stood and reached for my hand.

19

THE COOL AIR FROM INSIDE THE AIR-CONDITIONED BANK HIT me like a wall as soon as I opened the door. Briefcase in hand I walked directly to the receptionist desk.

"Good morning, how may I help you today?" the perky blonde lady asked me.

"Jack Perry. I have an appointment to see Joanna Lunden," I answered.

She turned to her computer screen, punched a few keys. "Yes. Mr. Perry. Please have a seat. I will let Ms. Lunden know you've arrived." She motioned to the small waiting area to the right of her desk as she picked up her phone. "Can I get you anything?" she asked.

"No, thank you," I replied.

Five minutes passed before I could make out Joanna's form walking out from behind a private hallway directly behind the receptionist desk.

"Jack. How are you?" she greeted me, with a firm handshake. She was dressed smartly in a tailored cream suit. I estimated Joanna to be in her early fifties. "Please. Let's go back into my office," she gestured with her hand.

I followed her through the doorway, down the private hallway, into her office at the end of what seemed like endless doorways leading into endless offices.

Joanna had been my personal banker for over ten years. She had moved branches twice in that time and I moved my accounts with her. She currently worked at the Santa

Monica Branch.

"So, Jack. I haven't seen you since last year. How have you been?" she asked as we sat.

"I'm good now. I had a challenging year, but I think I'm coming out of it." I hadn't been to see Joanna since I settled Stephen's estate.

"Got to love online banking," I said nervously.

"So what brings you by today?"

"Couple of things. First, I want to set up two trust accounts."

Joanna started taking notes.

"In the amount of a hundred thousand dollars each. I want restrictions that funds can only be withdrawn to pay school tuition. If they are not used for school tuition, I would like the funds locked until the thirtieth birthday of the person named on the account."

"Who are these for?" Joanna looks up.

"Sorry, I guess I jumped ahead slightly. They are for Stephen's nephews," I reached into my briefcase and handed Joanna a spreadsheet listing the pertinent information about each of them. She scanned the information.

"These boys are just seven and eight. I suggest we put the funds in a locked high yield CDI educational account until they're eighteen. Then transfer the funds to a lower interest account, unlocked, of course, so the funds can be withdrawn easily. Given the amount of money you are opening the account with, these funds will grow substantially in the next eight to ten years," she stated.

"Sounds good," I replied. I knew I was doing the right thing. Even though Stephen had barely talked to his brother in the ten years I was with him, I knew he would want his nephews looked after.

"Given the restrictions you want on this account, I'm assuming you are trying to protect the funds from the boy's parents, correct?"

"Yes. Stephen's brother isn't the best money manager. I want the boys to have the chance to go to whatever school they wish, and if they don't continue their education, I want them to have something saved," I finished.

"Then I would suggest we put restrictions that the bank will disperse funds directly to any college or university; we shouldn't list a guardian on the accounts."

"Perfect," I replied.

"I'll set these accounts up with the main branch of our institution in Dallas. Where do you want the account statements to go to?"

"To Stephen's parents. Their information is listed on the sheet, as well. Can you also send them direct notification that the accounts have been opened?" I asked.

She looked up. "You don't want to notify them yourself?"

"No. Since you were privy to the details of Stephen's estate, you know better than anyone that they didn't have the best relationship."

"I have to list you on the documents for the accounts. They'll know this is your doing." she said, looking over her glasses at me.

"I know. I just don't think they'll accept this coming directly from me," I said with a little sadness in my voice.

"Okay. I'll instruct the Dallas branch to handle all correspondence with Mr. and Mrs. Ross, outlining that they should contact the branch representative assigned to the accounts directly."

"Thank you, Joanna."

"I should be able to have the papers drawn up and ready for your signature towards the end of the week."

"Perfect."

"What else are we doing today, Jack?"

"I would like a certified cashier's cheque in the amount

of two hundred thousand dollars made out to The Hermosa Beach City Fire and Rescue Team Foundation. And this one *needs* to be anonymous."

She looked up, punched some keys on her computer. "Which account do you want this withdrawn from?"

"Savings."

She picked up the phone and pressed a couple numbers. Then, she gave my instructions to another employee to prepare an anonymous bank draft.

When she hung up, she said, "Cheryl will bring it in as soon as it's prepared."

I nodded.

"What else am I doing for you today?" she asked.

"I need your advice on my investment portfolio."

She punched more keys on the computer. "I see you made a sizable deposit into your savings account two weeks ago via the branch in Hermosa Beach. A very sizable deposit."

"Payout for my studio contract. *Chamberlain Heights* was cancelled a couple of weeks ago."

"Jack, I'm sorry. I hadn't heard." She touched my hand.

"I'll spare you the details, but I need you to know that I may not be working for a while. A very long while. I need to figure out an income."

I felt very nervous now, scared of my options or lack thereof. She took her hand from mine and turned back to her computer.

"Let's review all your accounts. Chequing account balance $43,050.16. Savings account balance, with the deposit you made last week, two point one million dollars, and change."

Part of that figure was insurance payout from Stephen's death. Joanna had tried corresponding with me numerous times over the last year to add it to my investment portfolio, but I couldn't bring myself to transfer the funds.

"The investments we've chosen for you have been doing quite well. Since you haven't been withdrawing dividends from the accounts, the money you have made each year has automatically been reinvested into the account. Current balance: three point two million dollars, and change."

The number didn't surprise me, because I scanned my account statement regularly. I just didn't know how the numbers would work if I had to start drawing on them.

There was a soft knock on the door. A petite brunette came in and handed Joanna a couple of items.

"Jack, please sign at the bottom, authorising the withdrawal from your account," Joanna said as she handed me one of the documents and a pen.

I quickly signed and handed it back to her.

"Thank you, Cheryl." Joanna handed the document back to the petite young lady and she left as softly as she has entered. I put the cashier's bank draft into my briefcase when Joanna handed it to me.

"Let's continue," Joanna said. "Let's look at what you owe now. Credit card balances all at zero. Line of credit at zero. No car payments, correct?" I nodded. "Good. Mortgage account balance is eighty-three thousand dollars. This is attached to the condo property in West Hollywood."

The beach house was insured and the mortgage was paid in full when Stephen died, leaving me the house with a clear title. The condo in West Hollywood I had purchased before meeting Stephen, and although we both lived there together after we met, we never got around to adding him to the title.

"Is the condo still rented?" Joanna asked.

"Yes. The rent is covering the monthly mortgage amount and maintenance costs, but that's it."

Joanna continued punching keys on the computer, her eyes moving quickly across the screen. She sat back and took her glasses off. "I would say you're in very good shape."

"Am I? Even without an income coming in for an indefinite amount of time?" I asked nervously.

"Yes." She sat back up. "This is what I'm going to suggest. We take the full balance of your savings account minus a hundred thousand dollars, and deposit it directly into your investment portfolio. We leave the mortgage on the West Hollywood condo as it is. It's locked in at prime plus one percent for three more years, which the monthly rent covers. There's no benefit in paying off the mortgage; let the renters do that for a while. The amount added to your investment portfolio from your savings account will give you annual dividends of around two hundred thousand dollars. Given the fact that you have no debt, I think you're going to do just fine. I would, however, suggest any leftover, unused funds from the annual dividend be re-invested into your portfolio to ensure its continued growth. You never have to work a day in your life again if you chose, Jack."

I sat stunned as she finished. I never thought the total invested amount would give such a large yearly dividend. "I trust you completely. Make the changes."

"I'll need a couple days to have the paperwork drawn up. Today is Tuesday. How about you come back Thursday around noon? When we're done with the paperwork, I can take my favourite client out to lunch," she said, smiling at me.

"I would love nothing more than to have lunch with you. Thank you," I replied, standing.

She came around from behind her desk and gave me a hug.

"It's so good to see you," she said as she opened the door for me.

*　　*　　*

" MR. PERRY, HOW ARE YOU?"

I turned from the window and faced Manuel. I was at my second stop of my day.

"Great," I replied and put my hand into his outstretched one.

"I see you're still driving the Beamer. Here to trade it for a real machine?" He gestured through the window at my car, with a laugh in his voice.

I smiled. "No, I need you to sell the one that I have here."

Manuel was the assistant sales manager for the Porsche dealership in Santa Monica. Stephen bought his car from Manuel four years ago. We both fell immediately in love with his genuine personality and heart. The day before Stephen's accident we had dropped the car for its regularly scheduled maintenance appointment. After the accident I left the car here, paying a monthly storage fee to the dealership, not wanting to bring it home.

"Let's go into my office, shall we?" Manuel gestured towards the stairs that lead up to his office on the second floor. "Are you sure you want to sell the car? It's a magnificent piece of equipment," he said as we settle into his office, which overlooked the showroom floor.

"I'm sure. It was Stephen's car. It's time for someone else to enjoy and love it the way he did," I replied as Manuel started typing on his computer.

"I should be able to sell it for around forty thousand dollars, given its low mileage."

I nodded.

"The dealership will take a three percent commission off the top for the consignment sale," he added.

"No problem," I said.

"I will need the papers for the car and the documents

supporting that ownership was transferred to you."

I reached into my briefcase and handed him an envelope I had prepared yesterday.

Manuel gave the papers a quick scan. "Perfect." He started typing on his computer.

"Manuel?"

He looked up.

"I have one small request."

"Yes," he replied.

"When the car sells, I would like the cheque made out to The Los Angles Gay and Lesbian Community Centre, naming Stephen as the donor. Will that be a problem?"

"No. Not at all. I'll just add that information to the sales agreement. I can arrange to have the cheque couriered to their office if you like."

"Yes. I would like that. Thank you," I replied gratefully.

The printer behind Manuel came to life, printing out the agreement to sell Stephen's car on my behalf. Manuel went over the agreement in great detail with me before I signed it.

"Do you want to see the car one last time, Mr. Perry? I think there are some personal items in the car," he said.

I paused, unable to make a decision.

"Mr. Perry?"

"Sorry," I said when Manuel broke the silence. "Yes. Yes, I would like to see the car one last time."

"Please follow me," he said.

Manuel led me back down the stairs to the showroom floor. We went outside, where Manuel unlocked the door that led to a gated compound. We walked towards the very back, stopping at the form of a car protected beneath a cloth covering. Manuel pulled off the covering, revealing a sleek silver machine. The lights flashed and I heard the gentle clicking of the doors unlocking.

"I'll wait for you inside, Mr. Perry," he said handing me

the keys.

I opened the driver's door and folded myself into the car. I ran my hand along the steering wheel, the dashboard, the console. I swore I could smell Stephen's scent. I looked through the glove compartment and centre console for any items left in the car. I found a cell phone charger, gum, a pen, and a few CD's— nothing of great importance.

On the visor, I found a picture of Stephen with the car. The picture was taken by the dealership the day he picked the car up. Taking the pen, I wrote, *I hope you get as much enjoyment out of this car as he did.* I put the picture back in its place on the visor. On impulse, I put the key in the ignition and started the engine. It roared to life without any hesitation. The sounds of Tina Turner immediately filled the small space as she belted out the lyrics to *You're Simply the Best.* I sang along, going back to the memory of our road trip to Las Vegas, the day we had picked up this car.

"Let's just go for a little drive. I have to drive around in my new car," Stephen had said excitedly.

That little drive ended in Las Vegas. We ended up having one of the greatest weekends of our lives.

"Good times, Stephen, good times," I said. I pushed eject on the stereo and retrieved Tina's CD.

Then, I shut the car off and locked it remotely when I got out. Tucking the Tina CD into my briefcase I made my way back into the dealership. Manuel was waiting for me by the reception desk.

"Please give any remaining items in the car to anyone who may want them," I said as I handed him the keys.

He nodded. I turned to go.

"Mr. Perry."

I turned back to Manuel.

"I never got the chance to give you my condolences on your loss. Please accept them at this late time."

"Thank you, Manuel." I smiled and made my way out

of the showroom, out to the visitors parking area. I put in the CD that was in Stephen's car. Cranking the volume, top down, I turned onto Pacific Coast Highway for the drive home.

20

I'M AMAZED AT HOW THE SUMMER IS FLYING BY, I THOUGHT AS I looked out at the water. It was now the first week in August. I found myself having fallen into a daily routine of running, working out, and enjoying the beach. Rick and I had fallen into a similar comfortable routine as well. He spent his days at school, rushing home so we could hang out. We loved doing things together: making dinner, rollerblading, watching movies, and of course eating on Friday nights at Joe's. On the weekends, travelled in and around Los Angles, doing the things tourists do when they come to Los Angles, things I hadn't done in years. Rick and I were starting to get truly close, sharing with our thoughts and dreams. I found he was challenging me constantly.

* * *

UNFORTUNATELY, WHILE RICK AND I WERE HONEYMOONING, Julie hadn't returned my calls. I left her messages a couple times a week, to no avail. Neither she nor Max had been in touch with Rick either. I hadn't seen Vivian or talked with her once on the phone. I suspected she was still in a funk over the cancellation of our show.

Surprisingly, the person who did stay in touch was Daniel. I saw him every week. Last week, he and his wife Jocelyn had Rick and I over for dinner at their home in Brentwood. Daniel was becoming a very close friend. He

214

had already been picked up for another show for the fall, replacing a director in a current successful medical drama.

"Jack, I would love nothing more than to bring you on board," he said to me one day at lunch. "But Goldman proved good on his threat. He ruined your name."

I thanked him and assured him I was unsure if I even wanted to get back into the regular grind of a weekly series. For the first time in my life I was okay with doing nothing.

The shrill electronic ringing from the phone inside interrupted my thoughts. I ignored it; It stopped after fours rings, automatically directing the caller to the voicemail server. Judging from the sun's position in the sky, I estimated the time to be pushing 5 p.m. Rick could be home within the hour. I decided to go into the house and start the preparations for dinner.

The phone rang again as I pulled out the items I needed to start dinner.

"Hey you," I answered on the second ring, knowing from the caller ID that it was Rick calling from his cell phone.

"Hey. I'm going to be late tonight. Professor Geller sprung a surprise interactive lecture tomorrow, with the all the faculty members of the department," Rick said.

"That doesn't seem fair," I said.

"It doesn't, no. But he says given our chosen profession we'll need to expect surprises like this. I need to stay with the group for a while. You'll be okay on your own?"

"Yes. Of course. I'll just miss you. When do you think you will be home?" I asked.

"We shouldn't need more than a couple of extra hours. We'll work over dinner. I should be there by nine."

"See you then," I said.

"Okay. Got to go. Bye."

I pushed the off key on the phone. Not wanting to cook

for myself, I put back the previously retrieved items into the fridge, deciding to head to Joe's for dinner. The voicemail light caught my attention as it flashed on and off on the phone. Hoping it was Julie I decided to check the messages before I left. I pushed the voicemail button on the base of the phone so I could listen via speaker.

"Hi, Jack? You don't know me, but I got this number from your sister, Julie."

The voice of a young woman filled the room.

"I'm looking for Rick. I haven't been able to get a hold of him for a few days. He's not returning the messages I left on his voicemail. Can you please tell him to call me?"

Sure. Tell me who you are, I thought.

"Thanks for your help, bye. Oh, sorry. I forgot to tell you who I am."

Not the brightest girl, I think to myself again.

"I'm Tanya. Rick's fiancée. Thanks for your help."

I listened to the message two more times.

"His fiancée," I said to myself.

I could feel the blood cooling in my veins, my head starting to spin. I grabbed the counter to steady myself. I felt like I was going to pass out at any second. I lowered myself onto the floor.

"It's a joke. Someone is playing a joke. That has to be it," I said. "She mentioned Julie, though. And my home number is unlisted." On the handset of the phone, I scanned the incoming callers list I found a number listed with the Washington State area code. The time received was shortly before Rick's call.

"Fucker!" I threw the phone across the kitchen floor. Putting my head in my hands, tears started to flow quickly.

* * *

"JACK?" I HEARD RICK CALL OUT AS ENTERED THE HOUSE. HE

dropped his bag by the door. The house was completely dark and quiet.

"Jack, are you here?"

He turned on lights and saw me sitting at the dining room table, glass of wine in one hand, a half empty bottle in front of me.

"What are you doing sitting in the dark?"

I lifted my head and looked at him.

"What happened?" He rushed over at the sight of my tear-stained face.

"Stay away from me." I got up and put distance between us.

"What's wrong?" he asked.

"What's wrong? You can actually casually ask me what's wrong? Wow!"

"You're not making any sense." He tried to move closer to me.

"Stay back." I put my hand up.

"Tell me what's going on here," Rick begged.

"I'll tell you. No, I'll show you." I made my way to the phone base on the kitchen counter, and I activated the speakerphone. Tanya's voice filled the room. I watched Rick as he listened to the message. His expression changed from concern to shock. His skin colour visibly paled at the sound of her voice.

"Do you have anything to say?" I asked when the message was over.

"I can explain."

"Good. I'm listening," I said, my voice trembling.

"Well. Where to begin?" He rubbed the back of his head as he talked to himself.

"Well, you can start with how you neglected to tell me you are engaged." The tremble in my voice was now replaced with anger.

"I was going to tell you, but it just never came up," he

said.

"Nice. Good answer." I gave him the thumbs up sign.

"Um. Uh."

"Is that all your going to say? Um. Uh? Maybe I should lead this conversation, then. I'll start it with thanks for lying to me."

"I never lied," he said.

"Omission is the same thing as lying." The anger in my body was building.

"I don't agree," he said.

"Okay. Fine. When were you going to tell me? The night before your wedding? Your first anniversary? When?"

"I… I didn't think I was ever going to need to tell you," he replied.

"Nice answer. So I guess I was just an experiment to you after all?"

"No!" he said quickly.

"Just a summer of fun then, maybe. Someone to ensure your sexual needs were satisfied," I spat.

"No," he replied.

"Okay. So as I see it, from what you're telling me, and what you aren't telling me, you were going to finish off the summer with me and then go home to Tanya."

He was silent.

"You little bastard. How dare you fuck with me like that?" I yelled, my voice seething with anger. I turned to leave the room.

"We never agreed we were exclusive, Jack," he called after me.

I turned. "Pardon?"

"We never agreed to be exclusive. Actually, we never labelled what our relationship was, remember?" he said, his finger gesturing back and forth between us. "You're just as much at fault here."

"This is how you're going to justify your actions? By

blaming me? How original. Let me tell you something," I said, pointing at him. "Not labelling us and having a secret fiancée are two completely different things. And who didn't want to label us? I think that was you," I said.

"Get off your high horse. You didn't want to label us, either. Then you would have to admit you're in a relationship," he argued back.

"Usually people who are in a relationship are in it with only one other person. Not two," I replied.

"*Ya.* I know. I'm tired of having Stephen in whatever you want to call us."

I noticed the colour had returned to his face, his eyes clear with anger.

"How dare you turn this into something about Stephen?" My heart began to race.

"Why not? He's part of this, too."

"He's the reason you hid your engagement from me?"

Silence.

"Tell me!"

"You have a past. I have a past," he smugly answered.

"No, Rick. I have a past. I have a past with Stephen. You have a present with Tanya. She is here. Alive. And she's your fiancée."

"But I live in this house," Rick said. "*His* house. I sleep in and make love to you in what was once his bed. I see reminders of how important he was to you in this house." He walked over to the fireplace and picked up the crystal anniversary bowl by its rim.

"Rick. *You* put that there."

"I know, but I didn't expect it to upset me as much as it does."

He shook his hand angrily, and I watched as the bowl released from his grip and fell in slow motion to the floor. It hit the hardwood floor with a loud crash, breaking into a cascading shower of hundreds of shattering pieces. They seemed to fly everywhere in the room.

My hand covered my mouth, stifling a scream. My breath stopped.

"Oh, Jack. I'm sorry. I didn't mean for that to happen. Oh fuck." He looked at me, surprised. I struggled for air. He stood stunned, looking at the mess at his feet. Minutes passed. My body went numb.

"I want you out of my house," I calmly said when I was able to catch my breath. "And I want you out of it right now."

I picked up my glass of wine from counter that was next to the phone and walked upstairs.

*   *   *

"HELLO."

"John. It's Rick."

"Hey, dude. What's up?" John asked.

"I kind of need a place to stay. Can I bunk in your dorm room?" Rick asked as he drove out of Hermosa Beach and toward the freeway.

"Sure. Not a problem, dude. When you coming?" he asked.

"Should be there in like thirty minutes. Is that cool?"

"Cool. I'll meet you at the lobby door. It's already locked for the night."

"Thanks. See you in a flash." Rick ended the call by flipping his phone closed. He slammed his foot down hard on the accelerator as soon as he hit the 405, hoping that the sooner he got away from Hermosa Beach, the sooner he would stop feeling guilty for what he'd done.

*   *   *

"SO, TELL ME, DUDE. WHY DO YOU NEED TO CRASH HERE?"
John asked as Rick dropped onto one of two twin beds in
the room.

"Complicated," Rick responded as he covered his eyes
with the back of his hand.

"Complicated? You had a lover's quarrel?"

Rick removed his hand from his eyes and sat up.

"What?" was all he could get out.

"I think you heard me the first time," John said. "I'm
not stupid. I can see the writing on the wall, so to speak."

"How? When?" Rick was stuttering.

"How did I figure it out?"

Rick nodded.

"Let's see. You've been blowing me off ever since we
got to L.A. You're in an unusually good mood all the time,
which I relate to regular sex. The signs are pretty clear.
Why would you be spending so much time out at the beach
with that guy unless you were involved with him?" John
finished.

"You're okay with this?" Rick asked.

"You're my bro. I could care less who you're sleeping
with. Doesn't change who you are," John answered. "So are
you gay or what?"

Rick nervously laughed. "I don't know."

"How can you not know? You're sleeping with the
dude, right?"

"*Ya*. I'm sleeping with Jack."

"Then you, my friend, are a gay, dude," John replied
with a smile in his voice.

"I'm not so sure. I still like girls," Rick answered.

"Oh, dude. You're a bi-sexual!" John said as he jumped
on his bed.

"I don't know. I'm just kind of in this place, you
know?" Rick said.

"No, bro. I totally don't know. Honest. Can't relate,"

John said. "What was your fight about? Must have been a big one if he kicked you out."

"*Ya*. He found out about Tanya."

"Dude, you're still with Tanya? You are a dog. A big bad, such a shit dog." John's comments didn't help alleviate Rick's guilt.

"I know," Rick said.

"So what you going to do?' John asked.

"About what?"

"About the tooth fairy, you shmuck. What do you think? About this guy and Tanya."

"I honestly don't know," Rick replied.

"Are you in love with this *Jack*?" John asked.

"Maybe. I like him a lot. I think I may love him. I'm not sure. He is a really great guy," Rick answered with confusion in his voice.

"Do you love Tanya?" John asked.

"*Ya*. I do," Rick replied.

"You are so fucked, my friend," John said.

"That's your advice? No words of wisdom?" Rick asked.

"I know this. You can't be with both of them. And you can't be with one, if you are constantly going to think about the other. If you can't figure out which one is the one, you need to break it off with both of them."

Rick thought about this for a moment. "That's pretty enlightened for you, bro. You hooking up with Oprah in the afternoons?"

John threw a pillow hard at Rick, hitting him square in the face. They both laughed.

"We better go to sleep. We have a huge day tomorrow," John said as he reached for the light.

"Rick."

"*Ya*, John."

"Just so we're clear. I know my ass is totally

irresistible, but it is totally off limits to you."

"Go to sleep, you fucker," Rick said as he pulled off his clothes and climbed under the comforter.

21

THE HOUSE WAS TOTALLY QUIET AS I CAME OUT OF MY ROOM. I went into Rick's room and found the closet and drawers empty of his belongings, the bed perfectly made. I didn't hear him leave last night, so I was unsure if he actually did.

I walked downstairs. I noticed Rick's key sitting in the middle of the table next to the door as I retrieved the morning paper from the stoop. As I entered the kitchen I found a plastic Zip Lock bag filled with the pieces of glass, which I assumed were remnants of the anniversary bowl sitting on the island. I looked into the living room area and saw no glass on the floor.

He cleaned it all up. I still felt numb from last night, still unable to grasp the thought that Rick had a fiancée. I went about my morning, preparing coffee, flipping through the morning paper as I waited for it to percolate. The ring of the phone startled me, causing me to jump. I walked over to the counter and retrieved the handset from its base. I recognised Julie's cell phone number in the caller ID window.

"Hey. I am so glad you called," I said as I answered.

"We have an emergency." There was panic in her voice. "It's Dad. He was rushed to the hospital early this morning."

"What's going on?" I asked, giving her my full attention.

"I don't know for sure. Mom said he was complaining about chest pains and he was having trouble breathing. She

224

called 911 and had him rushed to emergency. They haven't told her anything except that he's critical, but stable for the moment. You need to get to Phoenix right away."

"Okay. Where are you?" Panic gripped me.

"In a taxi, almost at the airport. I was able to get on a flight that leaves in thirty minutes," Julie answered.

"What hospital is he at?" I asked.

"Phoenix Memorial."

"I'll get there as soon as I can," I said.

"Hurry."

"I will. I'll meet you at the hospital," I replied.

"Okay. See you soon," she responded and disconnected the line.

* * *

"THANK YOU FOR CALLING AMERICAN AIRLINES; THIS IS Alisha; how I may help you today?" the very pleasant voice of a customer service representative answers my call.

"I need a flight to Phoenix as soon as possible please. It's an emergency," I answered, panic in my voice.

"Okay, sir, I can help you. From what city?" she asks.

"Oh, sorry. Los Angles. LAX. Please hurry." The panic built within me.

"We only have seats on two of the available flights today," she says.

"I'll take the first one available," I respond. "Unfortunately, sir, the flight is scheduled for departure at 9:30 a.m."

I looked at the oven clock: 7:30 a.m. "Book me. I will be there."

"I'm sorry, sir, I cannot do that. It is the airline's policy not to book flights that close to departure unless the passenger is already present in the departing airport. I can book you on the later flight at 3:30 p.m. this afternoon.

Would you like to proceed with that, sir?" she asked.

I took a deep breath to calm my voice. "Alisha, right?" I asked.

"Yes, sir."

"I really need to get on the 9:30 flight. It's an emergency. My dad was rushed to emergency in critical condition a short while ago. I live twenty minutes from LAX. I can be there in time for required sixty minute before flight check-in requirement. Can you please, please put me on that flight? Please?" I pleaded.

"I'm sorry; it's against policy," she replied.

"Please don't make me beg," I said.

She was quiet for a moment. "Okay. I will need you to buy a first-class ticket, and I will book you as a VIP; it's going to be expensive, but it is the only way the computer will allow me to process the ticket," she said compassionately.

"Not a problem," I replied.

She asked for my name and other pertinent details. I rattled off my American Express number for her to finish the process.

"Okay, Mr. Perry. Your ticket will be waiting for you at the American Airlines first-class check-in counter, in terminal one at Los Angles International Airport," she said after processing my credit card.

"Thank you, Alisha. I appreciate you doing this for me. You are an angel," I said with gratitude in my voice.

"My pleasure, Mr. Perry. I hope your dad is going to be okay."

"Me too. Thank you," I said as I hung up the phone.

*   *   *

IN THE HOSPITAL, I SAW JULIE IMMEDIATELY AFTER TURNING into the corridor that would lead to my father's room. She was slumped in a chair beside the last door in the hallway, dressed in jeans and an off-white sleeveless shirt. Her bright red hair was pulled back into a ponytail. My shoes echoed noisily as I walked down the silent corridor toward her.

"Jack! Thank God you're here." She jumped up and rushed to me.

I dropped my overnight bag on the floor and pulled her into my arms. We stood connected for a few moments.

"What's happening? Where's Mom?" I asked.

"She's in with Dad. It doesn't look good. He hasn't regained consciousness since he was admitted," she replied quietly, tears in her eyes as she broke our embrace.

"Have you seen him?' I asked.

"We're taking turns sitting with him. They're only allowing one person in at a time."

"What does his doctor say?" I asked as we sat in the chairs outside his room.

Julie blotted her eyes with a tissue. "Not much. They've been running tests, but without him regaining consciousness they won't do much more. They don't have much information, except to say we need to be patient and wait."

"That's not saying much. Who's his doctor? I want to talk to him," I said impatiently.

"Dr. Murray."

"I'm going to go find him," I said.

"Her. Dr, Murray is a *she*. They can probably page her at the nurse's station," Julie replied without looking up.

Just as I turned on my heel, the door to my dad's room opened.

"Jack, dear," my mother said, coming out into the hallway.

"I thought I heard voices," she said as she hugged me lightly. "How was your flight?"

"Good, I guess," I replied, stunned at her casualness. I

took a good look at her. Her complexion was slightly pale, without any traces of makeup. It was also completely free of tearstains. She was dressed in a black and light blue exercise outfit. Sneakers adorned her feet.

"You okay, Mom?" I asked.

"I'm fine. Thank you, Jack. I think you should go in and see your father. He'll like that," she said without any emotion in her voice as she sat next to Julie.

I pushed open the door to the private room, leaving Julie and Mom alone in the corridor. I walked in slowly, letting the door close softly behind me. The room smelled like a mixture of different disinfectants, all coming together but not producing a single distinct smell. My eyes took in the different medical equipment that surrounded the bed, all flashing various numbers, some beeping. I let out a small gasp, covering my mouth with my hand when I saw my dad beneath an oxygen tent, his skin grey, his mouth and nose covered with an additional oxygen mask. Various tubes and wires were connected to each of his arms.

I sat in the chair next his bed, the chair Julie and my mom had used for their vigil. Tears formed at the corners of my eyes. I reached down placed my dad's hand in mine.

How can this be my big strong Dad? I wondered.

"Hey, Dad. It's me, Jack," I said. "How are you doing? You sure know how to become the centre of attention, don't you?" I said with a small laugh. "Dad. You have to get better. Mom needs you. Julie needs you and I need you. You can't leave us. Please get better," I pleaded as I rested my forehead on top of his hand. "Please. You have to."

I jumped as his hand twitched. I looked at his face, but nothing had changed. He was still unconscious.

"Hey, God? Hello?" I said to the ceiling, giving a little wave. "I know I don't chat with you often— or not at all, for that matter. And I'm probably not one of your favourite people, but I have a small request." I held my dad's hand between mine. "Please make him better. Please let him be okay. I'm not ready to let go of him. You have already taken one of the two most important men in my life from me. Please leave me this one. Please." Tears streamed down my face as I begged. "I don't have anything to give to you in exchange, except the promise I will be a better person. I'll do anything you ask. Just please leave my dad with me."

"Jack?" a muffled voice broke my prayer.

I looked back to my dad. His eyes were open, full of confusion. He pulled at the oxygen mask covering his face and mouth.

"Jack?"

"Yes, Dad?" I answered, hope in my voice.

"Where the hell am I?" he asked, his voice gravelly and soft.

"In the hospital, Dad. Don't you remember?" I asked.

"Where is your mother?"

"Outside in the hallway," I answered.

"Go get her."

I released his hand and quickly obeyed.

"Mom. Julie. Dad is awake," I said as I opened the door. They both got up and rushed past me. My mom went to my father's side and took his hand.

"Julie, ring for the nurse," she instructed without taking her eyes from him.

"My beautiful lady," he said to her. "And my princess," he said to Julie. "What are you doing here? Shouldn't you be at school? It's not the holidays yet." He sounded exhausted.

"College was a long time ago, Dad," Julie replied softly, taking his free hand in hers, recognizing that he was confused.

He looked at her, her words not registering. "Jackie, my boy."

I stepped in closer and placed my hand on his leg.

"You ready for your game this afternoon?"

"Yes Dad," I said, not wanting to upset him.

"Your mother is going to drive you, okay?"

I nodded.

"I have a late meeting, but I'll be at the game. I promise you I won't miss it. Okay slugger?"

I nodded in agreement once again.

"Shirley. I'm so tired. Why am I so tired?" he asked my mom.

"Rest, darling. It's okay. Just rest," she replied.

He closed his eyes slowly.

A blonde nurse hurried into the room, her eyes widening to see us all gathered around his bed. "What is everyone doing in here? Didn't I say one visitor at a time? Everyone needs to get out."

"I'm sorry, Jennifer. We were all so excited because George woke up," my mom said to the nurse softly.

"He did?" she asked, surprised as she pushed Julie away from the bed and reached into the oxygen tent to replace my dad's mask. She checked the monitors and adjusted his IV drip.

"You all need to leave right now. The doctor is on her way in." She grabbed me and Julie forcefully by the arms, guiding us out of the room.

"You have ten seconds to take your hands off me," I said to Nurse Jennifer.

"You need to leave now." She continued to push Julie and me towards the door.

"In case you didn't hear me the first time, I told you to take your hands off me," I said angrily as I forcefully peeled her grip from my arm.

"Ouch! You're breaking the rules," she said.

"Fuck the rules," I said, glaring into her eyes.

"Jackie!" Mom scolded me.

"Who do you think you are?" the nurse asked, meeting

my glare with one of her own.

Ready for a fight, I prepared to stand my ground, but my father did it for me. "He's my son. And I wouldn't piss him off if I was you."

Everyone in the room turned to my dad. His oxygen mask was pulled down to his chin. I smiled.

"Nurse Jennifer? Is there a problem here?"

"Yes, Dr. Murray. These people are breaking the hospital rules," she said as we all turned our attention to a very attractive African American lady standing in the doorway.

"Sometimes rules are meant to be bent a little now and then, aren't they? I'll first suggest that you release this woman." Dr. Murray gestured to Jennifer's hand, still gripping Julie's arm. "We don't want her to think we're uncaring and abrasive at this hospital, now do we?"

Jennifer released her grip.

I liked this doctor already. Her presence was filled with grace and caring.

"Hi. I'm Dr. Murray." She reached an outstretched hand toward me.

"Jack Perry; nice to meet you, doctor," I said as I shook her hand.

She moved toward my father. "Mr. Perry. Nice to see you awake."

"Who are you?" Dad asked gruffly.

"I'm Susan Murray. I'm your attending physician," she replied as she unzipped the oxygen tent the surrounding my dad's upper body. She pulled out her stethoscope and gently placed it on Dad's chest.

"How are you feeling?" she asked as she listened to his heart.

"Very tired," Dad answered her.

"Mrs. Perry. Julie. Jack. Would you all mind giving me some time with Mr. Perry? I need to run a couple of minor tests now that he is awake. Can you give me thirty minutes with him?"

"Yes. Of course," my mother replied. "Darling, we will be back in a few minutes," she said, kissing my dad's hand. "Jack. Julie. Let's go get some coffee or something." She put her hand on my arm as we went out into the hallway.

"Jennifer. Page Dr. Jorge," I overheard Dr. Murray say to the nurse as the door closed automatically behind us.

* * *

WITH A CUP OF COFFEE IN HAND, I NOTICED THE BLUE flashing light immediately as we turned into the corridor my dad's room was adjacent to— flashing above his door. During my time writing for *Chamberlain Heights* I often had consulted with doctors and hospitals to accurately write story lines that pertained to health. I knew that a blue flashing light meant CODE BLUE. A patient in distress.

My fingers released the Styrofoam cup I was holding; I hardly noticed when it fell. I brushed past my mom and sister, running to my dad's room. The door was open and I entered quickly. The room was calm.

Dr. Murray and Nurse Jennifer were at the head of the bed, as well as another doctor I did not know. An additional nurse was also by the foot of his bed, putting items back into what I presumed was a crash cart. Nurse Jennifer was busying herself by turning off the monitors hooked up to my dad.

"What's going on?" I asked, dazed.

"Jack. I'm sorry. We lost him," Dr. Murray said compassionately as she made her way to me, putting my hands in hers. The room began to spin.

"But how? He was fine when we left. We weren't gone that long."

"Daddy!" Julie screamed before Dr. Murray could

answer my questions. "Daddy!" She rushed towards him, grabbing his arm, placing her ear to his chest. "Jack! Oh my God. Daddy!" She looked up at me, tears streaming down her face.

"Mom," I turned and tried to pull her close.

She avoided my embrace and calmly made her way to the head of the bed.

"Mom! He's gone!" Julie sobbed as she pulled my mom into her arms.

"I know, dear," Mom said to Julie as she patted her back. "I know."

Tears were flowing uncontrollably down my face, and my vision was beginning to blur. "How…? What happened?" I asked as I wiped my tears with the back of my hands.

Julie was beside me now. Mom was holding my dad's hand and was gently stroking his hair. I put my arm around Julie.

"Your dad went into cardiac arrest shortly after you left. His heart wasn't strong," Dr. Murray softy said.

"Did you give him a shot of adrenaline? Did you shock him with the defibrillator?" I asked.

"No. We didn't. We honoured his DNR," Dr. Murray replied.

"What's a DNR?" Julie asked.

"Do not resuscitate," I said. "Why would my father have a DNR if he was just brought into the hospital this morning?"

Dr. Murray paused and looked toward my mom. The nurses had left the room. The other doctor was now standing beside Dr. Murray.

"Mrs. Perry. Would you like to comment on Jack's question?" Dr. Murray asked.

She shook her head.

"Someone better tell me something right now!" I said.

The other doctor cleared his throat. My mother introduced us to him. "Jack. Julie. This is Dr. Jorge, a cardiac specialist. Your father's doctor. I'm going to let him explain."

"I'm sorry for your loss," he began. "To say this as simply as possible, Mr. Perry had a virus in his heart— like a cold, so to speak. The virus was actively damaging the interior walls of his heart."

"This didn't *just* happen, did it?" I interrupted.

Both doctors looked up to my mom.

"Mrs. Perry?" Dr. Jorge asked.

"Go ahead, doctor. Tell them," Mom replied.

"No, you're right. This just didn't happen. I've been treating your father for about ten months now. The virus accelerated its growth in the last three months, causing irreparable damage. It was only a matter of time before his heart gave up on the fight. He was on a heart donor list, but one was never found," he finished.

"You knew about this, and you kept it from us?" I directed my question at my mom. I couldn't help but be angry.

"Jack." Dr. Murray put her hand on my shoulder. "Don't be mad at her. It was your father's decision not to tell you and Julie. He knew he was dying and that it was a matter of time. He didn't want you or your sister constantly worrying about him during this last year. He wanted to enjoy you both without this hanging over your heads."

"It's not fair. I should have been told. We should have been told. We could have spent more time…" my voice cracked.

"George didn't want that. He wanted you both to have the memory of him being healthy and strong," my mom said from her place beside my dad. "Goodbye, my love," she said as she softly kissed him on the lips. "Goodbye."

She quickly blotted the tears in her eyes, straightened herself up and made her way over to Dr. Murray and Dr. Jorge. "Thank you both for taking the best care possible of my George." She took both doctors' hands in hers, then turned to us. "Jack. Julie. I'll wait in the hall for you."

She left. Shock, sadness, and anger were all floating through my body. Julie pulled away from me and went to the hospital bed.

"Goodbye, Daddy," she said as she kissed him on the forehead and stroked his hair. She picked up her purse and suitcase which were neatly tucked in the corner, touched my arm, and walked out into the hallway.

"Can I be alone with him?" I tearfully asked Dr. Murray and Dr. Jorge.

"Of course you can," Dr. Murray replied, and they both walked toward the door.

I sat on the edge of the bed and took my dad's hand in mine. Strangely, the colour of his skin looked less grey than before.

"Well, Dad. I should be totally pissed at you right now, but I'm not. I'll respect your wishes of keeping your illness from Julie and me. That's the least I can do for you given everything you have done for me in my life. Thank you for being my dad. You were the best ever!"

Tears were flowing freely down my face now. "I have one more favour to ask of you, though. When you get to wherever you are going, please find Stephen. Please look after him for me. Please tell him how much I love him. How much I miss him." I rested my head on his chest. "I love you, Dad." I gently kissed him on the cheek before getting off the bed. I picked up my overnight bag from the floor and tossed it onto my shoulder. Then, I gently closed the door to his room as I went into the hallway to join Mom and Julie.

22

"I'M GOING TO BED NOW. I PUT FRESH TOWELS IN YOUR bathroom," Mom said from the doorway to my father's study.

"Thank you," I mumbled.

"Try to get some sleep. We have a busy day tomorrow."

"Okay. I will," I responded without looking up.

She paused, started to add something, then thought better of it and was gone from the doorway. I held a Bavarian crystal tumbler up to the light, musing on the amber-coloured liquid inside before downing the entire contents. The liquid burned my throat as it passed by on its way to my stomach. My body shivered and yet, it was immediately warmed. I refilled the tumbler for the fourth time from the bottle of my dad's favourite forty-year-old Scotch. The plate of dinner Mrs. Johnson from next door fixed for me was untouched in front of me on the desk.

We all had gone our separate ways when we arrived at my parents' house earlier in the afternoon. Julie went to her room. Mom sat at the dining room table, phone in one hand, address book in the other. I could faintly hear her all afternoon and early evening, calmly explaining to family and friends that my dad was no longer with us. I spent the day here, in my dad's study, sitting in his chair behind his massive cherry desk. Just sitting, occasionally turning to the window, staring out into the afternoon, and then into the evening.

Somewhere around dinnertime the phones in the house started ringing uncontrollably. Annoyed at the constant interruption I unplugged the extension on the desk and opened my dad's bottle of Scotch. I didn't even like Scotch. But I couldn't seem to stop myself from repeatedly refilling my glass.

"This room used to scare the shit out of me," Julie said from the doorway. "Remember when we were kids? We were never allowed to come in here. Only when we were in trouble."

She walked around the room, touching the bookshelves and the furniture. She picked up a picture from on top of the mantle, stared at it for a moment, and then put it back in its place.

"You going to pour me one of those or what?" Julie asked as she sat in the wingback chair directly opposite me.

I reached over to the side table for an additional glass, filled it, then handed it to her. She downed the Scotch in seconds.

"Fill it again," she said as she placed the empty tumbler on the desk. I did.

She lifted her glass in toast. "To Dad."

I clinked my glass with hers.

"Do you think it's kind of weird Mom is so calm?" I asked her as I refilled both our glasses. "I mean, outside of the few tears she shed at the hospital, she has registered no emotion whatsoever. I heard her on the phone all afternoon. She never broke down once, just calmly informed everyone about Dad. When I asked her if I could help her with calls, she said flatly that it was her job to inform everyone and she didn't need any help."

"She's in shock," Julie responded.

"No. I don't think that's it. She's very clear. Very clear and calm," I said, looking into my glass.

"I don't know. She's a rock," Julie answered.

"It's confusing to me how she can appear to have no emotion. She just lost her partner of forty-four years," I said.

"Maybe she's putting on a front for our benefit. Maybe she doesn't want us to see that she is dying on the inside," Julie answered

"You're probably right. I just compare it to losing Stephen, and what a mess I turned into," I said.

"You two have some nerve gossiping about me in my own house."

Julie and I both turned our attention to our mother standing in the doorway.

"Mom, we're not gossiping. We're just concerned," I said sheepishly.

"You're trying to analyse me, and I won't stand for it. Not in my house," she responded with fury in her voice.

"That's not it…"

"You listen to me and you listen to me good," She interrupted me and took a step into the room. "Not everyone has a complete meltdown when their spouse dies. Not everyone turns into a pill-popping zombie. Not everyone needs booze to get through their day, Jack."

Slap! Her verbal attack stung me harder than a real slap.

She went on. "You're right. I just lost my partner of forty-four years, and it hurts like hell. But I refuse to turn into the mess *you* let yourself turn into. I will not be that weak. I will not." She was screaming now.

"Mother!" Julie exclaimed.

"Everyone grieves in their own way, Jack. I respected yours. You need to respect mine."

"I think that's enough, Mom," Julie said softly.

"You think I liked watching you fall apart? Liked watching you try to kill yourself? Liked worrying that at any moment you might try it again? Do you? Answer me!"

Her eyes were glassing over with tears and rage.

I said nothing.

"I will not be a burden on you or Julie. Or anyone, for that matter— the way you were on me. I just won't. So you can sit there and analyse me all you want, but you don't know me the way you may think you know me. I'm very different to you. Very different."

I sat stunned in silence.

"Say something!" Mom screamed, coming closer to the desk.

"I think you've said enough for both of us," I said, looking directly into her eyes.

I stood, picked up the bottle of Scotch and opened the French doors that led out to the back patio and pool area. "You lost your husband today. I lost my father. Thank you for kicking me while I'm down," I said as I closed the doors behind me.

* * *

"OKAY, I FINALLY GOT HER CALMED DOWN," JULIE SAID AS she sat next to me at the pool's edge. She hung her feet into the pool next to mind.

The evening was hot. Summer in the desert.

"Well, you succeeded in making her cry," she said as she took a pull from the bottle of Scotch. "Kidding, Jack. Kidding," she said as I glared at her.

"I guess I didn't realise what a burden I've been for everyone," I said remorsefully.

"Don't listen to what she said. She's grieving. She didn't mean it."

"Sorry for being such a burden on you," I said, looking into the water.

"Don't you dare apologise." She grabbed me by the shoulders. "That's what family does. They look after each other. You have done the same for me."

All I could do was nod. We sat in silence for a while, sharing the remainder of the bottle of Scotch.

"So, about my last visit to your house—"

I put my hand up for her to stop. "Don't worry; it's over. Rick moved out."

"He has? When? Not because of me?" she fired the questions.

"Because of Tanya," I answered.

"Oh. Sorry about that," she replied.

"Don't worry about it. It was bound to come out eventually," I said.

"I'm sorry, Jack. I shouldn't have got involved. It's none of my business. I just saw red that day, and I was protecting Max," she paused. "So what's going on?"

"Nothing anymore," I responded.

"So, is my stepson gay?"

"Don't know. He won't put a label on himself," I said, looking at her.

"That sounds like him: noncommittal. You did sleep with him? Didn't you?"

I nodded.

"Then, label or no label, he's at least bi, in my opinion," she said firmly.

"Whatever. Not my concern anymore," I responded.

"You sure about that?" she asked.

"Pretty sure. We both said some mean things to each other," I answered.

"Well, *we* have said some pretty mean things to each other over the years, and look at us. Still together." She pushed against me with her shoulder.

"This is different." I looked away, not wanting to talk about it anymore.

"Okay," she said, standing up. "We better go to bed. Big day tomorrow." She held out her hand.

I placed mine in hers and she helped me up off the ground.

* * *

"HONEY? YOU UP?" I COULD HEAR MY MOM ASK SOFTLY through the closed door.

"I'm up."

"Is it okay if I come in?" she asked as she opened the door a crack.

"It's your house," I answered, rolling away from the door towards the window.

"You just wake up?"

"No. Been up for a while," I replied as she sat on the edge of the bed.

"Jack."

"What?"

"Can you please look at me?"

I rolled onto my back and faced her.

"I want to apologise for last night," she said remorsefully.

"No need. You made your feelings perfectly clear," I said flatly.

"You're mad at me."

"No. Not mad, but it still stings a little," I said.

"I'm so sorry. May God strike me down if I ever talk to either of my children the way I talked to you last night ever again."

I remained silent.

"I didn't mean the things I said."

"You probably did, Mom, or you wouldn't have said them."

She looked down and ran her hand across the sheets, smoothing them. "You're right. I probably did mean them. I just want you to know that I was wrong in how I said them. I was in pain, and I needed to take my pain out on someone. You just happened to be in my line of fire. I love you, and I worry about you every second of every day." Her eyes were glassing over.

"No need for that, Mom."

"I don't know who I am without your father. I spent my whole adult life with him. It scares me to death to move forward without him." She rested her hand on my arm.

"Mom you are going to move past this, trust me. Okay, don't trust me. I'm not a very good example in this department. But, like you said last night, you *are* strong. As Dad would say, 'you're a tough broad, Shirley'," I said with a small smile, touching her hand.

"Thank you," she replied, cupping my face with her free hand, half smiling. "I'm going to go make us all some breakfast. Any requests?"

"Pancakes with bacon smiley faces?" I asked.

"Pancakes with bacon smiley faces it is," she replied as she got up off the bed and moved toward the door. "We have lots to do before everyone starts arriving tomorrow," she said from the doorway.

"Mom?"

"Yes, honey?"

"What about Dad?" I asked.

"He's all taken care of."

"He is?" I asked surprised, raising myself up onto my elbows.

"When he found out he was sick, he pre-arranged his funeral. He looked after all the details. All I had to do was place one call to the funeral home. We're having a small graveside service the day after tomorrow, followed by a catered lunch here at the house. Oh, and he wanted you give the final words at the service."

"He does?" I asked, choking up.

"Yes. He was so proud of you, his son, the successful

writer."

She turned and disappeared out into the hallway.

23

"WHAT'S IN THERE? STRAIGHT VODKA? YOU HITTING IT PRETTY hard there, buddy?" Daniel asked as he pulled my hand toward him and took a smell of the liquid in my glass.

"Just straight water, my friend," I replied.

"Water? Seriously?"

"The other night my mother commented on how much she thinks I drink. Made me think maybe she's right," I answered.

"Have you talked to him yet?" He gestured across the guest-filled living room of my mother's house at Rick, who was in deep conversation with Maria.

The room was buzzing with conversation and with waiters in pristine white uniforms weaving in and out of small groups of people, serving appetisers off sterling silver platters. I could see my mom deep in conversation with Vivian just inside the opened doors to the back patio and pool area. Julie seemed to be having her time monopolised by Uncle Harry. She kept inching away, trying to make a run for the front hall where Max was charming Mr. & Mrs. Johnson from next door.

"Not yet. Just a brief hello when he arrived this morning," I replied as I continued to survey the crowd of people.

"You're avoiding him, aren't you?" Daniel asked.

"Just not sure how to start a conversation, given where we left off," I said.

"*Avoiding.*" Daniel said before taking a sip of his drink.

"Okay, if you're so smart. How do you suggest I start the conversation? So Rick, how's Tanya? You remember Tanya, don't you? She's your secret fiancée? The girl you've been cheating on with me."

"Whoa. I'm not the one you should be mad at," Daniel said, raising a hand.

"Sorry. So much has happened in the last few days. I feel confused about everything," I said.

"No worries. You'll talk to him when you're ready. And if that's when he's thirty, then that's okay," he said, smiling.

I punched him lightly in the arm. "You're such a bastard."

"And you love me for it," he answered with a smile.

"You're right," I said. "Daniel, thank you so much for coming today and bringing Vivian with you." I swallowed a sob.

"Wouldn't have missed being here for you. I'm glad you called." He put an arm around my shoulder, gently squeezing it. "Gotta tell you, that send-off speech you gave for your dad— I didn't even know him and you had me crying like a baby. Not a dry eye to be found anywhere. He's looking down on you, so proud. I know it."

"Thank you." I leant my head on his shoulder.

* * *

"I'VE CONVINCED MARIA TO SPEND THE NIGHT. I'LL HAVE TO put Rick in with you, on the rollaway cot, so she can have the guest bedroom. Is that okay?" Mom announced as she came into the kitchen where I was straightening up.

All the guests had gone. People who travelled to attend my father's funeral were either on their way to the airport to catch late flights home, or checking into the nearby Hyatt where Mom had made special arrangements.

"I thought you only wanted our immediately family to be here tonight?" I asked as I turned to face her.

"Darling, I think she is our family," she said, patting my cheek.

"Come now. You must join the rest of us on the patio," she said, grabbing my hand and leading me out to the living room, then through the open doors to the back patio. Julie and Max were sitting together on the outdoor sofa; Maria was sitting on a chair near them. Rick was standing by the pool's edge, looking down into the softly lighted water.

"Okay, Max, we're ready now. Open up that bottle," Mom announced as we made our way across the patio.

My eye caught sight of a bottle of champagne and six glasses on the side table near Max. Max did as he was told.

"Everyone, come close," Mom said, gesturing with her arms.

The bottle of champagne opened with a loud *pop*. Julie helped Max catch the flowing liquid with the glasses. Mom handed a glass to each of us as they were filled.

"Okay. Everyone have a glass? Good."

She paused and looked at us.

"George bought this bottle so we could send him off with a farewell toast. No tears now. Only smiles for him. Okay?"

We all nodded in agreement.

"To my wonderful husband." Mom raised her glass to the clear night sky. "I couldn't have asked for a better, more loving partner or father for my children. You were my teacher, my lover, my friend. My life was enriched in ways I never knew possible from the touch of your life. We celebrate the life that was yours. To George," she finished, clinking first with Julie.

"To Daddy," Julie said.

Mom touched my glass next. "To Dad," I said.

"To George," Max said at his turn.

"To Mr. Perry." Maria clinked with Mom.

"To Mr. Perry," Rick said.

We all followed Mom's lead of raising our glasses high to the clear night sky before taking the first sip.

* * *

"YOU OKAY WITH ME STAYING IN HERE?" RICK ASKED AS HE closed the door.

I nodded without looking up from my magazine. He lay down on the rollaway cot, still fully dressed in his dark suit.

"You know, not only have you not spoken to me today, but I don't think you've looked at me, either," he said.

"I looked at you," I responded, still not looking up from the magazine.

"When?"

"I don't know. Earlier," I answered.

"Glancing at me while talking about me with Daniel doesn't count."

I looked up from the magazine.

"Didn't think I noticed, huh?" he said rolling onto his side and facing me.

"What do you want me to say, Rick? I've had a few rough days. I'm not sure if I'm up to making sure you're okay," I responded.

"Geez, Jack. Maybe I want to know if *you* are okay, regardless of what happened between us a few days ago. You know how hard it was for me not to scoop you up into my arms the minute I saw you today? All I wanted to do was to help you, and you wouldn't even give me the time of day," he said.

"I'm still pissed about Tanya," I replied.

"Fair enough," he responded, sitting up.

"I'm confused about us, about what happened. I'm not sure about anything," I added.

"I'm confused, too. I should tell you that I've broken it off with Tanya."

"Your broke off your engagement?" I asked, my full attention directed at him.

"John told me that if I couldn't decide how I felt about either of you–"

"You told John about us?"

"He guessed. He's totally cool."

"He is?"

"*Ya.* Now you going to let me finish?" he asked.

"Sorry," I replied.

"As I was saying. John told me that if I couldn't decide how I felt about either of you, I owed it to both of you not to be involved with either of you. You following?"

"Barely," I answered.

"His point was that I should be honest and not lead anyone on until I have clear intentions of what I want," he said.

"Did you tell this to Tanya? Are you still in love with her?" I asked.

"I told her that I had met someone. I didn't tell her it was you. I told her I couldn't marry her, and that she shouldn't want to marry me unless I am one hundred percent for sure with her, and I'm not there right now."

"You didn't answer my question. Are you in love with her?' I asked again.

He paused and looked down at the floor. "Yes and no. I love her. But am I in love with her? I'm not sure. I'm also not sure how I feel about you," he added, looking up. "I have feelings for you, but are they love feelings? Not sure. I need to figure this out for myself. Along with who I truly am, and what I want."

"Sounds like you have a big job ahead of yourself," I said.

"Can we hang out once you're back in L.A.?" he asked.

"Let's see where we're both at when I get back. I'm not sure when that will be yet. It might be a good idea to stay here and help Mom for a while. The change in scenery might help lift the fog off my confusion, as well," I answered.

"I understand."

"You're welcome to stay at the house if you want," I added.

"Nah. I'm okay staying at the dorm with John. There's only like two or three weeks left of the internship anyway." He got up and went into the bathroom. He came back a few minutes later, dressed in a tank top and running shorts. "Can you set the alarm for 5 a.m.?" he asked.

"Why?" I asked, surprised.

"Dad booked me on the first flight back to L.A. I could only get excused from classes for the one day," he said as he pulled back the covers on the rollaway and climbed between them.

I set the alarm and turned out the light.

"Goodnight," I said as I settled into my bed.

"Goodnight," he replied.

"Jack?" Rick asked in the darkness.

"*Ya?*"

"I didn't tell you how sorry I am about your dad."

"Thank you," I answered.

"Jack?"

"Yes?"

"I'm sorry I was such a little bastard to you," he added.

"Thank you." I answered.

"Jack?"

"Yes, Rick?"

"Can I sleep with you?"

I paused.

"Yes. Yes, you can."

I watched his shadow get up from his place on the rollaway by what little light was coming in from the window. I felt the covers being pulled back on the opposite side of the bed, his body weighing down on the mattress. I felt the warmth of him as he slid close to me, wrapping his arms around me, pulling me to him. I drifted off to sleep in seconds.

*   *   *

I OPENED ONE EYE AND LOOKED AT THE BEDSIDE CLOCK. 7:35 a.m. Stretching, I realised I never woke when Rick left. I didn't even hear the alarm go off. I felt rested, like I had slept for a couple of days solid.

I threw on a t-shirt and shorts and made my way down the hallway toward the kitchen. Freshly brewed coffee stimulated my senses the moment I opened the kitchen door. Sitting in the breakfast nook, Mom and Maria were drinking coffee, deep in conversation.

"Good morning, sleepy head," my mom said when she heard me enter the room.

"Morning," I replied lifting my arm in wave.

"How did you sleep?" Mom asked as I reached into the cupboard for a coffee cup.

"Great. Like a rock. I didn't even hear Rick leave," I replied as I filled my cup with coffee and sat in one of the empty chairs surrounding the round wooden table. "How did *you* sleep, Mom?"

"Not like a rock, but I did sleep some. What would you like for breakfast?" she asked.

"I think I'll just make some toast. I'm really not that hungry."

"I'll get it for you," Mom said as she stood up and

moved toward the far counter.

"What time is your flight?" I asked Maria.

"11:15 a.m."

"I'll drive you. That is, if my mom trusts me with her car," I said, looking over at Mom.

"Actually, I'll drive *both* of you," Mom said, turning towards the table.

"Huh?" I said.

"I've booked you on the same flight as Maria. You're going home with her, Jack," she said as she sat back down at the table, taking a sip from her coffee cup.

"I am?" I asked, shocked.

"You are."

"I really think I should stay for a few days at least," I protested.

"No, my darling son, you shouldn't."

I opened my mouth to protest more, but was stopped with the raising of her hand. "You need to go home. I need you to go home. I know you want to stay and help, but your staying will only prolong my grieving process. I need to do this now. I need to start walking on my own today. Don't look so hurt, Jack," she said, patting my head. "This isn't about you. It's about me, and this is what I need to do."

"Okay, Mom," I replied as she got up at the sound of the toaster popping.

"What about Julie? Does she get to stay?" I asked.

"Julie is already gone. She got the same speech. She caught the first flight out with Max this morning. She's probably home by now," Mom answered.

"I want to stay," I said, pouting.

She set a plate of buttered toast in front of me. "I know you do, darling, but you're not going to. Besides, you need to get home and figure out what you're going to do about your career and about Rick," she said, reaching for her cup

I looked at Maria. "You told her?"

"No, she didn't tell me. Nobody told me. You would have to be blind not to see that something is going on between the two of you. You went out of your way to avoid him yesterday, and he moped around behind you like a love-sick puppy. The only person who didn't pick up on it was Max, and that's because he's so into himself that he can't see anything past his nose," Mom said, chuckling.

"He's not in love with me. And nothing is going on between us," I said, playing with my toast. "At least, I don't think it is."

"You owe it to yourself, and to him, to find out what it is," she said.

"You don't think it's weird?" I asked.

"Why would it be weird? The age difference? Please, Jack. Get over yourself," she replied.

"No, not the age difference— well, maybe that, too. But he is Max's son."

"That's precisely it. He's *Max's* son. Not Julie's. Max's. I am far more open-mined and liberal than you give me credit for. All I want is to see is that you are happy. And if that means being with Rick, if he's what makes you happy, then I am all for it." She patted my hand. "Now, hurry up and eat. You need to pack and get ready. We can't have you missing your flight."

24

"YOU'VE HARDLY SPOKEN A WORD SINCE WE LEFT PHOENIX. What's going on in that pretty little head of yours?" Maria asked beside me in the back of the town car we hired at Los Angles International Airport to take us home.

"Sorry?" I responded.

"Don't be sorry, Jack. Do you want to talk about anything?" she asked.

"I think I'm getting clear," I said.

"About what?" she asked.

"About everything. The things my mother said to me this morning and over the last few days have really resonated." I turned to look at her. "I've floated for the last year. Just existed. I don't want to just exist anymore. I need to find happiness from within. I need to find my purpose."

"Are you saying what I think you are saying, Jack?" Maria raised an eyebrow.

"I think so. I think so."

We rode in silence for a few moments.

"Maria?"

"Yes?"

"Is the offer to stay at your house in Tuscany still open?" I asked as the car stopped in front of her house.

"You're leaving?" she asked.

I nodded. "I think it's time."

"Just say when and I will place the call to the caretakers and have it opened up for you," she said as she got out of

253

the car.

I pulled her back in and hugged her tightly. "Thank you."

She wiped a tear from her eye and got out of the car.

*   *   *

WALKING INTO MY HOUSE, I FELT CALM AND HAPPY. I LEFT MY bag by the door and took a tour of my home. I went to each room, taking in its essence, feeling so fortunate to have had such a beautiful home. I knew was time to let it go and let someone else experience its beauty.

Sitting at the desk in my office I picked up the phone and dialled the number I had just retrieved from my address book.

"West Shore Realty. How my I help you?"

"Is Dominique Bernard available?' I asked.

"She's out of the office, but I can connect you to her cell phone if you wish," the perky voice replied.

"That would be fantastic."

"Can I tell her who is calling?" the voice asked.

"Jack Perry."

"One moment, Mr. Perry," she said before my call was placed on hold.

Dominique's voice came on the line a moment later, her charming French accent accentuating every syllable of her words. "Jack. How are you?"

"Good," I replied.

"To what do I owe this surprise call? Don't tell me you're thinking of selling?" she asked.

"That's exactly why I'm calling. I want to list the house, and since you referred so many clients to Stephen over the years, and you sold us the land we built the house on, I want you to list it," I replied.

"Are you sure?" I could hear the sound of traffic in the

background as she spoke.

"I'm sure. I want to sell it as quickly as possible," I said.

"Houses in your area are listing at around one point two to two point one million. I would say we could list it at the high end of that range. Probably sell in sixty days," she replied.

"Where can we price it to make a quicker sale?" I asked.

"Why the hurry, Jack?" she asked.

"Dominique, it's time to move on. I need to move on," I replied.

"Okay, Jack, I hear you. If we list the house right in the middle, let's say around one point six or one point seven million dollars, then I can probably sell it in a few weeks for the full asking price," she said.

"Let's do it. How soon can we get this rolling?" I asked.

"It's two-thirty now. I could come by around five, get you to sign the paperwork, put up a sign, and take pictures for the website. Does that work?" she asked.

"I'll see you soon. Thanks Dominique, I really appreciate it."

She clicked off the line.

* * *

"WHAT'S WITH THE SIGN?" RICK IMMEDIATELY ASKED AS I opened the front door to greet him.

"Come in. We need to talk," I said as I closed the door behind him.

He followed me into the kitchen.

"Beer?" I asked.

"No. Why are you selling your house?" he asked, his face full of puzzlement.

"This was Stephen's and my house. I need to let go of it. I need to leave it behind."

"It sounds like you made up your mind," he said.

"Let's sit in the living room." I grabbed his hand and led him to the sofa.

"Where will you go?" he asked.

Since I didn't know how to start the conversation I needed to have with him, I took the easy way out and answered his question, "Italy."

"Italy! As in Italy that is like halfway around the world Italy?" His face flushed.

"The one and only," I answered.

"How can you move to Italy? Why would you move to Italy? What's going on? How long are you going for?" he fired questions at me.

"I feel like it's a good place for me to start my life again," I said.

"What about us, Jack?" he asked, hurt creeping into his voice.

"Is there an us, Rick? Really?" I asked.

He looked down. "I came here today to tell you I love you, Jack, and that I want to be with you," he said, not looking up.

"Rick. You don't love me. You may think you do, but you don't," I said.

"Don't tell me how to feel. I know how I feel." He looked up, anger in his eyes.

"If you were really in love with me, you would have known it without question. You wouldn't have needed to think about it during the last few weeks."

He remained quiet.

"I love you, Rick," I said, taking his hand in mine. "But I'm not in love with you."

"You're just scared. The pressure is too much. So what does Jack do? Packs up and runs." His voice was filled with hurt and rage.

"I can't tell you how wrong you are. For the first time

in my life, I'm not running, or hiding. I'm moving forward. And I owe you so much to you, Rick."

His eyes softened, just a bit.

"You showed me how to open up to someone again, and how to say goodbye. For that I will be eternally grateful to you, always." I stroked his hair.

"Screw you," he said, pulling away. "I changed my whole life for you. I broke up with Tanya for you, and this is what I get?"

"You didn't break up with Tanya because of me. You did it for yourself," I said.

"Don't tell me that. You don't know," he stood.

"Rick, I do know. You told me in Phoenix," I replied calmly.

"You can't leave. You need to stay here with me, I love you." He sat, pulling me into his arms. "You can't leave."

"I have to," I said as tears filled my eyes. "You need to finish exploring who you are, and you can't do that with me here."

"I know exactly who I am, Jack," he said, pulling away. "But I love you. Doesn't that mean anything to you?" he asked, holding me by my shoulders.

"It means the world to me. But it doesn't change the fact that you are not in love with me," I said.

"Fuck you!" he said, standing, hurt and anger in his voice. "You made me fall in love with you and now you're going to leave me. You're an asshole!" he screamed, holding back tears.

"Rick, listen." I stood.

"I'll never forgive you for this. Never!"

I reached out to touch his arm.

"Don't fucking touch me!" he said, slapping my arm away. "Don't fucking touch me or talk to me, or anything ever again you narcissistic fuck!"

He turned and walked towards the front door. "I hope

you'll be fucking happy in Italy," he said sarcastically, his voice trembling.

"Well, that went well," I said as he slammed the front door shut.

*   *   *

"HE REALLY CALLED YOU A NARCISSISTIC FUCK? SERIOUSLY?" Daniel asked for the second time in a row.

"Yes. He really did," I replied, not looking up from my menu.

"I would have paid money to have seen that."

I looked up and raised one eyebrow.

"Well, think about how funny it is. You of all people, *narcissistic*? It's a joke. You're one of the very few in Hollywood who isn't narcissistic. It's hilarious," he said.

"Ha. Ha. I'm so laughing with you," I answered as I took a drink from my water glass.

"Really, Jack, knowing you, don't you find it the least bit funny?" he asked.

"Nothing funny about hurting someone," I replied.

"He'll be okay. Like you said, he really isn't in love with you; once he realises that, he'll be okay," Daniel answered.

"So, is this really our last lunch together?" Daniel asked.

"It is." I nodded.

"Are you really sure about Italy?" he asked.

"As sure as I am about anything right now."

"Do you think it will be permanent?" he asked.

"I don't know. What I realised on the plane back from Phoenix is that I really don't know who I am right now. Or what I'm supposed to do," I said.

"You think you'll find that in Italy?" he asked.

"I think it's a good place to start."

"I admire you, Jack. You've brought yourself back from

hell, took a stand, and are moving into the future without a plan. You're a brave man, Jack Perry. A brave man." He lifted his glass and took a drink of his Chardonnay.

"Well, wait till you see me cry like a baby at the party tomorrow night," I replied.

"Brave men cry, Jack," he replied.

"You're one of the few people I am really going to miss, Daniel," I said, a tremor in my voice. "I can't tell you what your friendship has meant to me over the last few weeks."

"It's not like you're disappearing off the face of the Earth. You think I'm going to let my new BFF off the hook that easy? No way. We'll email. We'll call. Jocelyn and I will visit. You'll come back and visit, or live. It's not the end, Jack. It's just the beginning." He looked down at his menu.

25

I STOOD LOOKING OUT TO THE OCEAN FOR THE LAST TIME FROM my bedroom window. The last three weeks went by in a blur. I couldn't believe it was the first of September, fall just around the corner.

The house sold in three days, the new owners accepting a quick closing date. Just yesterday, I left my car in the caring hands of Manuel to sell on my behalf. The artwork from the house went on display at a gallery in Santa Monica for commission sale and my furniture was currently being loaded into the back of a truck headed for an auction house.

My eyes felt sore from crying at the going away party Maria and Joe threw for me last night. Vivian made me cry the hardest, hugging me, not letting me go until Daniel pulled her off me. Then, I shared tears of happiness with Michael and Sheila as they announced they were newly pregnant. Mom had flown in for the party and flown out early this morning. She was doing remarkably well without Dad. I admired her strength. Saying goodbye to Maria, Joe, and their family nearly killed me. They were my family and they were Stephen's family.

I got a note from Stephen's mother, thanking me for the items I sent to her and for the fund I set up for Stephen's nephews. It wasn't friendly, but it was polite.

After taking one more look at the picture of Stephen on the day of his surfing competition win, I placed it into my suitcase.

"Excuse me, Mr. Perry."

"Yes." I turned to face one of the five men moving out the furniture.

"All we have left is what's in here. Can we take it?" he asked.

"Yes. Of course," I replied as I zipped the suitcase closed and placed it on the floor out of their way.

They moved quickly. They disassembled the bed in minutes and carried it and the remaining furniture out, leaving me in an empty room.

Tears filled my eyes as I looked around the room for the last time. But I wiped them away. And then I picked up my suitcase and walk out into the hallway. I glanced into both of the guestrooms, lingering at the one Rick occupied.

Downstairs, I walked first into the kitchen. I ran my hand along the empty granite countertop and touched the wood of the cabinets. I took one last look out the glass sliders, past the deck, past the beach and out to the ocean.

"I can't believe you sold our house. How could you do that?"

"Hello, Stephen." I wiped a tear from my cheek as I turned to face him.

He was standing next to the fireplace that visually separated the dining area from the living room.

"It's time for me to leave you behind," I said, my voice choking.

"This is our home. We have memories here," he protested as he walked around the empty living room.

"I'm taking those memories with me, every single one. Don't you worry," I responded, my eyes clouded with tears.

"You're really moving on, aren't you?" he asked, coming close to me.

"I'm really moving on," I answered.

"Dance with me one last time?" he asked, touching my face.

U2's "A Beautiful Day" started playing softly from the ceiling speakers. Stephen held out his arms. I fell into them, letting him lead me around the room slowly.

"Goodbye, Stephen. Goodbye, my love. Goodbye, my everything," I said as I looked into his eyes as the song came to its end.

Releasing me, he kissed my hand and walked towards the far wall, disappearing before he reached it.

"Who you talking to?" Julie asked as she came into the house.

"No one. Myself," I said, wiping tears from my eyes.

She came over and put her arms around me.

"It's hard saying goodbye to this house, isn't it?" she asked.

"Yes. It is. I had a whole life here, lots of memories."

I pulled away and we both took a last look at the empty room.

"Hey. Am I interrupting?"

Julie and I both turned at the sound of Rick's voice.

Julie smiled at him. "No, not at all, hon. I'll wait outside," she said to me as she walked towards Rick. She paused and placed a hand on his shoulder before picking up two of my suitcases and moving out the door.

"The place looks totally different without anything in it," Rick said to me.

"I know. It looks so big," I replied, offering nothing further.

Rick walked closer to me.

"I don't know where to start," he said.

"Start with why you came," I replied.

He paused, uncomfortable. "I came…" He paused again. "I came to apologise to you. I was a total asshole to you a couple weeks ago, and I'm really sorry," he said.

"Thank you. It's okay," I replied.

"No, it's not. I shouldn't have been that harsh with you. I really am sorry," he added.

"You were hurting. I understand," I said, compassion in my voice.

"You were right, Jack."

"About what?" I asked.

"I can't truly love someone until I know exactly who I am, and I'm not there yet. You know when you said to me that I helped you and you were grateful for it?"

"I remember," I answered.

"Well, I'm grateful to you, too. You showed me different experiences in life. You helped me open up to someone. I've never have been as open to anyone the way I have been with you. So thank you." He came close and pulled me into his arms.

I meet his embrace and held on to him tightly. He lifted my head and kissed me gently on the lips. Our last kiss.

"I needed something to remember you by," he said, smiling as we parted.

"So what's for you now? The internship is done, right?" I asked.

"Yup. I was offered one of several positions, one at a private school in South Africa."

"You going to take it?" I asked as he held my hand and led me toward the front door.

"*Ya*. I think so. It's only a two-year contract. Probably be great experience for me," he said.

"I think that's a great idea."

He looked around. "I guess I'll let you say goodbye on your own," he said, releasing my hand, picking up the last of my suitcases, heading out the door. I looked around the main floor one more time.

"Goodbye, house. Thank you for sheltering me through the happy times, the stormy times, and the calm times.

Thank you for protecting me through life's changes." I
softly closed the door for the last time and walked out into
the afternoon sunshine.

* * *

"I DON'T KNOW HOW TO DO THIS. I DON'T KNOW HOW TO SAY
goodbye to you," I said to Julie as we stood on the curb
beside her car at the terminal for international departures.

"Just say I'll see you soon," she said as tears filled her
eyes.

"This is so hard. I don't know if I can do it. I've
changed my mind. I'm not going," I said, my voice cracking.

"Don't be silly. You're going." She wrapped her arms
around me.

"I'm only a phone call away. And anyway, Mom and I
are coming at Thanksgiving," she said.

"I love you so much." I hugged her tighter.

"I love you, too, my darling baby brother. Now go.
You'll miss your flight," she said, releasing me.

"Go!" She pointed to the entrance to the terminal,
wiping the tears from her face.

I followed the porter pushing my bags on a cart into the
terminal. I turned one last time. Julie blew me a kiss, turned,
and got into her car.

* * *

"WOULD YOU LIKE SOMETHING TO DRINK, SIR?" THE PRETTY
blonde first-class flight attendant asked me as the plane
reached its cruising altitude.

"Sparkling water, please," I responded with a small
smile, as she took my attention away for the copy of the
L.A. Times I was reading.

Six Months Jail Time for Ashley Sinclair, the headline

screamed. I quickly scanned the article outlining Ashley's sentence and Christina's sister Marissa's full recovery from her injuries. I reached under the seat in front of me and pulled out my carry-on bag. I took out my newly purchased laptop and turned it on.

Maria's words rang in my ears: "Write what you know, with your heart, and it will be spectacular."

I reached for the keyboard and typed:

CHAPTER ONE
STEPHEN

One year after Stephen's accident, Rick came to stay with me.

CPSIA information can be obtained at www.ICGtesting.com
Printed in the USA
239813LV00001B/219/P